To Danny

Tayli

Divergent Omegaverse: Paranormal Gay Romance - Book 2

JP Sayle

Editing Lucas Cornelius

Proofread by Virginie Toulon

Book Formatting by JP Sayle

Trigger Warnings:

Some of the content of this book contains sexually graphic scenes, with the use of explicit language, adult situations, and violence.

Story Outline

Taylin doesn't have a clue how the universe works, but he believes that given the right conditions in which to flourish, love can conquer everything. He is about to put that belief to the test.

Divergent. It's a dirty word in society, and it's also the reason those who should love him unconditionally have cast Taylin out. One act of bravery changes the course of Taylin's life, and he counts his blessings every day.

Years later, his life is set to change once more when his adoptive parents announce they're retiring, putting him directly in Hollis Adice's path—Taylin's one true temptation.

Only one problem.

Hollis has shown zero interest in him for five years!

Coming home, a change in dynamics for their working relationship...

Will it all lead to Hollis finally seeing what is right in front of him—Taylin?

Only time will tell.

Taylin's Temptation is book 2 in the Divergent Omega-verse series, (book one is a prequel to the series about the founders of Starling Enterprises, and a freebie when you sign up to my newsletter) it's a twist on shifters versus non-shifters. With steam, heat's, cuteness and an alpha who just wants to be loved for who he is.

Dedication

The journey of creating a book comes from many things, but sometimes it comes from someone who just loves your crazy mind. Monica, thank you for being my sounding board, my alpha reader and mostly my friend.

To Tal, you were a star. Thank you for working with me to create artwork that fits my boys and made me swoon.

Contents

Prologue

Taylin

Taylin's fingers drummed on the boardroom table, his only sign of agitation. Dust motes danced in the bright sunlight streaming through the window, warming the large space. He wasn't sure if holding interviews in this room would intimidate the candidates or not.

Cream walls held dozens of fashion magazine prints showing the rise of Starling Enterprises in the fashion world. The company's name was synonymous with quality and inclusivity. 'Fashion for all' was exactly what his fathers had set out to achieve. Taylin was proud of the small part he had played in the business since he'd left college and joined the family, paying back a little of what he'd been lucky to receive.

"Why are your lips pinching together like that?" Lane, his Popi, sat forward and eyed him, much like he always did. It was clear that he'd miss nothing of what Taylin was thinking about. Popi was excellent at picking up things regardless if Taylin wanted him to or not.

"Are you sure about this, Popi?" Taylin waved his hand to where the glass of water they'd put out for the first candidate they were interviewing. The position was lead PA, who would assist Lane, Taylin, and his brothers with the branches of the business they managed. "Why would you want me to be part of the interviews for this post to replace Ren? I mean, look how that turned out?"

They had recently discovered in a most horrible way that little omega wolf, Ren, was a supporter of the 'divergent haters'. As a divergent himself, Taylin, had been subjected to some of Ren's hateful vitriol.

It was nothing new. His own family had been unable to grasp that his inability to shift into a wolf had something to do with their genetics. They had subjected him to years of abuse before he'd escaped.

Lane, Taylin's adoptive father, who liked to be called Popi, reached over to him and took hold of one of his large hands to squeeze it. He directed a smile at Taylin that lit his eyes and made him appear much younger than his years. Age sat well on him, regardless of the dark gray hair that he claimed was because of his son's antics as children.

Eight alphas in the same house brought with it a lot of rough and tumble, along with quite a lot of broken furniture.

"Ren deceived us all. Me and your father as well. Fortunately, we figured out his game before he did too much damage." He squeezed Taylin's hand a little tighter. "You have good instincts, don't let that little shit make you believe otherwise."

Hearing Popi curse, something he never did often, Taylin chuckled. "Don't let Dad hear your potty mouth."

Popi rolled his eyes to the ceiling. "Like he doesn't use worse language. I might not shift, but I'm not deaf!"

Popi let go of his hand and reached for the small pile of files sat in front of him, taking the first one. "I've gone through these, and the background checks Derick insisted on. This first one, Hollis Adice, has just finished his Masters in business with a focus on fashion." He glanced up from the page, a look in his eyes that gave Taylin pause for reasons he couldn't pinpoint. "He came in about a year ago requesting a meeting to talk about the history of the company for his dissertation. His questions showed genuine interest in the business, so I gave him our card and told him to get in touch when he was looking for a job."

Taylin listened with interest as he took the offered file. His thoughts scattered as his heart jumped hard enough to knock the breath from his lungs when his gaze landed on the photo clipped to the top of the page. The black-and-white photo captured the attractive man's... *vulnerability.*

It was there in the enormous eyes that stared back at him from behind clear, plastic, square rimmed glasses. For a fleeting moment, Taylin got the sense the other man used them as a barrier. He shook off the silly notion and continued his perusal of the picture, noting Hollis had styled his dark hair to part on the left side.

Taylin couldn't deny that it gave Hollis a professional look, only for some strange reason Taylin had mixed feelings about it. The hair looked thick and luxurious and his fingers tingled with the sudden desire to run them through it, muss it up and test his theory Hollis would look hot all mussed up.

"How old is he?" Taylin murmured absently, his head tilting to change the angle of the picture his gaze lingered on.

"He's twenty-three. Young, but he's worked to support himself through college, showing a solid work ethic for such a young man."

Seven years younger than him.

"Hmm," Taylin replied, never lifting his gaze. When Taylin dated, he went for men around his own age. He wasn't after someone who wanted to play the field. He wasn't like his brothers. Jupiter, in particular, liked young and impressionable, making it easy for him to move on. His 'love em and leave em smiling' motto didn't work for Taylin.

There was a tap at the door and a chuckle from Popi that drew Taylin's gaze up.

Taylin looked at Popi, blinking him into focus, confused as to the reason he was laughing.

"Come in," Popi called, his lips quivering as he looked anywhere but at Taylin.

What had Taylin missed? With no obvious answer, he glanced at the door, holding his breath.

A second later, Hannah, Popi's blonde, bubbly secretary, appeared through the gap in the now open door.

"The first candidate is here, Hollis Adice. Should I get him to wait at the reception area on this floor?"

"Thank you, Hannah." Popi glanced at me. "Are we ready to start?" Back were the quivering lips and a look of obvious amusement glinting in his eyes.

A loaded question for sure with the impact Hollis's picture had on Taylin, which he now suspected was the reason for Popi's amusement. He released his breath in a measured way and forced a smile as he nodded. Everything narrowed down to the open door. Taylin used it to stop his gaze from drifting back to the picture he was still holding.

"As I'll ever be," he answered, unsure if he was talking to Popi or himself.

"Wonderful. Hannah, you can bring him here."

A fluttering started in the pit of Taylin's stomach as Hannah disappeared. Moments later, he rose along with Popi when the door opened fully and Hollis stepped into the room behind Hannah, looking cool and professional.

A suit of charcoal accentuated a lean body, though Taylin assessed Hollis had to be a good half a foot shorter than he was. Underneath the jacket was a white shirt that didn't have one wrinkle. The tie, with a perfect Windsor knot, was a soft baby pink. Black loafers with a high shine finished the look.

His glasses differed from the ones in the picture. These had a thick black frame in the same square style and didn't detract from the huge chocolate brown eyes staring at him with polite interest. It didn't lessen the punch to Taylin's solar plexus or how his heart rate picked up as he stepped to the young man and offered his hand.

"Hello Mr. Adice. I'm Taylin Starling." A soft palm touched his when Hollis came forward, reaching for Taylin's offered hand.

Taylin's six-foot-four-inches dwarfed Hollis and brought out a protective urge to sooth the other man when he dipped his gaze, and a flash of color filled his chiseled cheekbones.

Words that were there on the tip of his tongue disappeared when Hollis clutched his hand with trembling fingers.

"Thank you for inviting me in for an interview," Hollis replied in the gentlest of tones, as if trying to calm an upset child.

The fluttering happening inside Taylin increased at the soft lilt of Hollis's voice. It was delicate and very appealing.

Taylin searched for something, anything, to say to get him to speak again. They stood for so long holding hands, Taylin felt heat creep past the collar of his shirt, but he was unwilling to let go.

The sound of a cough broke the extended silence and Taylin glanced at Popi wide eyed, having forgotten he was in the room.

Oh shit!

"Thank you for coming in today, Mr. Adice. It's nice to see you again," Popi said, giving their joined hands a pointed look, getting Taylin to let go when he noticed Hollis was tugging to escape.

Smooth. Real smooth, asshole!

"Take a seat," Taylin suggested in a pleasant, totally non-weirded out tone, giving Hollis a smile that he'd been told could melt an icy heart in seconds.

When Hollis didn't return the smile, just took the seat indicated to him, Taylin bit the inside of his cheek to stop the sigh at Hollis's obvious disinterest. He was probably thinking Taylin was some sort of weirdo.

He's too young for me, anyway.

The words were hollow as he returned to his seat and gratefully sat.

My best smile and nothing! Not a glimmer of a smile in return.

He'd been well and truly shot down in flames, his one consolation being that his brothers weren't there to witness his humiliation.

Popi relaxed in his seat and offered an encouraging smile to Hollis. "Could we get you a coffee? A soft drink, before we start?" Popi pointed to the glass of iced water, giving him an encouraging smile. "There is water if you need it."

"No thank you Sir, I'm fine." Hollis crossed his legs, his palms together as they rested in his lap.

Popi shook his head. "Please call me Lane. Sir makes me feel old. And do you prefer Mr. Adice or Hollis?"

"Hollis is fine, S—Lane," Hollis quickly corrected, a slight pink hue appearing over the bridge of his nose as he kept his gaze on Popi.

Popi's attention shifted to Taylin and an eyebrow rose, his eyes widening as he tilted his head in Hollis's direction. All the questions Taylin had thought to prepare disappeared into the black hole of his mind.

Seconds ticked by and an awkward silence ensued until Popi's chest deflated as Taylin struggled to find anything to say that would make him come across like the professional business person he actually was.

"Shall we get started?" At Hollis's stilted nod, Popi gave Taylin an encouraging look before asking Hollis. "Tell us a little about your interest in the fashion business. What about it appeals to you?"

Minutes ticked by and Taylin's tongue stuck to the roof of his mouth, wishing he'd thought to get himself a glass of water, as he listened intently to Hollis speak with a passion that matched his own for the fashion industry. He consoled himself at the man's apparent lack of interest in him with how they had a shared commonality for the business. He could work with that. Although, could he, when Hollis didn't spare him a glance?

Too young. He's way too young for me!

It was poor consolation, and he knew it, but it was for the best. An ache developed in the center of his chest and he resisted rubbing at it as Popi glanced at him, giving him a pointed look. "So your area of interest is the same as Taylin's."

Rolling his shoulders, he gathered his scattered thoughts and offered a polite smile, taking the cue. "What accessories are causing a stir in fashion week right now? That 'must have' that will translate down to the big high street stores?"

Chapter One
Hollis

Five years later

Why did Lane want me here with his and Derick's sons, but no one else?

Hollis was getting a feeling of dread in the pit of his stomach. Lane had always made Hollis feel like he was part of the family... but this? No, this was something else.

Lane Starling, an omega divergent, was the joint owner of Starling Enterprises with his husband Derick, a wolf shifter who'd defied society's views about mating with a divergent. Society deemed alphas, betas or omegas who had an animal spirit but couldn't shift into their animal form, as 'divergent'. The term got treated like a slur since it had become apparent that there were two differing species in the last two centuries: divergents and shifters.

As the decades passed and more divergents emerged, the divide grew. Derick Starling had flouted society's expectations and married Lane forty years ago, creating a company that was renowned for accepting everyone, despite what they might or might not be.

Hollis was proud to work for such a trailblazing company... *when I don't have to work with a certain son.*

Taylin, since the first moment he'd laid eyes on him, had knocked him off balance. Five years and still he had the ability to make Hollis forget his sensible nature. It took concerted effort to act like Taylin being in the room—hell, inside the building—didn't make Hollis super aware of the attraction he felt.

Taylin's masculine scent was musky with hints of forest fruits. It was enough to distract Hollis's animal half to the point he sometimes had to excuse himself from meetings just to get a grip of himself and have words with his animal, ones the pesky brat ignored.

You want to lick him too.

Easier to pretend he hadn't heard and focus on the other men at the table, all wearing varying looks of concern.

Lane and Derick had eight sons, three of their own and five they'd adopted. He observed them from under his eyelashes as he returned his attention to the reason for the meeting. He easily picked up that something important was going down. It was in the air that vibrated with a kind of tension that made Hollis sense a potential threat, but to what? Him? Lane's sons?

"So what you're saying is that in the past, when you've delayed me, it's cause of the impact on another part of the business?" Julian's question was met with a wide smile from his father, Derick.

"Exactly." Dark penetrating eyes moved over everyone at the large boardroom table and Hollis noted his inclusion. The growing storm of nerves in his stomach swirled together like a tornado. "What I want is for you all to take on my role, work with each other to reach a common goal."

Derick's statement drew involuntary words from Hollis. "Good luck with that." His whisper gained attention from the shifters in the room.

Hairy balls!

What the heck was wrong with me speaking aloud?

He resisted checking just how hot his cheeks were when he felt the sweat gather at his hairline. Instead, he dropped his gaze to his trembling hands, which he folded to hide his reaction. He'd spent years with these men and understood just how hard this was going to be for them all, and for himself, when they didn't play nice.

He didn't dare shift his attention towards Taylin to see his reaction. In the five years Hollis had worked to establish a barrier between them, it was currently at its pathetically thinnest. The infuriating man had a habit—a dreadful habit—of aiming his stunning smile at the drop of a hat, at the unsuspecting. Him, usually! Hollis was wise and hadn't fallen for such nonsense.

"Hollis, that's where you'll come in."

Derick's deep voice carried past his thoughts and Hollis's head popped up. His eyes hurt at how fast they widened. How had he got anything to do with this? "Sir?"

"There are eight casting votes, so they will need a majority vote to carry through a motion. That will be you. Lane has been giving you increased responsibility and he trusts you to be the one to step in when it's needed."

"He does?" Hollis burned with embarrassment at how squeaky the words came out. Convinced he felt the weight of Taylin's stare on him, Hollis refused to look in that direction to check and see if he was right. Because right now, Hollis was freaking out, and it took all his years of experience to hold all his emotions in check, keeping his expression from revealing just how much he wanted to slink away.

How could they want him to be the voice of reason between the brothers? Were they insane? Had they lost their freaking minds?

The rest of the men stared at Derick like he might have lost his marbles, that the bag that held them when he came into the room had somehow ripped open and they were now slipping all over the floor, waiting to trip up an unsuspecting employee—him.

"What! How can he make those types of decisions?" It was impossible to read Silas with how restrained he was being, but Hollis bristled at the implication that he wasn't capable of what Derick was suggesting, when he most definitely was!

Was he backtracking? Yeah, he was, but he'd keep that to himself.

Lane moved around the table towards the seat he'd vacated to get up and hug Jupiter when he'd gotten upset at the beginning of the conversation. He was a loving father and had—it seemed—an innate need to make sure everyone was alright, including those he worked closely with. Hollis was positive Lane would adopt all the PAs he worked with if he could, including Hollis.

"Hollis is more than equipped to rationalize what decision is required. He has a business management masters and has been working alongside me for the past five years. He's perfect for arbitrating if *it's required.*" When Lane stopped next to his husband, he rested a hand on Derick's massive shoulder, his fingers flexing. "As the base of operations is here in Hazardville, you will all need to relocate back in town."

"You gotta be shitting me!" Kodi ground out, bouncing out of his seat, pursued by his twin brother, Kari, but Hollis wasn't listening because he was reeling from this second blow. They were all going to move back to Hazardville?

All eight brothers were going to be here!

Under one roof!

All the time!

Oh gods, how was he going to cope with that and the PAs. They were going to freak.

You're doing enough of that for everyone, his animal side pointed out, enjoying itself way too much in Hollis's opinion.

This is going to make my life—

It's going to shake up your boring existence, is what it's going to do.

Unsure how long he'd zoned out for, he jolted to his senses at the scent of sex wafting down the table towards him.

"Have you got any questions? Anything you'd like to say?"

Lane was looking at Hollis, so he felt compelled to reply honestly. "Not right now." He kept his tone soft, working to refrain from being squeaky again. "I'll need to consider everything first. But I'd like to say thank you for trusting me."

He counted in his head, working to meet every brother's stare, recalling exactly how hard he'd worked over the last five years. These men weren't going to ruin how much he loved his job—they weren't.

He sucked in a breath and set the boundary he was positive the brothers would cross because he'd worked with them. But he wasn't going to be a pushover, no siree. His Mamma didn't raise no fool. "I'd like to make something clear here and now. I won't allow anyone to bully me into something I'm not sure about, so be warned. I'm no pushover."

Taylin's head dipping caught Hollis's eye, and he noted him paying more attention to his tablet than to what Hollis had said. The hurt that came got pushed to one side to be explored in private at a time when every pair of eyes, bar Taylin's, wasn't focused on him.

Fine, if Taylin wanted to play it like that, then he was going to find Hollis was more than a match for showing indifference. He was a damn professional!

The conversation was over minutes later as the scent of lust increased and Derick all but dragged Lane out of the boardroom, leaving their sons and Hollis alone. He at least kept his thoughts about what might or might not be happening when Derick and Lane reached one of their offices to himself. Their sons, not so much, which signaled it was time to leave.

Hollis stood, his mind whirring with everything, and the potential impact on his organized life. He reached the open door before someone called his name. He twisted in the doorway to look back at the men who remained sitting around the table, all showing varying degrees of interest in him.

“Yes?” He quirked up his brows, unsure whether it was Kodi or Kari who’d spoken. They were too similar to say.

“Where are you going? We need to discuss what this means. How are we going to deal with this situation if you leave?” Kari asked impatiently.

Hollis cast his eyes over the alphas—*men*—he was now going to be answerable to. Showing weakness as an omega was the last thing he wanted to do. His animal form was a pygmy slow loris. A big-eyed ball of cuteness and he’d often gotten taken for a ride because of it. He’d learned his lessons a time long ago.

He turned around fully to face them. Back ramrod straight, he chanted, *don’t show weakness. Don’t show weakness.* He might look adorable and harmless, but he wasn’t defenseless. He was venomous and had a nasty bite if he felt threatened.

“As I advised Lane, right now I need to consider this information. When I have, I will check your calendars and schedule a meeting that works for y’all. I’m sure y’all have a lot to sort in the next couple of days before your fathers step down from the company."

How would that change things? Starling Enterprises' fashion business was world renowned for many reasons. These eight men were now in charge.

God help them all!

Met with what appeared to be stunned silence, Hollis nodded and made a quick exit, feeling for now like he might have just dodged a bullet. For how long though, was anyone's guess.

Hollis made his way down the hallway, moving silently on the plush carpet, keeping his gaze down, unsure of who was aware of what they'd just discussed. He was good at being invisible; it was a skill. He went straight to Monica, suspecting that as Derick's trusted assistant and what Hollis often referred to as 'the librarian of all things Starling', she would know what the heck was going on.

She had worked for the company for the same length of time as Hollis, employed only a week apart. They'd become close friends as the newbies, although it would seem not close enough for her to give Hollis a heads up.

Long dark hair curtained gorgeous features as Monica's dark, expressive eyes lifted from the computer and met Hollis's gaze over her overflowing desk. No matter how silent he was, she never got caught unaware. Perks of being a vampire bat.

A grin appeared on her face before he reached her desk. "I wondered how long it would take you to come see me."

She rose gracefully from her cherry red seat, casting a glance at Derick's closed office door. Slim fitting, black trousers gave her the appearance of having long legs, but she barely reached five feet tall in stocking feet. It was something she often moaned about and why she wore five inch killer heels in her favored red.

The forest green blouse she wore floated about her as she came and took his hand, dragging him back the way he'd just come, heading it would seem, to the coffee lounge that was on this floor.

Every floor had one. Their bosses were very generous and wanted their staff to have every amenity that helped them be productive, including copious amounts of coffee, soft drinks, and snacks.

Met with the scent of sugar and fruit, apple if his nose was correct, Hollis held back his groan of complaint as his tooth cleaning tongue roamed over his teeth, already anticipating eating a slice of cake. Few people realized his animal had two tongues, one of which was abrasive, and used like a toothbrush to help with all the fruit he liked to eat. It was full of sugar, much like the cake always in this coffee lounge. He hated to admit when it came in cake he had a particular weakness for it.

The door clicked shut behind them and Monica's hair flew around her slim shoulders when she bounced up and down. "Well, did you say yes?"

"I—"

"I really wanted to say something, but they barely gave me time to adjust to the news. I mean, how the heck am I going to keep all eight hotties in check?"

"I—"

"They all like to get their own way and I'm not sure they'll try to steamroller over me. Derick was clear though, I'm not to take any nonsense from them. Do you think they'll listen to us?"

This time Hollis waited to see if she was going to start with more questions. When two seconds ticked by he reckoned the firing questions part of the conversation was over for now. "I haven't really said anything, other than that I won't be a walkover. And that I was honored, 'cause I am. As for keeping them in check, you've been doing that for years. As for listening to us… that's tricky to say when we barely get to see them, except for important meetings and new business that relates to their particular area of interest. Then it's usually just one or two of them, not all eight."

She nodded sagely. "You're right. We need a plan."

The door opened and Frey came in, his gray-green eyes narrowing as he glanced between them. His normally smooth brow wrinkled as he strolled towards Hollis, who swallowed the sigh of displeasure at what Frey might have overheard.

Frey, a fennec fox, had excellent hearing. "What you two gossiping 'bout?" Frey rested his hip causally against the counter and plucked up a piece of cake, his gaze moving between them and the white chocolate and jammie treat he held.

Dressed in casual chic, he could have been a model on any magazine cover. He liked to wear the line of clothing the firm sold that targeted the 'hip and trendy' workforce.

As he glanced down at his suit, his favored attire for work, Hollis scowled. He was clearly neither hip nor trendy.

Frey's features were strong, yet he came across as a delicate flower with full lips and wide expressive eyes that never hid his emotions. Expressions fleeted over his face as he continued to watch them both.

"We aren't gossiping," Hollis stated in a hoity-toity tone, hating that he'd been doing exactly that and got caught out.

Frey rolled his eyes at him. "If you say so." He bit into the chocolate and moaned, his free hand going to his throat. "Goodness, this is better than sex," he exclaimed loud enough that Hollis was sure those on the corridor would hear.

Monica's giggles came with a snort from Hollis. "Then your sex life can't be any good," he snapped waspishly, instantly regretting it.

Frey batted long, blond eyelashes at him as he took another bite, the moan this time more obscene. One fit for a porn movie that Hollis would never own up to watching when he was going through a heat.

A chuckle from behind them got a flash of heat rolling through Hollis when he scented fruits of the forest. Feeling like he might expire recalling exactly what he'd said, he turned and found himself staring directly at an amused looking Taylin.

Could this day get any worse?

"That's a theory that maybe needs testing," Taylin directed at Frey, bringing out the big guns as his smile turned seven shades of wicked.

It seemed it could!

Being utterly still was one of Hollis's abilities, and right then, not even an eyelash flickered at how Taylin flirted openly with Frey. Hollis wanted nothing more than to lick the venom his body produced on his arm and bite Frey when he licked his lips and held out the treat.

"Wanna try... some?"

Chapter Two

Taylin

"Where the hell are you slinking off to?" Booker questioned as Taylin made his way to the door.

"None of your business," Taylin replied, offering a toothy grin that would irritate Booker and get a rise out of him.

Before Booker could respond, Laken jumped in with his enormous feet. "He's going after Hollis to see if he can get in first and charm him. Not that it's ever worked before" Laken gave him a knowing look. His smirk was all knowing and fucking irritating because it was true.

Lifting his middle finger, Taylin flipped Laken off and kept going out the open door. Sometimes having brothers was a pain in his backside.

"I don't know why he keeps trying," Laken added with a throaty laugh.

Taylin's nose twitched, his wolf tracking Hollis's scent and leading him to the coffee room. Outside the open door, he paused, eavesdropping.

"Then your sex life can't be any good."

Taylin's animal spirit surged at Hollis's comment. Who was Hollis having sex with? Taylin had heard no gossip from the other PAs about Hollis dating anyone. Had he missed something?

He often justified listening to gossip by claiming that it kept him knowing when his staff weren't happy.

Yeah, that's the only reason.

The voice sounded distinctively like Laken and Taylin pretended not to hear it. Popi had taught him that happy staff were more productive and loyal. Which was true... only this was Hollis. Hollis, a man who, after five years, still held all of Taylin's attention. It was sad and pitiful.

Unable to resist the pressing urge to find out more, he stepped into the coffee lounge at Frey's next throaty moan and chuckled at the man's over dramatized expression.

"That's a theory that maybe needs testing." His comment was out before he could think about it, his thoughts still worrying over who Hollis might be having sex with. To make matters worse, and dig an even bigger hole for himself, Taylin used his sexist smile and stupidly aimed it at Frey.

Taylin blamed Hollis for this, thoughts of the man with anyone but him turning him into a hot, jealous mess. Hollis tormented his dreams and kept him awake at night after they'd occupied the same space and Hollis's scent lingered in his nose.

It had been years and he'd still found nothing to breach the hard exterior that Hollis used to keep folks at a distance. Taylin was a nice guy—people often said he was—and the reason Hollis couldn't see it, he figured, was because he hadn't gotten the opportunity to really get to know him.

He keeps you at a distance, cause you act like a damn dork! The snappy retort came—absolutely—from his wolf half.

For a while, Taylin had tried dating other men and his wolf's spirit had made it impossible when it came to touching them. It was hard to convince someone how attracted Taylin was to them when his body didn't respond the way it should. Or when his wolf side didn't like their smell, or their taste and that was that, so Taylin had given up and stuck to bachelorhood.

The bombshell his fathers had just dropped, Taylin—unlike his brothers—saw it as an opportunity to finally get under Hollis's skin and figure out why he didn't like him. A proximity he'd been unable to gain in the past due to work had now presented itself, and Taylin would not waste it.

Unlike his brothers, worrying about how this was going to change things, he saw altering the status quo as something positive... he hoped. His fathers had given him an opportunity, and Taylin was excited about it. It was why he'd kept his head down during the conversation so as not to reveal just how happy he was.

So acutely aware of Hollis, Taylin noted immediately when Hollis went into 'invisible mode' right in front of him. Every fiber in Taylin's body screamed with the need to reach out and touch him. It took a split second to realize that

Frey—who was cute but not what Taylin was interested in—was offering him what he held in his hand with an expectant expression. If it had been Hollis, Taylin would have all but bitten his hand off.

He sighed in his mind and struggled to keep the smile attached to his lips. Taylin shook his head, trying to come up with a valid reason not to nibble on the treat. If Hollis was offering...

"A sugar high at this time of the day would make me useless in about an hour," he waffled, which was utter nonsense, not missing how Monica folded her lips into her mouth, probably to stop herself laughing at his ridiculousness.

Frey batted long blond eyelashes at him. A flirty smile added wattage to the obvious interest. "That's okay, I can come revive you as many times as you need."

Monica, who had kept silent up to now, giggled, then stifled this behind her hand while Hollis's expression went stoney.

"Frey, don't you have a full calendar of meetings today that require your attention?" Hollis's icy tone could have cut through metal.

Frey appeared unconcerned and hip swayed his way to the doorway Taylin stood in, his fingers curled around the remaining treat he held. "Sadly, I do..." he winked at Taylin as he brushed his body against his, making his wolf very unhappy and him struggle not to flinch away. "But there's always after work."

A chuckle teased its way up Taylin's throat at the blatant overture. Frey was persistent, Taylin had to give that to him.

He was to blame for having encouraged it, even if not totally on purpose, so he needed to fix this.

His lips parted right as Hollis snapped, "Taylin is busy this evening." Hollis's teeth clacked together on the words and drew Taylin's narrow-eyed gaze.

He tilted his head and watched Hollis closely, looking for something to explain the waspish sting to his reply. Was he jealous?

Frey remained close enough for Taylin to feel the heat coming from his body and inhale the sweet chocolate and jam treat.

Taylin caught Monica staring at Hollis with an expression that revealed a curiosity that made him wish he'd cultivated more of a relationship with her, to understand what she was thinking.

Taylin kept his tone light. "I am?"

Hollis blushed a delicate shade of pink, looking a little flustered when he glanced at Taylin. "Of course. With the changes coming and your requirement to return to Hazardville to start work here on Monday, I'd say you have little time to... *to do anything more than pack and arrange to move home.*"

Could that be the only reason he was snapping at me like an alligator at a fresh piece of meat?

Taylin felt the hope surge in his heart. *Maybe he was jealous after all?* If he was, then all bets were off! Taylin had been called tenacious when he wanted to achieve a goal.

Could the angry snap and glittering light in Hollis's eyes when he glanced at Frey, whose mouth hung open, be a clue to Hollis not being as averse to him as he thought?

"Changes? Why is Taylin moving to HQ?" Frey asked, sounding confused as he lost interest in Taylin, his attention on Hollis.

"Who's moving to HQ?" Bowie's gaze swept over everyone, and his nose wrinkled as he moved past Taylin. "Are you having a party here and no one invited me?"

Bowie, a PA who Taylin had worked with frequently, elbowed past Frey next, eyeing the hand holding what appeared to now be melting goo.

Bowie put enough hurt into the question that in the next moment, Taylin watched wide eyed as Hollis rushed to reassure him. "Of course not, Bowie. Frey was, as usual, here first to get his hands on what you brought in."

Frey held up the hand holding his treat. "This is better than sex, Bowie. I need the recipe for when I'm having a dry spell." He stared pointedly at Taylin, licked his lips, then left, his hips working hard to make his ass sway like he was doing a rumba.

Hollis made a hissing sound whereas Monica's hands went to her middle when her gales of laughter boomed out.

Bowie looked around with a bewildered expression. "Why is it I always feel like I'm three steps behind the herd?"

Hollis slipped an arm around Bowie's rather broad shoulders and attempted to hug him closer. "You aren't. Frey was just being his *usual self.*"

The latter appeared aimed at Taylin, who thrust his fisted hands into his trouser pockets, counting in his head like he'd learned to do when Hollis showed any affection towards someone that *was never him.*

"Foxy and flirty," Bowie supplied, causing Hollis' lips to curl down.

"Yes."

The need to get Hollis to move away from Bowie wouldn't abate. "I'll leave you to it." He nodded at Monica and Bowie.

"Hollis, when you have a moment, I'd like a word," he said, far too sharply for his own liking.

A flash of what looked like temper came and went before Hollis answered, "I'll set up a meeting with *everyone* once I'm ready."

A firmness to his statement suggested discussing it further was pointless. Often referred to as having 'a laid back' personality, Taylin considered it a real possibility that Hollis was the only one able to push his buttons. Rather than argue in front of an audience, something that had started in the last year *for some reason,* he kept silent.

Not for 'some reason'. You know why! You know he's ours so stop messing about and claim him.

Easier to nod and pretend he didn't hear his wolf spirit, Taylin exited the room feeling steam coming out of his ears.

He breathed through his open mouth all the way back to the office he seldom had cause to use.

His secretary, Alma, peered at him from behind her spectacles, looking over the top rather than through them. It was a habit she had that made her look rather stern when, in fact, she was anything but.

"I wasn't expecting to see you." The surprise was obvious in her voice.

Her gaze swept over him from top to toe in a motherly fashion he was used to. "No, it was a sudden change." He ran a hand through his hair, working to contain his frustration. "Can you please come into the office, and I'll explain."

Her notebook in hand, she rose and came around the desk. Her navy dress nearly touched the floor as it swirled about her legs. Taylin opened his office door and held it wide for her to enter.

The room smelled of leather and pine. The latter came from the gift Alma had given him last year for Christmas. A jar of incense that she refilled regularly. A bank of windows offered him a view of the city beyond. Windows in the surrounding tall buildings shimmered from the sun. He stood for a brief second, taking in the changes of the place he'd found a home in.

He loved Hazardville despite it being an industrial town. He'd found love and acceptance here. He let those thoughts settle in his heart as he swung back to shut the door.

Alma walked to the seat across from his desk, her petticoats rustling. She liked to wear them under her long flowing dresses to make the skirt flounce out. Her fashion sense was based much around the swinging sixties, and it suited her and her hour-glass figure.

His thoughts returned to Hollis with someone that wasn't him and his shoulders sagged when he went to take his seat across from Alma.

"What's up, sweet child?"

Despite his mood, his lips curled at the motherly term. One Alma had used often when Taylin got frustrated or upset with his brothers... *with Hollis.* He had no recollection of her not being here, of working for his fathers. She, like him, was divergent and had found acceptance within the walls of Starling Enterprises, like so many others.

Taylin took the seat behind his desk, tugging up his pant leg as he crossed his legs. Alma was his confidant. He trusted her implicitly. "Hollis."

"Is that why you are home and looking glum?"

He shook his head at her compassionate gaze. "Popi and Dad have decided to step down and retire. They want us all to come home and base ourselves here."

If he'd expected shock, he didn't get it but then Alma was around a similar age to his fathers, though he'd never be rude and ask exactly how old that was.

Then a horrifying thought struck. *God's, would she be thinking of retiring next?*

Alma, unaware of his sudden panic, perched closer to the edge of her seat, a smile touching her eyes. "What great news. You'll be here, right under Hollis's nose, showing him what a wonderful boy you are."

Thoughts of her leaving fled with the need to figure out if Hollis was actually seeing someone that wasn't him. "Is Hollis dating anyone... Bowie, for instance?"

Her bark of laughter jolted him. "Silly boy. Hollis isn't interested in Bowie, or anyone else that isn't you, for that matter."

It was something she'd often said to him, and Taylin had never been able to substantiate. The doubt came with the fresh memory of Hollis cuddling Bowie. "Are you sure?"

Her tut came with a narrow-eyed stare, making him squirm like a naughty child speaking back to a parent. "I've the spirit of a crow inside me. When have I ever missed anything that's going on when it comes to those who I work with?"

She was right. She missed nothing. "Sorry, I shouldn't have doubted you."

"No, you shouldn't." Notebook on her knee, she rubbed her hands together. "So, what's your plan to get your beau?. And do you need my help?"

"You'll help me?" he exclaimed, unsure whether or not he should be scared of the offer.

The layered, salt and pepper colored hair shifted around her tiny, wrinkled face as she nodded eagerly. "Of course. You setting up camp here is perfect. You'll be right under Hollis's nose. I know someone that can help us," she answered absentmindedly. "Though it's best if you don't know who that is. Wouldn't want you trying to act when you aren't any good at pretending to be something you're not."

"What! I got picked two years in a row to play the lead in a high school Christmas play."

As if he'd not spoken, she continued, "But that's okay, I've got you covered like I always have."

He got the feeling he'd just been steamrolled, but as he'd failed for years doing it alone, how could a little help make things worse?

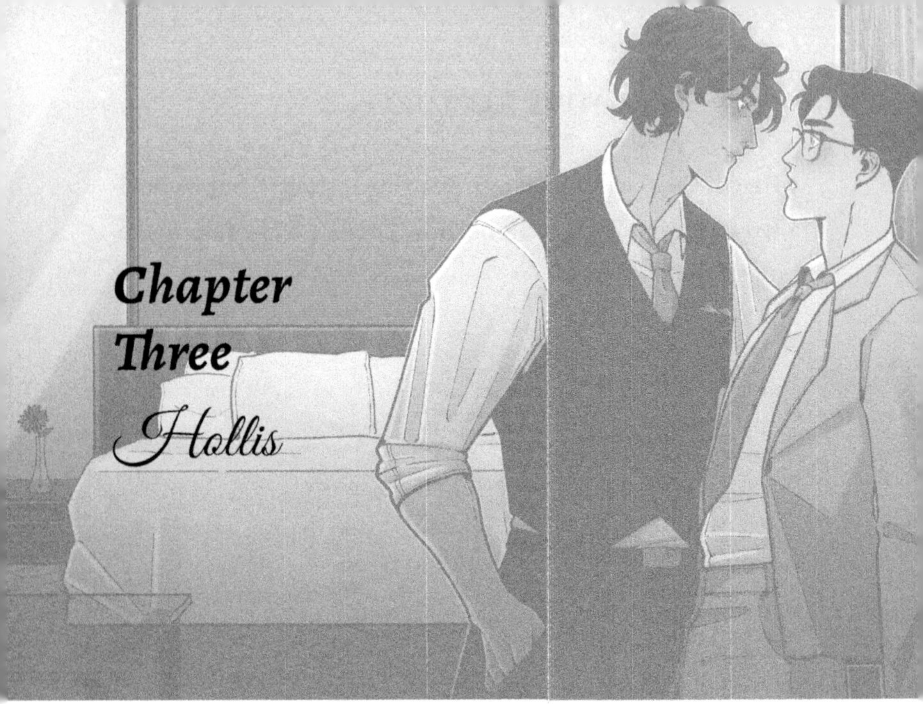

Chapter Three

Hollis

Although Hollis had expected this invasion that crowded into his office the next morning, he'd hoped for a little more time to gather his thoughts before being confronted by his team of PAs. However, they didn't need to know that, or that he'd spent most of the previous evening evading his own thoughts about a certain someone and focusing his attention on how he could move forward and get his team to work with him—and with the brothers—in close quarters.

He'd gone through their WhatsApp group chat and figured things were going to be rocky for a while, once he assigned the PAs to the brothers they didn't enjoy working with for extended periods of time. They were all in for a sharp shock at his strategy to keep the brothers in line.

What the brothers felt about him and his new role was the least of his worries. He eyed the men crowding his office and speaking over each other and sighed in frustration. It went unheard because of the multiple questions they peppered him with.

Giving up, he lifted a hand to draw attention to himself, waving his fingers at everyone other than Ziggy. Their newest recruit, an omega snake shifter, was the only silent one in the group who just watched Hollis.

Hollis had been convinced—initially—that Ziggy wasn't the right person for a PA job when he'd interviewed him with Lane. He couldn't see Ziggy working closely with any of the brothers. Alphas really hated to be challenged, as Hollis had learned very early on. Ziggy's appearance had confused him and others into thinking he wasn't an omega. Big and muscly, with a shaved head save a small strip of dark hair on the top of his head, neck tattoos, and piercings added to Ziggy's overly macho appearance. He looked more suited to being in a biker gang than working for a billion dollar company.

Looks could be deceiving.

Ziggy was very much an omega with an analytical brain that could fathom out problems quicker than anyone Hollis knew. In the few weeks he'd worked at the company, he'd so far kept to himself and only spoke when absolutely necessary. Hollis liked him for that alone, once he'd got used to his appearance.

"Why weren't we told our bosses were retiring?" Isley, a tiny sugar glider, muttered, wearing a sullen frown.

"Are they retiring or are you just making an assumption, as usual?" Frey asked, rolling his eyes when Isley glared back at him.

"You were the one who mentioned the brothers were coming to take over the business," Montague, an otter, who everyone called Monty, pointed out to Frey. Monty's scowl was about as terrifying as a butterfly flapping its tiny wings.

Lennon rolled his eyes heavenward, revealing his irritation. His vampire bat half wasn't tolerant of bullshit. "Didn't Bowie say that it was Taylin who was moving back here?"

Bowie nodded, but no one looked at him. They were all focused on Hollis, who used his hardest stare to create a semblance of order and authority. Some days were harder than others!

"If you want me to answer your questions, then I'd suggest you stop shouting over each other." Hollis added enough force to his voice to get everyone's full attention.

Silence descended, and he released a shuddery breath, hoping no one noticed he was shaking a little while still struggling to come to terms with what this would all mean to him—to the company.

"Let's take this to the coffee lounge. There are more seats there and we won't feel crammed in like sardines." It was how he felt with his team crowding him.

A bunch of over excited men who loved to gossip as much as they liked to work got encouraged out of Hollis's space and down the corridor. Other members of staff working on the floor stopped as they passed, curious looks aimed their way, which Hollis ignored.

There would be an all staff bulletin put out to let everyone know what was happening. But with how things were with his team, he didn't have the patience to field all their questions until that occurred. They would be incessant, prying out all the answers until they had the full picture. A trait which was part of the reason they'd been hired for the roles in the first place. A trait Hollis admired, even when it irritated him when their tenacity was aimed in his direction.

Hollis was fairly certain they wouldn't come across any of the brothers as their offices were on the floor above, something that had thrown him when he'd started working for the company. Lane had explained the PAs' role in the firm was slightly different to other companies. There were secretaries assigned to each of the brothers to manage their day-to-day office requirements, and they were on the same floor as the brothers' offices. Even with the brothers spending little time in Hazardville, their secretaries remained based here working alongside the PAs.

When Hollis first started at the company, he'd expected the PAs would do the secretarial work as well. He'd quickly got dissuaded from the notion that he would have time to complete office work, type letters, make appointments, and so on. Lane had explained the PAs role was far broader and much more challenging—especially with how demanding the alphas were. One week in the job had proven just how silly his notion was that he could do everything.

Hush fell when everyone took colorful, padded seats around the coffee scented room that held a hint of sweetness to the air too. Hollis suspected that it came from whatever was in the white confectionery boxes on the far counter, next to the coffee machine.

Tension rolled through Hollis as he closed the door, not wanting anyone else to overhear what he was about to disclose. The group looked expectantly at him as he rested his ass against the counter and put his thoughts in order, figuring out where to start. "Lane and Derick are retiring. They have asked all their sons to return to Hazardville and run the company jointly."

The dry chuckle that came from Monty, a cunning otter, held no humor. "As if they'll be able to do that!"

"Yes, well, that's not for you to worry about." Hollis grimaced at Monty, who wasn't wrong after what Hollis had seen and heard the day before. "For now, your biggest concern is that for the transition to happen smoothly, you will each find yourself allocated to one of the sons who work in the area of your expertise."

"What... no... you can't be serious," stuttered Bowie, a furious blush coating his cheeks.

Frey waggled his thumb at Bowie. "What he said! You know I—"

"I know perfectly well your opinion of a certain brother. You have made that abundantly clear. As I have said before, that is not my issue. My job is to ensure that my team, who are paid a princely sum to do their jobs," he met each man's stare, "do it. If you are unhappy, then I'm sure there are other firms looking to hire."

"Hollis, do you really need to be an A-hole?" Frey asked, lounging back on his chair. The hand resting on the arm of the chair moved continually, belying his relaxed posture.

Hollis bristled, his lips thinning into a tight line as he gave Frey a stare that expressed his displeasure.

"Leave him be, Frey. This applies to him too," Bowie pointed out, looking at Hollis sympathetically.

Hollis worked hard not to think about changes to his role, because if he did, he'd break out in a cold sweat. "My role is changing—"

"How so?" Isley questioned, paling. "We aren't going to get a new boss, are we? I like working with you, even when you're bossy."

The backhanded compliment slid off Hollis like water off a duck's back. It was the weight of the following silence that followed Isley's question that got him responding.

"No."

Being the deciding vote if things got out of hand shouldn't affect his team too much, but Hollis hadn't dwelled on that. Because how did you measure something when it hadn't happened yet?

"I'll still be your boss. Although there might be times when I can't stop what I'm doing to deal with your issues, like I have in the past." His gaze landed on Monty and Bowie. The two men often came to his office to bitch about working with certain sons.

"Hey, why are you looking at me?" Monty muttered, shrinking down into the seat as if trying to make himself invisible.

Frey rubbed a hand over Monty's shoulder. "'Cause we all know that Tweedle-dee gets irked when you spend any time sorting out his lengthy line of wannabe models that think if they shag him, their asshole will be better than a gold-coated heaven and become the next Mr. Starling."

Chocked laughter came from everyone, including Ziggy.

"Please, the only thing Jupiter is interested in is getting his end away in—"

"Enough, Monty," Hollis snapped, doing his best to contain his own amusement. "It's bad enough in the group chat. At least there I can skip by your comments. Now, shall we get back to why we're here?"

Chapter Four

Taylin

A quick boot to close the door behind him and Taylin dropped two heavy suitcases with a grunt. His head tilted as he listened out for any noise. Met with nothing but silence, his brows furrowed as he called out, “Popi. Popi.”

He’d messaged from the airport to say he’d landed and would be home within the hour. Had his dads gone out?

Taylin expected Popi to hang around waiting for him like he usually did and it was the reason he always messaged when he landed. It was a tradition, one of many they had. It wasn’t like Popi to change one.

Scratching his head, he left his suitcases where they were and strolled in the sunroom’s direction, discarding his suit jacket as he went. Could they be having breakfast without him? Again, they’d normally wait for him, or any of his brothers, to arrive if they knew they were coming.

An unsettled feeling formed in the pit of Taylin's stomach with thoughts of the retirement bombshell not being the only thing that was shifting in his world. Frown lines deepened around his eyes as he checked his wristwatch. Heading through the large, open living room, he couldn't smell anything other than wood polish and Popi's fragrant flowers sat in a vase on the far table.

Almost every Saturday morning his fathers predictably ate breakfast in the sunroom that overlooked the large, landscaped garden Popi had designed. All year round they had blooms that would flower, making the sunroom Taylin's favorite place to sit and read or listen to music when he was home.

His shoes clipped faster on the marble floor, his frown deepening at the house's silence. He stepped through the open door leading from the formal dining room, which was only used for family get-togethers and special occasions, and paused at finding the sunroom empty.

Unsettled, Taylin felt the tension gather at the base of his neck, causing his shoulders to draw up. Dad and Popi's stability—routine—had gotten him through some of the worst days of his life. Days when he'd thought death would be better than struggling and fighting for his next breath.

Before he could shut out the past, images flashed through his mind fast enough to steal the air from his lungs. They punched at his psyche like they always did when his mind decided traveling back to the events that brought him to his found family was a good thing.

A tremor ran through Taylin at the effort it took to stave off what he didn't need reminding of when his body bore the scars. He shut his eyes, slowly drawing in a breath. He clenched his stomach muscles tightly, holding them and taking several deep, even breaths, releasing each one slowly as Popi had taught him to, to get his focus on nothing but breathing.

"Why, Master Taylin! When did you sneak in?"

His eyelids darted open, and a grin formed at being caught with his eyes closed by Bessie. Round, flushed cheeks, bright eyes and a mop of gray curls framed a face that was homely and welcoming. She was one of Taylin's favorite people. Their longtime housekeeper's motherly tone never failed to make Taylin feel deep affection.

She smelled of lavender and baked bread—of home. Taylin, glad of the distraction, looped an arm over her shoulder and gave her a side hug. "I texted Popi over an hour ago to let him know I was coming. Where is he? I expected him to be hanging around waiting for me like usual, or here having breakfast? I know it's been two months since I was last home, but..." he swept a hand towards the empty room, "I've never known my dad's to break from routine."

Bessie's giggle was definitely naughty, as was the light in her blue eyes. "Your daddies... well, they... aren't behaving... like themselves," she finished, looking anywhere but at Taylin.

His smile disappeared. "What do you mean? Is their retirement because of something else? Something serious?" He didn't need to tighten his stomach muscles this time, they did it all on their own as fear crawled through him at thoughts they might not have been honest about their reasons for retiring.

"No, silly boy. I'm meaning they've had a... *new lease of life...* if you catch my drift?"

This time she met his gaze and Taylin realized exactly why she was flustered. Relief flooded through him, and his lips twitched. "Oh, you mean—"

"Yes, you don't need to be going and sayin' such things, Master Taylin. Now, let's change the subject." She bustled him out of the room and towards the kitchen. "I take it you'll be wanting my pancakes for breakfast?"

Fleetingly feeling like the fourteen-year-old boy she had mothered, he grinned and nodded. "You know it's my most favorite part of coming home." He kissed the top of her silky hair and inhaled her familiar scent, letting it help settle him.

Her arms came around his waist, and she hugged him hard. "You were always the sweetest boy."

Emotions caused his throat to clog, making it hard to swallow when an ache developed at the back of his eyes. She'd always had the ability to make him demonstrative, much like Popi. He hugged her back, careful not to squeeze too hard. He sniffed and blinked back the moisture forming at the corner of his eyes.

"It's good to be home, Bessie," he murmured softly, meaning every word.

Several hours later, Taylin wasn't so sure that statement still held with Booker, Silas, Kodi, Kari, and Rue's arrival. The house was noisy and nothing like his own peaceful apartment.

His dads had finally come out of their bedroom, reeking of sex, about two hours ago… it was disconcerting when Taylin wasn't sure how he felt to be home and two doors down from their room. Something Silas had pointed out not so kindly when he arrived three hours after Taylin and their dads hadn't put in an appearance.

Taylin wasn't the only one struggling with this new dynamic. Booker had spent quite some time staring sullenly at the twins, who'd arrived together. None of them had all lived in the same space for over fifteen years. Silas and Booker were the first two to leave, quickly followed by Taylin and Jupiter, the others following suit soon after, leaving Popi with an empty nest.

Popi eyed the bickering men around him with an indulgent smile. Taylin, on the other hand, wasn't feeling so indulgent and pondered if he'd made a mistake leasing the apartment he had bought several years ago, aiming for independence. He wasn't sure how he felt to be—even temporarily—left here with his brothers in such close proximity.

He loved them, would fight to his last breath to protect them, but sitting listening to their bitching... that was a big ask, even for him.

"Is this how it's going to be until we can all find places to live? If so, then I'm thinking a hotel has got to be better than hearing Booker and Silas argue just because they're in the same room. Or listen to Kodi, Kari and Rue bitch about Hollis's assignment of permanent PAs to them," he stated, unsure anyone would hear him over the din in the room.

They'd all received a group email from Hollis at four-fifty-five pm on Friday advising who they would work closely with for the transition home and to aid with the added responsibility of running the company together. A true hit and run if ever there was one and Taylin had to smile at Hollis realizing it was probably the only way to escape questions until Monday, giving his brothers time to cool down.

Silas jabbed a finger in Taylin's direction, a scowl gracing his handsome features. "I've got a ranch to run, and being here isn't conducive to doing that, especially when I get the newbie. What's his name?"

"Ziggy. His name is Ziggy and darling, he's going to be an asset to you, you'll see," Popi supplied, his head resting on Dad's wide shoulder, looking relaxed and unconcerned by the conversation. Dad intertwined his fingers with the hand Popi rested on his thigh. The move was casual, yet it demonstrated a level of connection that Taylin had witnessed a thousand times. A connection he one day hoped to have with...

"What kind of name is Ziggy, anyway? Is it even real?" Booker's comment broke through Taylin's thoughts.

Booker got up and walked to the roaring fire in the massive fireplace, lowering himself right in front of it on the thick rug. One Popi had bought when he noticed how Booker liked to nest in front of the fire. When home, it was Booker's favorite place to make himself comfortable. The sweats and T-shirt strained to fit his enormous frame as he stretched out.

Popi had worked with designers to create a clothes line for men like Booker when, as a teenager, they'd struggled to find anything to fit him. A bear shifter, Booker was the same size in both forms. Though part of what drew folks' attention to Booker was his size, it was his dark, styled hair, chiseled features, and magnetizing, gray-green eyes that got the most attention. He could have modeled but attracting that kind of attention always made his brother uncomfortable. It never failed to secretly amuse Taylin that such a big alpha could blush like a schoolgirl when folks stared at him for too long.

"Yes, it's his real name," Lane said, with an indulgent tone.

"Whatever his name is, I've got more balls to juggle than the rest of you," Silas snapped with enough bite to get Dad to give him a stern look. "It's true," he continued, the anger a little less noticeable but there in the tightness of his clenched jaw and the tension rolling off him.

"We all have lives outside the company," Kodi pointed out, his blond brows arching as he rubbed at the designer beard that was trimmed to frame his jawline. "Some of us just don't bitch about it like others."

As blood brothers, the twins and Silas could and would get into more arguments than with their adoptive brothers.

Taylin settled back, getting ready to watch the fireworks he didn't want to be in the way of, or the fallout when one of those fiery sparks hit a target. Anyone could go up in smoke when they started on each other. Taylin absently rubbed at the scar on his left wrist from when he'd stepped in to stop a fight between Kodi and Silas, only to be the one with a wolf bite, courtesy of Kodi.

"Boys, behave!" Dad growled, his alpha power bringing silence to the room. The only sound was that of the wood crackling on the fire. He shifted forward in his seat, getting a grimace from Popi, who had to move his head. "I understand that this is a big change for you all." He paused, aiming a pointed stare first at Silas, then Kodi before his gaze swept the room. "That being said, you are no longer rambunctious teenagers who need to learn how to behave. Get a fucking grip and act like the men I raised to take on new challenges without fear."

Lane grinned at them all. "The PAs are there to help you. They'll be the making of you all, mark my words."

Taylin searched Popi's expression when he got an odd feeling in the pit of his stomach at how—pleased—*smug* he sounded.

What did he mean 'they'll be the making of them'?

Arching a brow at the uneasy feeling settling inside him, Taylin glanced at his brothers to see if any of them noticed anything off with Popi's comment.

Only Kari met his gaze with a worried frown. At the questioning look that developed as Kari continued to hold Taylin's stare, Taylin shrugged, not sure how to answer the unspoken question. Popi wasn't into random statements.

Taylin shifted his gaze to Popi, the odd feeling they were missing something increasing. Was this another change they'd need to adapt to?

He released a pent up sigh.

Only time would tell...

Chapter Five

Hollis

Hollis shuffled the papers in front of him before slipping them into the file he'd spent hours preparing for the upcoming meeting. One he'd scheduled after deciding to send out the PA assignments first, to give the alphas time to digest the decisions he'd made. Or rather, give them time to calm their asses down.

He'd done that on Friday then put his out of office on his email and work phone. A smile teased his lips at how that got Lane texting him privately with a thumbs up at the move. It had been decided, during the formal dinner Derick and Lane invited him to on Friday evening so that he could formally accept the position, that he would keep them in the loop until he was satisfied things were working as they should be. They'd both been supportive and they were going to keep this bit of information to themselves. Hollis was happy with that as he didn't want to make a dick of himself.

He also didn't like surprises so he'd gotten approval from both men and now he was 'going in prepared for battle'. He nodded his head at his empty office as he rose. Checking his suit jacket sat properly and that his shirt and tie were as they should be, he gave another nod of approval. He looked like a professional. Creases were not acceptable, not when he wanted to project an air of confidence.

'Show no weakness.' Lane's words rang through his mind as he tucked the file under his arm and exited his office.

On the same floor as the other PAs', his office was situated closest to the lift. He sighed in relief when he didn't encounter anyone. That would come later, once they figured out who they'd been assigned too. Something he'd not shared as yet, knowing he'd not escape the inquisition before his nine-thirty meeting in the boardroom. And if he knew his foe they might insist on changes. Ones Hollis was adamant wouldn't be happening!

His fingers tapped absently on the file tucked under his arm, his thoughts on everything he'd decided upon as he entered the lift. Up to this point, the PAs were allocated on a needs basis, based on who was available. Hollis decided that wasn't going to work when all the brothers were now at head office. He was aware some, like Silas, had other investments that required some of their time to be utilized in the working week. Working on that principle, he'd decided—for good or bad—that each brother needed a designated PA to prevent a catch up game for the PA and the alpha. It made total sense to him and Lane had beamed so happily when he'd suggested it, Hollis felt he was off to a good start.

Although he wasn't stupid enough to consider that the brothers wouldn't be testy with him and by extension, the PAs he managed. To circumvent some of the issues early on, he had given much thought over the weekend on how to handle the meeting he was about to have with the brothers.

What he'd avoided thinking about was Taylin and how it made total sense for him to be assigned to him.

You are so silly. He'll know you don't want him anywhere near Frey!

It was hard not to snap aloud in the empty lift when it came to a stop and the doors opened to reveal the man in question stood a few feet away.

Hollis's scowl was all for his animal but got aimed at Taylin, whose smile dimmed when he noticed who was in the lift and gazed at his face. Hollis resisted the temptation to explain something that would only make him sound foolish, and clutched the file tighter.

It was then he registered how handsome Taylin looked as his gaze swept over the handsome man. Oh, where's the CPR machine! Hollis's throat made a clicking sound as he gulped. Then, gathering himself, he plastered on a professional smile.

"Morning," Hollis murmured, pleased when his voice didn't have a tremor to it, despite his insides quaking at how well the charcoal suit fit Taylin's broad frame. Or how the array of brown, tumbled curls framed his gorgeous face. His jaw held a hint of dark stubble and highlighted its squareness as eyes not quite blue or gray got crinkly lines at the edges. They revealed Taylin's amusement when he stepped aside, and Hollis took more than a few seconds to gather himself while licking at his dry lips.

The elevator door starting to shut brought him to his senses and he stepped out blushing furiously, nearly getting sideswiped by the doors.

"Morning Hollis. I like those new frames. They are much like the ones you wore for your interview."

Taylin's husky voice brought him up short, and he answered without thinking. "My animal broke the arm of my main pair, so I had to use my spares."

Taylin took hold of his elbow in a move that was both sweet and sexy, to guide him down the carpeted hallway towards the boardroom. A fluttered feeling in Hollis's stomach was joined by the urge to lean into the touch and get a better smell of Taylin's scent. Yet, another part of him wanted to yank away like he had gotten burned, trying to figure out what Taylin's game was.

"Why did he break them?"

At the genuine interest, Hollis' feet faltered, a smile tugging on the corner of his lips at how sulky his animal had gotten. "Because I had restricted his fruit consumption."

The hand never moved from the crook of his arm and heat was spreading to places it had no business going when they entered the boardroom.

"Why'd you do that?" Taylin asked, sounding curious despite his chuckling.

Hollis forgot himself at the weight of Taylin's gaze when they came to a stop. The intensity of his focus on Hollis had sparks of excitement ride on the train heading south.

"Getting in early I see, brother, to make sure Hollis is swayed to vote for you, hey?" Booker asked, jarring Hollis from his daydream that the attraction between was real and not just one sided.

A further blush deepened the heat coating Hollis's cheeks and made sure no one missed his discomfort. He tugged his arm free and stepped away, doing his best to keep his head up and his spine straight at having gotten so spectacularly caught ogling Taylin in front of... all his brothers.

Great start! He chastised himself when it registered all the other brothers were seated around the boardroom table, entertaining themselves at Hollis's expense.

That would never do.

Spine stiffer than a metal rod, he strode to his seat and placed his file down in front of him. He gave himself a few seconds pulling out copies of what he'd outlined for the meeting. He looked at Silas first as he was directly to his left and offered the sheath of papers. "This is the outline for the meeting. You'll see that I've highlighted in each the PAs' skills and experience—"

"Yeah, let's start there! What's this crap about the allocations." This came from Jupiter.

Hollis continued on like he'd not so rudely been interrupted. He'd deal with Jupiter later, and kept his thoughts about why Jupiter was ready to protest to himself.

He was aware that Jupiter had a preference to work with Frey. He was almost sure that they'd been intimate, but that was none of his business as long as Frey did his job. "I've matched each PA to your area of expertise. It makes more sense when your workloads will increase from now on."

"How will it help when I have to keep explaining things!" Booker growled, clearly remembering his past run in with Hollis about this same thing when he'd gotten Wilder one week then Isley the next. This was why this would be better for all of them long term, *if they gave him a damn chance to explain.*

He turned to Booker, feeling the sting of anger as he gave Hollis a hard eyed stare that was something Hollis had trained himself not to turn away from. "If you let me finish? This will keep that from happening—"

"Unless they have a heat." The comment from Kodi got an indrawn breath from where Taylin was seated.

Hollis didn't look away from Kodi and held up his hand when Rue gritted out, "That's a low fucking blow, Kodi."

"No, it's a valid point and as Kodi has had call to have issues with this before, I've given you all access to the calendar that the omegas use to show what days they won't be available to you."

His gaze traveled around the table, making sure to hold each man's stare. He wasn't embarrassed, more uncomfortable talking about something so personal but it was something they needed to talk about, despite the accusatory tone in which it had been said.

"Accessing the calendar will allow you to plan around those absences. If there is an issue, then you will need to let me know and I'll work to find a solution that works for you."

Silas squirmed in his seat and Kari slumped next to Kodi, who still didn't look convinced. Hollis continued to lay out how things were going to work from now on. This was his area of expertise and Lane entrusted him to make it work. And by heck, he would.

There were no more interruptions until he got to the part involving the vote he'd need to make if they couldn't decide.

"Now, I suggest a board meeting once a month to discuss any upcoming decisions that impact beyond your own areas."

"Who died and put you in charge?" Laken muttered.

"Powers gone to his head!" Kari said at the same time.

Taylin pushed back his chair with enough force it rocked as he stood, his hands forming into fists that he shoved into his trouser pockets. "Give the fuck over. He's only trying to figure out the best way to get us to work together."

He might as well have been talking double Dutch because Hollis's gaze was eye level with Taylin's crotch, where his slacks were emphasizing the bulge of his cock.

A groan inadvertently slipped out.

"Something caught your attention, Hollis?" Rue's voice held a wealth of amusement and snapped through Hollis's thoughts. A surge of heat ran from his toes right through to his ears at super-fast speed.

"Yes! That we are losing track of what's important."

"Taylin's cock," Booker murmured quietly, but Hollis and the others never missed it.

It was hard to resist looking at Taylin to see his reaction, but he managed to keep his expression neutral—as much as anyone could with a radiator heating his face—and rose slowly.

"I can make this process easy or I can make it hard. The decision is yours." Hollis scooped up the papers and shoved them into the file with hands that weren't quite steady.

"You had to open your big mouth, Booker," Taylin stated in a flat tone. "We're sorry Hollis."

He didn't acknowledge the apology with how hard it was to gauge Taylin's overall feelings about what had happened. He swung on his heel to a deafening silence and marched to the door. He paused, glancing back and got a smug feeling at the shocked expressions.

"When you're willing to stop behaving like spoiled children, then and only then will I arrange another meeting. Until then, my time is too valuable to waste on you."

He left, his heart hammering against his ribs in a fast tattoo, heading to Monica. He needed to hide out and regroup because he'd *just stood up to eight alphas and survived.*

Ignoring the fact you got caught ogling Taylin's cock.

"Oh, shut up!"

Chapter Six

Group Chat – Cake & Vent

Three days later…

***Frey:** Has anyone seen what Jupiter is wearing? You'd think he was getting ready to go out and party rather than work and he smells like he fell in a bucket of aftershave. EWW*

Bowie: *More like he didn't go home last night and has come to work in his pulling gear.*

Ziggy: *Seriously, pulling gear? What decade are you in Bowie?*

Bowie: *Don't we call it 'pulling gear' anymore? Why doesn't anyone tell me these things? Oh, and by the way, I left a box of brownies in the coffee room. I'm trying out a new recipe. Can you let me know what you think?*

Frey: *Yay for chocolate. I need some after the morning I've had with mr snippy pants who can't find his way out of the tiniest paper sack when looking for anything. When did alphas forget to look with their eyes and not with their hands?*

Frey: *Did you add the cherries like last time and leave out the nuts? You know I hate them.*

Isley: *Hands? Who's using his hands? Booker? And you are such a fibber! You love some nuts in your mouth… or on your chin… in fact, anywhere…*

Frey: *Pleaseeee… did you have to lower the tone Isley?*

Hollis: *You haven't forgotten I can see this, right? Don't you lot have work to do? Or is it more productive to talk about Frey's nuts?*

***Wilder**: Wasn't me…*

***Hollis**: But you are looking at your phone!*

***Isley**: We are all multitaskers It's what makes us so good at our jobs, and it's not gossip if it's true. We all know how much Frey loves nuts to nibble on, and not just his own.*

***Ziggy**: WTF! Frey, can you suck your own balls????*

***Frey**: That's a bit personal don't you think, Ziggy?*

***Ziggy**: Sorry…*

***Bowie**: Ignore him. He told us within weeks of him being with the company and he proved how flexible he was at an unforgettable Christmas party… don't ask how. I'm still traumatized!*

***Frey**: You're just jealous you can't reach your own junk with your mouth.*

***Hollis**: ENOUGH! I can't bleach my eyes. Now stop chatting and get to work… and thank you Bowie for the brownies. It's much appreciated when it was my turn to make cake and I forgot.*

Bowie: *You have been a little stressed these last few days, I noticed. Don't worry, we got you covered. Don't we guys?*

Frey: *Yep.*

Isley: *Always.*

Wilder: *Defo! Bowie you remember I prefer fruit based cake?*

Ziggy: *is it my turn next? I said before I can't bake for shit and wouldn't want to poison anyone. I'll buy stuff from the bakery close to me. And I think my idea that this group chat should change to*

Delicious & Vicious PAs is defo the way to go with what we talk about in here!

***Lane**: I love that Ziggy, Cake & Chats doesn't quite have the same ring as Delicious & Vicious PAs*

***Ziggy**: Ohhhh… Sorry if I've o…fended you.*

***Lane**: You'll soon figure out that what I say I mean, Ziggy. You need to go back as far as the chat allows and see I'm as bad as everyone else. Now I think I'll pop in for some of those brownies. Bowie, can you send me the recipe too?*

***Bowie**: Done!*

***Hollis**: WORK PLEASE!*

***Lane**: Oops, sorry Hollis, my bad!*

Chapter Seven

Taylin

“We need to consider a different supplier for the innovative designs that Booker sent through to me for the accessories, shoes, belts, and bags. The intricate design on the leather needs hand tooling and our current supplier doesn’t have the Artisans to do the level of detail we’ll need.”

Taylin blew out a frustrated breath at the extra workload Booker was causing for his department in less than a damn week. “Josh, the manager at Cross Leathers, the firm we usually use, emailed this morning and recommended a couple of smaller firms for us to potentially use. They focus on bespoke pieces. I’ve forwarded the email to you.”

Taylin turned his attention to the divine smelling man opposite his desk. His hair swept back more than usual, Hollis’s glasses were a navy frame today—suggesting he’d still not had his glasses fixed—adding something to the look of a professional businessperson. “If you could reach out to them and arrange on-site meetings, that would be great. We need to see their operation firsthand before we can make any concrete decisions on who we should consider, if any."

When Hollis never so much as spared him a glance, Taylin's lips thinned.

To distract himself, he picked up his tablet to make a note to speak to Booker about coming on the trip with him, not sure he'd remember otherwise. Because he needed his brother to see just what a mess he was causing by insisting on this specific designer for their new spring range. "I've expressed my concern about these designs and its impact on my division, but Booker isn't listening!"

"Yes, Sir."

Taylin ground his back molars. Hollis's damn polite tone sounded like he had developed a nasal problem with how stuffy he came across, but Taylin kept his snippy remark to himself. It was all his brothers' fault for goading him at the meeting on Monday. There was a standoff going on and Taylin had his money on Hollis winning. He just hated that he'd not noticed if Hollis had indeed been looking at him like his brothers ribbed him about after the man had left. Granted, there had been a brief pause while they all recovered from Hollis's parting threat.

Taylin had had to sit down to avoid anyone seeing his reaction to Hollis being all bossy. He had no clue he liked that sort of thing, but with Hollis it was very appealing!

Since the flirting with Frey incident—and in Taylin's defense, he'd only done it because of what he'd overheard and subsequently hadn't been able to clarify if Hollis was indeed dating someone—Hollis had used this particular tone when referencing him directly. Was it because of the meeting or the 'Frey encounter'?

Quite the conundrum for Taylin, when it could be either. As he placed his tablet down with care, he ran his hands through his hair and tugged hard enough to distract himself once more—a habit that was possibly going to make him bald—when instead of working, he was tempted to grab hold of...

Stop that line of thought right now!

Shouting at himself? Yeah, this was a whole other level of exasperation after a week with Hollis looking and smelling so damn tempting. Right now, Taylin wasn't sure if he wanted to punch something or kiss Hollis until he surrendered. Both vied for equal attention, not that Hollis appeared to notice any of his frustrations.

Am I that good an actor?

Hollis finally deemed him worthy of a glance as he shifted his attention from his lap where the tablet upon which he'd been making his own notes sat. The navy-rimmed glasses perched on his nose had slid down and Taylin suspected sexy wasn't the look Hollis was going for, but those big doe brown eyes peering up at him made his groin tighten and arousal swirl through the pit of his stomach.

Back was an irresistible itch—that was never far away—to yank the other man over his desk and kiss him until he saw sense.

Taylin looked away first. Kissing Hollis until he moaned Taylin's name, the same as he did in his vivid dreams, really wasn't on today's agenda.

It should be! exclaimed his animal side.

Give me strength or I swear I'll find a way to mute you.

With the dreams becoming increasingly frequent because of his wolf's spirit feeding Taylin's desire to make a move, it was making Hollis's closeness daily torture.

"Do you want me to invite Rue and Kodi as well? This is going to influence the launch of the spring range and we need to know we can source the materials needed, too."

Taylin got up and stalked around his desk, stomping to the window, seeing nothing, only the extensive list of problems that were already giving him a headache when added to his own personal dilemma.

"How the fuck did Dad do this and make it appear so effortless?" Taylin didn't wait for Hollis to respond as he spun back, his annoyance driving him to suggest, "Add Booker to the list to stop any complaining. From what I've seen in our joint calendar, towards the end of next week looks better for us all to travel—"

"Us?" Hollis squeaked, pushing up his glasses, a nervous habit Taylin recognized after years of observing the other man when no one was watching.

He stepped to the chair Hollis was sitting in to rest his hands on the leather arms, caging the other man in, throwing caution to the wind with his scent driving him to distraction as he inhaled. Taylin came close enough that when Hollis gasped, he scented the coffee he had drunk earlier and something sweet he must have eaten, his breath hitting Taylin's lips.

Their gaze met and something flickered in Hollis's eyes, then was gone before Taylin could assess what it was. "Why yes, *us*. This is part of a PAs role and as you assigned yourself as my personal PA, you get to travel with me."

His grin was predatory, because that was significantly better than a pathetic begging look, when that's more how he felt. "This means you'll be there *to assist me with whatever I need...*" The pause was very deliberate, wanting to get a rise from Hollis. Anything was better than 'politeness'.

Hollis's pupils dilated behind his glasses and his chest moved as fast as a hummingbird's wings. What could have been desire or...

Taylin wasn't sure what, and right then guessing wasn't an option with his wolf pushing at him, so he didn't.

A shiver ran down his spine at how his wolf surged with force, making him vibrate at being so close to Hollis. Taylin swallowed hard enough they could hear his gulp in the office's silence. Tension thickened the air the longer they held each other's stare. He scented... *arousal.* The sweet scent wasn't Taylin's.

Hollis is aroused!

Fuck! He's into me!

As it registered, his pounding pulse increased to supersonic speed. His tongue ran over his drying lips, a move Hollis tracked. A delicate flush appeared over the bridge of his nose, which flared.

Taylin faltered for a second, trying to bring his thoughts back to the thread of the conversation. "When it comes to business, you know that *includes travel*," he stressed, then realized he was repeating himself, noting Hollis's brow furrow.

For the first time in days, Taylin felt some amusement at the confused look Hollis now wore. Had he also lost the thread of conversation?

Hollis's facial armor—one that Taylin had grown to recognize and hate—slipped into place. For now, Taylin took that as a win because it proved that beside the scent, Hollis was working to hide his reaction to Taylin. He moved back, reminding himself he wasn't an aggressor and that diving in to kiss lush, tempting lips would only create a problem for both of them.

Sink your teeth into him and taste his sweetness, his wolf snarled. *Do it!*

Those same teeth ached in his gums, and it took sheer determination to not overstep when his pushy fucker wolf side made demands. The sweet smelling arousal filling Taylin's office heightened his wolf's baser need, making the large office feel he had no room to move—to breathe.

Hollis's head dipped and he stared fixedly at his tablet, his cheeks remaining a delectable shade of pink. Taylin desperately wanted to cup them and feel the warmth against his palms.

I'll not take what isn't offered freely! He added more for his benefit than for his pushy wolf side.

An angry growl was the response before his wolf began pacing inside his mind. *Then figure out how to get him to offer it freely before—*

There's no 'before' here. I'm in charge, not you, and he has to want us before I'll bite him and claim him the way you want.

We want.

"—so as I said I hadn't updated that part of the calendar, so I can't come. The other PAs can fill in for my absence and assist you."

Taylin's thoughts shifted back to Hollis as the man rose and his words registered.

"What... wait... no!" he barked, then took a breath to get himself back under control, pushing aside thoughts of losing out on the opportunity to have a trip with Hollis in the hopes they might spend some of their down time together... maybe a dinner out.

Hollis was clearly trying to wrangle out of it and Taylin could only guess at what excuse he'd come up with, having missed that part of the conversation while arguing with his wolf side.

See what you did, he snapped.

What would be a valid enough reason not to come with him? He rifled through reasons that popped into his head to prevent Hollis from traveling with him. Coming up with nothing that would warrant it, he stared at the man hovering in the middle of his office. Was this a 'boyfriend' thing?

Not liking that idea at all, an idea took root. His father had always looked at ways to keep traveling costs down. A suite would have separate bedrooms, yet still give Taylin closer contact with Hollis.

"Book four suites. One for us, Booker, Rue and Kodi and their PAs. I need you with me, and I'm sure we'll cope with whatever issues arise. *Together.*" He added the latter, hoping it would maybe tempt Hollis from his excuse—whatever it was. Happy he'd covered all his bases, he grinned.

"Seriously?" Hollis said, eyes popping wide. "You... want... me there... when..."

He didn't let Hollis finish, seeing no point in arguing when, in his mind, it was a done deal.

"Of course I do. I'm sure everything will be fine." He waved off the ridiculous idea they wouldn't be able to cope.

Taylin returned to his seat, feeling it was safer for some reason when Hollis, whose animal half had two tongues, they popped out of his mouth, licking at both corners of his lips at the same time. Another spike of arousal shot through Taylin, his mind heading straight for the gutter.

Hollis's tongues were a source of endless hours of speculation about the sexy things they could do at the same time.

"*Fine*... why..." Hollis' knuckles turned white, and he got a thoughtful look that actually made Taylin wary before he muttered, "Let's hope you're prepared because you have no idea what you're letting yourself in for!" His head snapped forward, eyes flashing a warning that Taylin couldn't grasp. "You've been warned."

On that, Hollis clamped his tablet to his immaculate navy suit jacket and, head held high, he sailed out of Taylin's office without a backward look, the door shutting with a definitive click.

"Prepared? Warned? What the fuck does he mean by that?" he spoke to the empty room, getting a tight feeling at the base of his neck that suggested he'd missed something vital.

Something important.

He stared at the closed door, stubbornly refusing to go after Hollis to ask what he meant after finally hoping he had a chance to break through the other man's barriers by sharing a space outside of the office for a few days.

Instead, he reached for his phone, opening up his WhatsApp to click on *Alphaholes* group chat. A chuckle tickled the back of his throat at Julian's last attempt to come up with a name that fitted them all.

Julian had created the group chat, saying it was too tiresome to individually message each one when he wanted to ask something that maybe one or more of his other brothers could help with. This name had stuck the longest because Jupiter had explained he'd overheard one of the PAs had called them Alphaholes—they'd called Julian Alphahole because none of the brothers were stupid not to know it wasn't them they were referring to. It was kind of funny in a weird sort of way, so instead of ragging on Jupiter for it, Taylin simply referred to it as the Alpha chat. It meant far fewer questions to answer when it got mentioned in polite conversation. The one time he had tried to explain it, he'd given up trying to explain Jupiter's sense of humor, which turned out to be an impossible task.

Alphaholes Chat

***Taylin**: Have any of you heard of any reason Hollis doesn't want to travel with me? And Booker you are a pain in my ass with your demands, so what's coming is all your fault!*

***Booker**: Christ Tay, why can't you just jump his bones and be done with it? You're pining worse than Jup did when he mooned over that skinny, cross-eyed Twink who took Milan by storm last year. And what the fuck are you moaning about? Is this to do with the impromptu trip that's just got added to my calendar?*

***Jupiter**: Fuck right off. And I mean all the fucks away, you jealous asshole. He was not cross-eyed! And I never moon. Not unless it's over a fit man who might want to eat my ass.*

***Rue**: Gross! And that explains the added trip to my calendar I can ill afford. Booker, is this your fault?*

***Jupiter**: It's only gross cause you ain't getting any little bro.*

***Rue**: How would you know what I'm getting?*

***Jupiter**: I've got eyes and ears…*

***Taylin**: Could you two stop having a pissing match for a second and answer my question?*

***Silas**: Ask Monica, she's his best friend. And I'm kinda with Booker, just ride him for a while then get off when his ass aches.*

***Taylin**: Silas what the fuck man… ride him… you've been at that ranch too long or it's Jup's influence! I'm not sure which* *is worse. But I blame you all for what happened on Monday! He won't even give me the time of day.*

***Jupiter**: Fuck, don't do the best friend thing. It'll come across as sadsville and desperate. About time I rubbed off on one of you*

***Silas**: Christ Jup, that's even low for you. Do not listen to Jup for dating advice.*

***Jupiter**: Why? Is that cause I'm always right… and I wasn't the one who said to ride him till his ass aches!*

***Kodi**: First, why am I getting dragged on a trip away too? And second, always right! Jup, you have a short memory, bro. I seem to remember a time you were very wrong and got your ass thrown in jail overnight and if Dad hadn't saved you, you'd have been ass fodder for all the big* *hairy alphas who wanted to play hide the sausage.*

Taylin: *I'd forgotten about that……*

Jupiter: *You can keep on forgetting it! I thought you wanted to know if anyone had any gossip about Hollis?*

Taylin: *Now you wanna change the topic of conversation. you hate to be called out. Rue and Kodi take it up with Booker, he's been the difficult one and insisting on using the designs our current manufacturers aren't skilled for.*

Booker: …

Jupiter: *You hate it when Hollis smiles at me… I might need to get an invite on your little trip just to show you.*

Silas: *Stop winding him up Jup, or I'll prove that Wilder prefers to ride cow-boys!*

Rue: *What wait… what am I missing here?*

Taylin: *Yeah, what's this?*

Jupiter: *Nothing!*

***Kodi**: Nothing, my cute little ass. You got the hots for our little raccoon? This is news. I thought it was our little fox you were…*

***Booker:** Yeah… what the fuck Jup?*

***Jupiter**: Give the fuck over. There is no ours. Now shall we get back to Tay's problem? Some of us actually have a ton of work to get done by the end of the day.*

***Taylin**: So, has anyone heard anything relating to Hollis dating?*

Chapter Eight
Hollis

Out of the office door, Hollis took a deep breath of air that wasn't contaminated by Taylin's fruity scent. The arousal in the air was not all Taylin's, and it had been hard to think straight with him looming over him. Hollis had somehow lost the thread of the conversation. Maybe they both had because Hollis was sure as flies like shit Taylin hadn't got what Hollis had been talking about.

Letting go of his breath, Hollis stomped down the corridor, away from the temptation to go back into the office and act unprofessional in the workplace. Something that he'd never considered possible until this last week, working so closely with Taylin.

Hollis had lofty theories about how he'd cope being around Taylin for more than a few days. A week in and his own need was there, stinking up Taylin's office. Screaming "let's get down and dirty" like Hollis had taken up a new career as a cowboy, seeking an alpha to ride!

He scowled at himself for his body's betrayal.

Taylin was—

Acting like his usual sexy self, supplied his animal helpfully.

It was getting worse. His animal was getting out of control. He knew it, but there was little he could do about it when he had to spend so much time in Taylin's company. Now he was demanding Hollis go away with him.

In theory, he knew this was part of the role, but he thought he'd have more time before they'd start taking trips. Time for him to get himself under control.

How would he manage that when he was going through a heat? How had Taylin not understood it really wasn't wise for him to travel at that time?

It wasn't like Taylin was a monster or anything, even if he had gotten a little too in Hollis's space today. He could still feel the warmth from the proximity of his body. So close...

You assigned yourself to him. Getting close was always your goal, his animal side said in a bored tone, showing just how over it he was at Hollis denying aloud what they both knew.

I'm the one with needs, Hollis pointed out testily.

I know, so why aren't we getting naked, hmmm?

Easier to direct his thoughts to what had happened in Taylin's office than go six rounds with his other half, Hollis shut out the voice taunting him to face the truth. Had Taylin heard a word he'd said? He had looked to have zoned out. *Was I that boring?* It wouldn't be the first time someone had accused him of being boring.

When that thought didn't sit so well with him, he shut it out too and went back to his original concerns. Okay, maybe he hadn't exactly spelled out what the issue was, but still, telling Taylin he'd be 'indisposed for three days' starting Sunday next week should have been clear enough. Shouldn't it?

His free hand rubbed at the renewed vein throbbing at his temple. If there was ever a time when one might consider a head could explode, Hollis reckoned he was the perfect candidate to watch. His skull actually hurt at how hard his brain pounded with all the thoughts running through his mind. Disbelief warred with common sense and a need to go back and check exactly what Taylin meant by *'we'll deal with whatever issues'*.

The response from his animal and the plumping going on with a certain part of his anatomy suggested they'd like Taylin's help... a lot.

He groaned, his grip tightening on his tablet until he heard a cracking sound and realized he'd reached his destination without noticing how he'd gotten to his office.

Inside, he went to his desk and deposited his tablet after checking he'd not caused any actual damage except to the case. He breathed a sigh of relief and took his seat. He purposefully set about starting on the list he needed to tackle for organizing the trip, doing his best to keep his attention from how snug his slacks were. He was the ultimate professional, he prided himself on it. Yet, for a moment, in Taylin's office—and if he was honest with himself, much longer than that—he wanted to jump over the highly polished, neat desk onto his boss's lap and show him...

So not going to happen!

Work, this is a working establishment!

His groin tightened to the point of pain at where his thoughts were determined to remain. Hollis's hands quivered as he typed into the calendar for the meeting appointments. Then he rang the first of the two companies to arrange the visits, followed by the second one. Next, he moved on to confirm the use of the company jet and finally sorting the accommodation they needed.

Suites!

This was going to be a disaster, and not just for him and Taylin. The other PAs were going to have a hissy fit when they found out they were going to be sharing a suite with their assigned alpha. Hollis resigned himself to the fallout and that he had no one to blame but himself for all of it.

You could have insisted you couldn't go.

The voice of reason got blocked out because Hollis was more than aware Taylin wouldn't force him if he had actually explained his problem better. He had no one but himself to blame...sort of...maybe.

Taking longer than it normally would to have everything in place, Hollis found he couldn't settle when his head continued to pound with erratic thoughts. Deciding he needed a sensible voice of reason—clearly not his own—he shut down his computer and rose.

He headed out of his office only to find himself confronted by Wilder, who wore a look of pain with how screwed up his face was. His usual cute smile was nowhere to be seen and his short, cropped curls were in disarray, like he'd spent hours tugging at his hair.

Jupiter!

Hollis didn't sigh, he didn't see the point in wasting his energy. "What did he do now?" Hollis didn't even bother to say the man's name. Wilder had been in his office no less than six times since he'd been assigned Jupiter, to complain about one thing or another.

Balled fists went in a wide arc, which resulted in Hollis ducking back, before they landed on skinny hips covered in tight fitting, red slacks. "What hasn't he done? He keeps sending me on damn errands and getting me to contact his boyfriends. I am not a pimp!"

Hollis bit the inside of his cheek at the overly dramatic way Wilder spoke. The raccoon was cheeky and often wore a cute expression that made others give in to him. It seemed Jupiter wasn't one of them.

One time Hollis had gone to visit Wilder when he wasn't well, and he got greeted by his animal wearing a bright pink onesie. Somehow Hollis had ended up peeling fruit and feeding it to Wilder while he sat in a baby rocking seat. Hollis still couldn't figure out how it had happened.

For now, he suspected that Wilder's frustration came because he wasn't getting the attention he liked from Jupiter. Although he wasn't going to point that out when he didn't want anyone saying anything about his situation with Taylin.

"Explain your role to him and follow it up with your terms of employment. You only have to work within those. If he's being unreasonable after that, I'll speak with him."

Wilder's expression brightened, the thundercloud that had seemed to hover over his head now gone. "I knew you'd have the answer. There is nothing in my contract that says I have to run around after his… play things!" He beamed at Hollis and blew him an air kiss. "You're so good at this."

Without another comment, Wilder swung around on his sparkly sneakers and waltzed off back the way he'd come.

Glad to have helped someone, Hollis headed to the elevator, then decided against it and went to the fire escape to take the stairs up to Monica's office, to avoid potentially running into anyone else.

He needed some common sense beaten into him so he could get a grip on himself. That, however, didn't stop him from circling back once more to why he hadn't made a stand in Taylin's office when he should have.

Had Taylin lost his goddamn mind, or was that him? Maybe the scent of Taylin had removed a part of his brain function. A scent lobotomy? Probably both for Hollis to consider traveling and staying in a hotel during his omega heat.

An omega's heats normally started when they hit twenty, which was full maturity for an omega. His heats, mostly, were predictable in two-month cycles, and he planned his work schedule accordingly. He had everything he needed at his house to get him through. His bedroom came with extra paneled walls to stop his scent escaping and his bedside drawers held all manner of toys he could use when the desperation took hold.

It was all he needed. He had never, ever considered using one of the popular clinics that supplied a willing alpha to take care of omegas who didn't have a long-term partner. Hollis didn't think too hard about the reasons behind that or how it would somehow feel wrong.

Cheating... you mean cheating.

Shut up, it's not cheating. We aren't a couple. If I wanted to book into a clinic, I could. I just don't want to.

Change the record. This one is getting boring.

He hissed once more, shutting out the annoying voice in his head.

As it was company policy to allow omegas to take the time off during their heat, Hollis reminded himself there was absolutely nothing stopping him from evoking the policy. *Nothing at all.*

So why hadn't he?

One thing Hollis hated was to feel like he'd gotten pushed into a corner against his will. Was that the only reason he was contemplating this madness? Because it was madness.

Had Taylin any idea what could happen?

What about you? Have you thought about what's going to happen? What if he rejects you?

Taylin was the one insisting on this trip, so rejection seemed way down in the list to worry about. This whole situation was... getting ridiculous?

What if Hollis incited a rut riot?

His blood ran cold at the very notion. Inciting a rut riot with any alpha who scented an omegas heat was not something Hollis considered would be in his top one thousand things he'd do—ever! He'd heard of it happening with omegas. Hell, only four months ago there'd been a reported case in the news of an alpha breaking into a hotel room in a wild rut after scenting an omega.

A strangled moan escaped as he reached Monica's office, trying to shut out images of his hotel door being forced open and Taylin having to fight off another alpha.

He flounced in after knocking and getting a shout of "come in".

Door shut behind him, he waited for Monica to lift her gaze to him before he announced, "I'm having a crisis and I need you to talk some sense into me before I incite a rut and need Taylin to fight off other alphas to protect me from myself."

She sat up a little straighter, flicking her hair onto her shoulder, and grinned widely. "Okay... but you need to explain why Taylin is fighting other alphas. Not that I don't love the idea of a little macho display. I just need all the facts first. Although I'm good with you giving in to temptation and getting to have some fun, if that's what this is about. It's been years, Hollis. Isn't it time to give in to your wild urges?"

Recalling just how bad Monica was at pushing him to step outside his comfort zone, Hollis sighed and flopped down into the leather seat in front of her desk. He could see exactly why he'd come because she wouldn't talk him out of it. She was the only one who witnessed this kind of behavior. "I'm doomed! I want to give in to this madness so badly!"

Her giggle was pure naughtiness. "Good, now spill," she demanded, resting her elbows on her desk and cupping her chin, giving him all her attention. There was an eagerness to her expression that made him groan aloud.

"Taylin has insisted I go away with him when I'm probably going into my heat."

"He's what?" She screeched, loud enough that those four floors below to have heard her.

He wiggled fingers in his ears. "Are you trying to deafen me?"

Up out of her seat, she came around her desk and wriggled in between him and it, crouching in front of him. "Sorry. Of all the things you might have said, that wasn't quite what I had in mind. You'll be in a hotel during your heat?" Hollis nodded. "Wow! That was the last thing I expected you'd want to do. But let's go back a step. Can you tell me how this happened?"

Hollis quickly ran through the conversation with Taylin, skimming over the part where Taylin had looked bored. He didn't need a reminder of that or why he was sure he hadn't pushed his point across.

"So you explained, and he still wants you to go? Wow! I mean, that's a ballsy move to get you"—her brows waggled at him—"into a naked, hot, and steamy situation. I always knew I liked Taylin the best!"

"Can't you take this seriously!" he gasped at her.

"I am. You want this to happen otherwise you'd have told him no, in no uncertain terms. I know you, Hollis."

This was why he'd come to her. She wouldn't let him hide from the truth and wasn't snippy like his animal half about it. "What should I do?" He hated how uncomfortable he already felt at what her response would be.

"This attraction has been simmering between you two for years. It hasn't gone away and judging by how you've been of late, I'd say it's worsened now you're working so closely with him." She placed a hand on his knee and rubbed it reassuringly. "Isn't it time to allow yourself to open up again? Allow him in. He is nothing like your ex. Yes, I know I didn't meet him," she jumped in before Hollis could make that point, like he'd done before. "But from what you've said, Taylin would never set out to dominate and humiliate you the way he did. It's just not who Taylin is." She stood and came to place a soft kiss on his wrinkled brow. "Give him and you the chance to see if you're as compatible as I think you could be... *in every area.*"

The wink she gave him was salacious and downright encouraging. "I bet he's a real demon when his alpha is in a rut."

Back to groaning at how his thoughts went where they had no business going, Hollis chastised her, "Stop that, you dirty minded bat!"

Her teeth gleamed as they dropped and she hissed, "You bet I am!"

"You're a bad influence," laughed Hollis, his bad mood easily turned around by her antics.

She reclaimed her seat, looking unrepentant. "That's why we're best friends. I help you cut loose, and you help curb my wild side."

"Thanks, I think."

When he left Monica, he was still grinning as he headed back to his office. Maybe he needed to cut loose, but was letting Taylin near him in a heat the answer? It was risky with how his animal could misbehave when Hollis had no control.

Seeing his mood was going to tank at just how out of control he'd be, he switched his thoughts to what he could control—work.

Chapter Nine

Taylin

"Have you packed my tablet? I can't seem to find it," Taylin asked Bessie from his position bent over the bedside drawers, where he was sure he'd put it last night.

"It's in your computer case with your laptop, where you asked me to put it not half an hour ago."

Bessie's reply held a wealth of amusement that didn't require him to turn to see her face to know that she was smiling at him. "Sorry, I'm just a little het up and trying to make sure I remember everything I need."

The reason for double and triple checking what he could usually do blind folded with one hand tied behind his back was Hollis. Since their meeting about this trip, his mood had shifted into...well, it was hard to put into words. Equal parts overly excited and terrified seemed to fit. Both were perplexing and left Taylin struggling with how to decide what, if anything, he should do to find out why.

Hollis appeared to have developed a tick at the side of his left eye, along with lips that curled up slightly at the edges. Was it a smile? A grimace?

It was pathetic that at one point, Taylin had convinced himself Hollis smiled at him like they were more than friends, more than boss and employee—and it was freaking Taylin out not knowing if it was real.

Was he reading too much into it? His brothers had been no help—again! This left him floundering, once more getting a feeling he was playing catch up with Hollis over whatever this was they had going on between them.

Now the trip was upon them, and they were leaving this evening and the out-of-control nerves were having a party in his belly and gathering momentum with every second that ticked down.

What should have been a simple trip was now more complicated. They were having to make an additional stop to pick up Rue and his PA in New York where they'd gone for a two day urgent trip to have meetings to sort out a few problems that couldn't wait.

Taylin didn't know the ins and outs, but it sounded like a ball ache for Rue, who'd been exceptionally grumpy in their group chat.

"You're worse than when you got wolf pox and couldn't focus for more than a minute. What's up, Master Taylin?"

Blinking rapidly, he brought his stare to Bessie, seeing an expectant look. It was hard to hold back the sigh of confusion, having possibly missed some of what she'd said. A state he appeared to live in these last few weeks. "Did I miss something, or are we still on the same topic?"

She laughed heartily. "You got a case of 'up inside your head'. I don't suppose it's got anything to do with that nice young Pygmy Loris I've met several times, does it? He's such a polite young man. Handsome too."

Nothing got past Bessie. He twisted to look back at the drawer he was rummaging in, blushing harder than a virgin getting naked for the first time. Or that was how he remembered it when he'd taken that plunge.

"What have you heard?" he mumbled, his hand going inside the drawer and plucking out random stuff while paying no attention, waiting for Bessie to answer.

"Now you know I'm not one to gossip, Master Taylin."

He sensed her 'but' as she paused for dramatic effect and drew his attention to the mischievous housekeeper's twinkling eyes. "But," he supplied, knowing her game as she giggled like a young girl.

"Silas and Booker might have mentioned that you have a particular fancy for Hollis and that you were pining after him."

He choked on his own spit at how she'd phrased it. "Pining! I'm not pining."

"Master Taylin, there is nothing wrong with a little pining over a love."

He blanched at her words. "I never said I loved him!" His voice was several octaves higher than normal, and as if the universe was lobbing bricks at him, Popi chose that moment to come into the room. His brows arched as he looked at Taylin with that knowing stare that suggested he'd heard their conversation and was aware Taylin had out right fibbed.

Popi had a built in bullshit radar, which he'd often put to good use when Taylin had been growing up. He didn't cower or hunch his shoulders, but it was a close call. He was a thirty-five-year-old man, for pity's sake!

"Popi, do you need me for something?" He offered an absentminded smile, aiming to deflect what might come his way. "I'm in a bit of a rush."

Taylin chose then to look at what he was holding and squirmed with embarrassment at the large box of condoms he'd plucked randomly out of the drawer.

Why me!

He dropped them into the open bag on the bed, purely as a reflex to hide them.

Popi chuckled at the move but thankfully didn't bring attention to the box peeking out. "Your car is here. I just came up to say Booker and Kodi are already downstairs and ready to go."

"Shit!" Taylin exclaimed, checking his wristwatch and seeing the time had gotten away from him. He hated to be late.

He eyed his travel bag, rifling through to check he had what he needed, zipped it, and reached for his computer carry case. "Sorry about the mess, Bessie. I'll tidy up when I get back."

"It's fine." She gave him a broad wink. "I like clearing up after my boys."

She bustled about the room, setting it to rights faster than he could as he headed to Popi to give him a kiss on the check. Taylin inhaled the scent of earth and flowers. The familiarity of it settled a little of his nerves. "See you when I get back."

"Make sure and have some fun," Popi murmured so quietly that for a second, when Taylin stepped away, he thought he'd misheard him until he got a load of the goofy grin.

"Work, Popi. I'm going on a working trip."

"Whatever you say, my sweet boy. Whatever you say."

Taylin made a quick exit to escape whatever innuendo Popi was getting at because it caused an inner tension to creep in. Had his brothers been feeding Popi and Bessie gossip about Hollis?

God, he hoped not. None of them were very good at holding their secrets around Popi, including him.

In the car minutes later, he tuned out of the bickering between Booker and Kodi. He'd had to relearn over the last couple of weeks to block it out. Hunting for an apartment was on hold because the mere mention brought a sad look to Popi's eyes, but he wasn't sure living with his brothers long-term was the sane thing to do.

Taylin rubbed at his temples and closed his eyes, running through the list of things he needed to do over the next few days. A separate car was collecting Hollis, Lennon, and Frey. Monty was already with Rue, so it meant the jet wouldn't be as full for the first part of the journey. However, what that meant was that he'd be in close quarters with flirty Frey, which he'd avoided since the coffee lounge incident, not wanting to give the man any more wrong ideas.

Taylin sent up a silent wish to get to the jet before the omegas so he could make sure he sat in a position to avoid Frey. The additional hours of the trip gave Taylin more concern than he liked. With how things seemed to have improved—if that was the right word—between him and Hollis, he didn't want to upend the apple cart. But knowing his luck, he'd end up flat out knocking the cart over, tripping on the apples, and ending up on his ass.

"Did you get my email containing the updated designs for the leather pieces for the fashion show? The Native American designer has come up with a whole concept to tie in the clothes and accessories. They are a little more detailed than the last ones, but boy, are they stunning." All enthusiasm, Booker's question sank past his thoughts, and it took a moment to reply.

"I did. But we need to see if either of these business recommendations fits with what you need. The designs might need to be adapted—"

Booker shook his head vehemently. "Those leather designs tie into the whole of the spring collection. We can't change them!" His growl was all bear. His jaw set rigidly as he glared at Taylin, as if daring him to argue.

Taylin sat forward, not intimidated in the slightest. "If we can't find someone to do the level of detail you need, it'll be a moot point. Then you'll have to compromise and switch out the shoes, bags, belts, and any other accessories that tie the collection together and go with something else or consider canning the whole spring line."

They wouldn't do that as it would cost them a fortune and the impact on fashion week would be a catastrophe for Jupiter with the hype he and Kari had been working on for months.

Booker's scowl spoke volumes. The deep lines etched around his eyes and bracketing his full lips said he wasn't budging on this. Tension radiated from his enormous frame, making the confines of the car shrink. "I'm not having this discussion now!"

Taylin didn't point out Booker was the one to start the conversation. Instead, his attention turned to the window when the car slowed and the sign for the private jet entry appeared.

A disheartened sigh escaped at seeing his evening was carrying on in the same vein when he saw another company car parked in the bay near their jet. There was no sign of the PAs which meant they were already on board.

"Lennon better get that no one else wants to listen to his incessant chatter," Kodi bitched as they pulled to a stop.

Booker's lips twitched. "Lennon never was a chatterbox with me. What about you?"

For the first time since he'd got in the car, Taylin grinned. "Nope."

"This is gonna be fun!" Booker hustled out of the car, following Kodi as Taylin rolled his eyes heavenward, realizing he was going to be limited to his seat choice because he'd gotten distracted and was now last getting on the plane.

Out of the car, he grabbed his bags from the driver and gave chase. Inside the jet, Thomas, their air steward, met him with a polite smile. Dressed smartly in a black shirt with the company logo adorning the breast pocket, and some smart trousers, he looked every bit the alpha he was. "Evening, Mr. Starling. May I take your bags?" He held out his hand, only Taylin's attention had switched to the seating arrangements.

Hollis was sitting in the seat Taylin would have picked and Frey was sitting on the other side of the aisle, one seat down, leaving a seat on either side of him. The wide aisle allowed plenty of room between the opposite seats, which could swivel to face each other at an angle so you could hold a conversation, if needs be.

Booker sat next to Hollis, whereas Kodi opted to take the seat next to Frey and not spare a look at where Lennon sat in the booth section they used for working, as it had a table to hold laptops. Lennon's eyes were downcast and he fiddled with the laptop in front of him. But there was a droop to his shoulders that wasn't his usual posture, which suggested something was amiss.

Problem was, Taylin, for now, was more concerned about avoiding sitting next to Frey and inviting three hours of flirty conversation. Seeing his best option was to sit across from Lennon, Taylin went and sat down in the booth, which unfortunately was furthest away from Hollis.

Booker's hearty laugh got him lifting an enquiring brow as Taylin dropped his bags down next to him on the empty seat. Booker gave a pointed look at Thomas, who appeared to have followed him, and was wearing a look of expectation.

Taylin eyed his bags and gave an internal groan at why Thomas had followed him.

Bugger it to all hell!

Taylin picked up the bag containing his clothes and stood to offer it to Thomas. "Thank you," he murmured, not looking at anyone as he retook his seat, cheeks glowing with warmth. He reached for his computer bag on the pretense he needed something inside it.

Dork!

You absolute dork!

There was a cough and Taylin glanced over at Lennon, who gave him a timid smile. "How's your fish doing?"

Chapter Ten

Lane

A massive big spread over Lane's cheeks, making them ache. "It's all going swimmingly,"—he glanced at his naked husband, who'd stretched out beside him. Derick looked glorious in the late afternoon sun, which caught in the strands of his silvery chest hair, making them shimmer—"don't you think?"

Derick reached up and tweaked his nose. "Don't go counting your blessings yet, my love. From what I've seen, things are about to get a little bumpy for some of our sons."

Lane rolled closer to the broad chest and laid his head down on the solid wall of fur covered muscle. "What have you seen in the group chat? Is Taylin still searching for answers about Hollis?"

The thud of Derick's heart remained steady as he chuckled. "I told you, I'm keeping out of it. You're the one who likes to meddle."

"They need it," Lane exclaimed gleefully. "They've all gotten complacent and possibly got stuck at always getting their own way for too long. It's time they saw what is right under their noses. I've vetted and found each of them the perfect mate."

Derick's chuckle turned to full-blown laughter. It vibrated against Lane's cheek, causing the hair to rub deliciously against his skin, giving him something else to think about.

Lane's groan was full of delight when Derick's strong fingers stroked down his back. His cock plumped as the fingertips stroked down the crease of his ass.

"That may be so, but they have to choose for themselves."

Derick, always the reasonable one, got Lane nodding absently as he pushed his ass back in invitation. His arousal thickened and scented the air at the delicate touch of his husband, who was clearly working on distracting him. "I know and although the plan initially wasn't to play matchmaker, I'm finding I like it. We have a long retirement to look forward to and a few grandbabies to bounce on our knees wouldn't go amiss."

Lane lifted his head and met his husband's heated stare as the pad of his fingertip circled his hole. "I have other ideas on filling our retirement." Derick ran his nose down the side of Lane's neck. "I can smell your arousal, my love."

In a swift move, they rolled and Lane found himself pinned to the bed, Derick's mouth temptingly close. Lane reached up and his fingers slid into thick, silky strands of silver hair. Taking a firm hold, he tugged Derick's mouth closer to him. Their son's future was in the hands of the Fates—and

Lane trusted them implicitly—but giving a helping hand? He could see nothing wrong with that.

He set aside—for now—ideas of grandbabies when his renewed hunger for his mate took president. Full, fleshy lips parted against his, giving Lane a taste of himself, and he moaned in delight.

The kiss deepened, and the conversation became the last thing Lane wanted. Retirement had a lot of benefits, and this was most definitely one of them.

Chapter Eleven

Taylin

The place smelled bad, nothing could disguise it. Not even the air fresheners hanging from shelves near where the omegas worked diligently, keeping their gazes on the task at hand.

Two days they'd waited to gain access to the factory, and it took Taylin all of two minutes to understand why. The place... it was a glorified sweatshop.

"As you can see," Amatus, the manager, said with a confidence that played on Taylin's last nerve with what he was seeing, "the quality of the work is exceptional."

The brown leather, hand tooled bag with the teal mandala on the front was indeed a beautiful piece of craftsmanship.

At what cost to the omega? That was what ran through Taylin's mind as he masked his emotions to ensure none of his anger escaped. Those with him stayed silent. Hollis and

Frey, who'd come in with them, stayed unusually close to him and Booker.

Booker, Rue and Kodi wore expressions that revealed none of their thoughts, but as their brother, Taylin could tell they were as angry as him. The rigid line of Booker's jaw line. The groves bracketing Kodi's eyes. Rue's fists that he'd thrust into his pockets when they'd started the walk through. All signs the asshole guiding them through the place hadn't picked up on, so confident it seemed that they could fool them about the awful working conditions for the omegas.

"Your workers are extremely talented. These pieces are absolutely stunning." Booker's voice projected loudly, and yet not one worker looked in their direction, sending chills down Taylin's spine.

He made a casual move of looking around as they continued on through the factory, pretending to be interested in what Amatus was spouting. He nodded at the appropriate times but his attention was on the alphas stationed above them on the upper floor. They all looked to be carrying something under their thick coats, the way the coat bulged unnaturally.

Were they carrying weapons?

The alphas dressed according to the cool temperature in the building, but that was not the case for the silently working omegas. They must be freezing their asses off. Another chill ran down Taylin's spine at the unnaturalness of the atmosphere and what it all meant for those working hard to achieve the high standard they could see in pieces sat on work benches.

Did Amatus and whoever owned this place think that because he couldn't shift into his animal form that Taylin wouldn't notice what the fuck was going on?

The tour took an hour and, because of the lateness in the day—the only time Amatus had given them to come after two days of avoidance—they had no choice but to leave and not confront the issue then and there.

In the car with his brothers, the PAs having gone in a second car, Taylin waited till they were driving away before he let rip.

"Asshole, motherfuckering shitheads!" he growled through teeth clenched so tightly, it made his gums ache. "Did you see those alphas? They were wearing something under their coats? Like a weapon of some description?"

Booker wore a disgusted look as he gave a stilted nod and took out his cell phone. His hand trembled as he punched at the screen clumsily until there was the sound of the ring tone for FaceTime. Taylin moved so he could get his head in the shot when Dad's voice came through the speaker with a greeting.

Dark eyes swept over them and the smile Dad wore disappeared. He came forward, his face taking up all the screen as he demanded, "What happened?"

Feeling dog tired and utterly gutted, Taylin's polished shoes dragged over the thick carpet as they followed the hotel concierge who, for some strange reason, wanted to take them to their hotel suite.

Booker, Rue, and Kodi were all on a lower floor, something Taylin didn't question. Between how occupied his thoughts were and how busy the place appeared when they'd arrived, it just didn't cross his mind. The last three days were long and had culminated in the disastrous visit to the factory Dad had discovered was *not* owned by Design Detailing & Co, but by a subsidiary of a large company that backed politicians who wanted to introduce laws to take away divergents rights.

The first of their two planned trips had turned into a fucking disaster.

Booker had gone closed-lipped after he'd explained the situation to Dad. It hadn't taken a rocket scientist to understand why the company had rearranged twice. This raised a big red flag in the first instance, which was confirmed no more than two minutes inside the place.

It was fucking terrible to consider how those monsters achieved the level of design detail to the pieces they'd seen. The dilemma now was what to do to help those omegas because help them, they would. They'd need to be careful so as not to alert anyone to their plan to buy the company and see if they could salvage something for the omegas by removing the oppression they were currently working under.

In hindsight, they should have paid an impromptu visit to the factory rather than ignoring the warning signs that something was up. When they'd entered the factory, no matter how hard those working there had tried to disguise what was going on, they'd seen the place for what it was, a glorified sweatshop. The working conditions made Taylin cringe whilst fueling an anger that drained him of all his energy as he'd interjected into the conversation with Dad about what he'd seen and felt.

Booker, who had been so impressed by the level of detail the company could produce in the samples, had been more than ready to find the funds to purchase the company. Dad had talked him down and spoke about the long game with these types of places. They didn't want them catching wind that they'd figured out what was going on.

Before they'd left Amatus, the manager of Design Detailing & Co was all but rubbing his hands together with glee at what an account with Starling Enterprises would mean to him.

Even now, Taylin had to forcibly relax his jaw to stop his teeth grinding together or a snarl from sneaking out at the images burned into his brain of omegas working under those harrowing conditions. Many, he'd noted, were so thin they looked like a strong breeze would snap them in two. Those who'd been brave enough to look at them had haunted eyes that skittered away way too fast. Marks on exposed skin along with gnarled, trembling hands left Taylin sick to his stomach.

Sacking those alpha fuckers wasn't going to be good enough for the terror they were inflicting, but it was a good place to start. Even now, hours later, at their second destination of the trip, Taylin was still brooding. This had to be why Taylin, after entering the room behind the concierge, had to blink several times to check he was seeing correctly.

What is this?

He lifted a hand, but it flopped back down by his side. He was at a total loss and he couldn't find words at the sight of the bed.

"There has to be some mistake!" he stuttered finally, his gaze never moving from the queen sized bed sat on a plinth, making it the focal point in the large, beautifully decorated *room*. This was most definitely not a suite!

The concierge smiled widely. "The room you requested."

Requested?

The man pushed the trolley holding their bags to the stand next to a large closet and unloaded them. "It comes with additional strengthened doors and sound proofing, along with excluders around the doorframe to prevent any scent from escaping the room. Windows are also triple glazed, but being so high up should mean that isn't an issue."

Seconds later he was pushing the trolley towards the door and Taylin, who'd already pulled out his wallet for a tip, handed over the money absently as the guy smiled assuredly, not getting that Taylin was still processing what the hell was going on.

What the hell was he talking about? High up? Frowning and cluelessly staring, Taylin's head attempted to play catch up when the door clicked shut and he remained alone with Hollis—and an enormous bed!

Why was the guy so pleased with everything he'd reeled off?

None of it was making sense.

Hollis walked to where the bags were and lifted one of his onto the bed.

One bed.

One big bed...

Why wasn't Hollis chasing after the dude and giving him hell for not sorting them with a suite?

Remaining at a total loss, Taylin walked towards where Hollis was, head down, digging through his bag, appearing as if he didn't have a care in the world. One glance at the bed and Taylin swallowed hard, changing direction to march over to the one other door. He swung it open, groaning when it confirmed Taylin's suspicions. The bathroom was nearly as big as the bedroom.

There was no hidden bed in there, clearly!

He swung back around and scrubbed tiredly at his face, trying to understand what he was missing and to figure out why Hollis still wasn't freaking out.

"This... mistake... erm... sure..." He shut up, realizing he wasn't making any sense at all. But who the hell could blame him?

"Sorry, you're going to have to do better than gobbledygook." A smile spread over Hollis's face, transforming it, and made it hard for Taylin to catch his breath. Never mind grasp the concept of how to string two words together.

Taylin pointed to the one bed. "That... one." That made sense, didn't it?

Hollis nodded. "Yes, one bed. Why would we need two beds now, with my heat due tomorrow?"

Taylin actually released a squeal of distress, one he'd have to think about when his brain wasn't so scrambled by the blow of Hollis's words, once they registered past his confusion. A sinking feeling came when the pieces slotted together, giving him a picture of what the concierge had been wittering on about. It all made terrible sense.

One bed...

Hollis in heat...

He gulped hard, his throat working to stop closing in panic. He attempted to wet his lips and unglue the tongue stuck to the roof of his mouth, trying to get it to cooperate in this bizarre conversation. Because it was bizarre. How else would one describe Hollis suggesting they share a bed during his heat?

"Ermmm... it's... yes... no... oh gods!" He plonked his ass onto the bed, his legs too weak to hold him up any longer, and dropped his head into his hands, willing his head to play catch up with his lips.

"Is there a problem?" Hollis asked sweetly.

Is there a problem? Too fucking right there is.

And *now* Taylin could clearly see the reason Hollis had looked at him like he'd lost his mind when he'd suggested this trip, after his wolf...

You shithead! You did this on purpose. You distracted me from what Hollis was saying! How could you?

I don't know what you mean.

The utter smugness coming from his animal spirit made his teeth ache as they ground together in frustration.

How was he supposed to resist Hollis? Resist what evidently was going to happen before they could get back to safety!

It's too late now.

Taylin looked at his watch and ground out a curse. The pilot and steward would have left. They had another trip planned with Jupiter, which meant they were stranded here with Hollis in… heat.

"Are you okay? You were the one who was adamant you would help me with any issue."

Was that a sarcastic bite to Hollis's voice?

He glanced up and caught the omega staring at him from behind clear rimmed specs that had slipped down his nose.

"Is this a setup?" Taylin asked, not sure whether to be relieved Hollis was pulling his leg, or gutted. Probably a bit of both—though gutted was edging ahead with how sexy the man looked right then as he peered over the top of his glasses.

"No."

That one word held a weight that hit Taylin right in the solar plexus, knocking him back a little. He jerked up off the bed, feeling at a distinct disadvantage because of his damn wolf side.

"You explained why you couldn't come, didn't you?" It wasn't really a question, but Hollis nodded. "I didn't listen, did I." Again not a question, but Hollis nodded once more while Taylin tried his best to hold back his excitement, even if his wolf had been a devious shit in the first place, when it registered Hollis wanted this.

Wanted him...

He ran trembling fingers through his hair, trying to force himself in to doing the honorable thing and leave Hollis—

You can't.

He disregarded his animal.

The moral thing to do was leave. It was. A heat was a very private and intimate thing. They hadn't even been on a date. Gone out to the movies. Nothing. Then why wasn't he running for the door?

Gazes clashing, Taylin—with effort—held Hollis's challenging stare. "Do you want me here for this?" Taylin didn't give Hollis a chance to answer when the next question popped out. "What do you normally do when you have a heat?" The likely answer made his whole body tense up.

Did Hollis use one of the agencies to help with his heat? The very idea—one Taylin had avoided thinking about for years so as not to make himself go mad—reared its hideous head. Hollis hiring an alpha or going to one of the many establishments that catered to omegas made him burn with... jealousy. It spread through him, eating at his heart.

For the first time, he was on board with his wolf. There was no way in hell he was going to let another alpha touch Hollis—*so not happening.*

Did Hollis understand fully what he was doing by inviting in the wolf? It was too late now. There was no going back for Taylin.

Chapter Twelve

Hollis

Light glinted off tumbling curls that gave a softness to Taylin's features. One that belied the mix of emotions that Taylin wasn't hiding. Dark, heavy-lidded eyes carried a wickedness that made it hard for Hollis to draw in air. He'd imagined Taylin looking at him as he was now a thousand times. Only nothing had prepared him for the all-consuming intensity of it. To be Taylin's entire focus was... hot... *scary*?

Why had he thought this was a good idea when he talked it over with Monica? Why? It had taken only a second into the conversation to twig that Taylin's animal was somehow the reason they were here.

Hollis couldn't decide if he'd initially seen a look of resignation from Taylin.

Where did that leave them? Him?

Hollis wanted to be brave and had been, right until he realized he was going to go into his heat whilst they were away.

For a while, he'd considered they'd be back home before it happened. The additional days they'd added in had forced his hand in Drinkwater.

A part of him he'd admit to no one but Monica, was dancing merrily at how the choice was here, now, away where no one could witness what was about to happen.

Except for Booker, Rue, Kodi and the PAs, his snarky side reminded him.

Any consideration his heat could be late, slid away when they'd gotten onto the plane and, having come over all hot, he'd gone to test his temperature. His first thought was that it was temper over the factory visit, but he quickly gotten dissuaded of that notion when he looked at the thermometer. He'd be lucky now to attend the visit at the next factory the following day, with how he could feel the continuing increase in his body temperature.

The idea and the reality of being with Taylin in this most intimate and vulnerable position an omega could find themselves in were miles apart.

Taylin's question hung between them like a red flag to a bull. Waving a warning that suggested Hollis's reply needed to be handled with care, once he could figure out how to respond. For once in his life, Hollis had gotten himself into a situation where he wasn't sure he'd cope with the fallout. His attraction to Taylin was real and yes, it was pretty obvious the wolf wasn't averse to him, but would his answer change everything?

Make Taylin view him differently.

Make him think Hollis was desperate enough to force the issue between them like this?

"How, Hollis?" Taylin asked, with a bite of impatience and something else Hollis considered and discarded as jealousy.

It was hard to hold Taylin's gaze, but Hollis managed as he answered, "I have a bag of supplies that I use to get me through the worst of it—if you need to leave."

The sudden feral light in Taylin's eyes was predatory and Hollis barely resisted taking a step back when there was no sign Taylin was leaving him alone.

"Show me?"

The sexy, raspy demand ran over Hollis's heated skin and he tugged off his suit jacket, glad of the opportunity to break eye contact. He dropped the jacket on the bedcover and rolled up his sleeves to the elbow, to give himself time to gather his scattered wits.

"Please."

That one word was more persuasive as it held none of the earlier demand, only desire, sending frissons of lust through Hollis.

Fuckity fuck!

He was in so much trouble if Taylin figured out what that tone did to him. Then he groaned, because his scent was already betraying him.

It was somehow easier to grab the bag that held his supplies and avoid looking in Taylin's direction. Hollis had lost count of the years since he'd had an alpha present during his heat, and having one interested enough to want to know what he liked was giving him uncontrollable urges. This was how his heat always started, his desire making its presence felt deep in his core.

He unzipped the bag with shaky fingers then took a steadying breath as he stepped aside, not wanting to witness what Taylin would think about what was inside. Hollis had a lot of toys he liked to use and when he'd packed, he'd catered to all of his proclivities.

When Taylin prowled towards the bag, showing none of the same hesitation as Hollis, he watched in a kind of horrified fascination. The kind that had a person watching a scene knowing something bad was going to happen, but they couldn't look away. Taylin upended the bag and emptied the contents onto the bed in one fluid move.

Air in the room simply disappeared at the growl Taylin released, and made every hair on Hollis's body stand to attention. He refused to be ashamed of the enormous dildo that had an inflatable knot at the base, which Taylin reached for first.

Even in his hand, the thing looked obscenely big. "How do you make the knot inflate?" he asked, not once shifting his gaze from the toy.

It helped Taylin wasn't paying him any attention, though the curious way he examined the dildo made it near impossible for Hollis to get his words out. "There's a small switch on the base."

Immediately, Taylin's fingers moved to feel under the base and the sound of buzzing filled the room a moment later.

Oh, shit on a stick!

Embarrassment warmed Hollis's cheeks as the sound filled the silence between them.

Could this get any more embarrassing?

"Nice," Taylin murmured. "I think my knot is bigger than this. Will that be a problem?"

The question came with such a genuine look of concern that Hollis became dumbfounded. Not only by the concern but at the visual of what Taylin would look like aroused, his knot exposed.

Thoughts tumbled over like pins in a bowling alley at the heavy ball striking them. So many replies came and went.

"Fuck, no."

"Give me all you got."

"Show me."

"Didn't know it came in a bigger size."

None of them left his parted lips as his tongues slipped out to wet the dryness that came with a heavy dose of lust.

His initial reactions probably weren't the right ones if he wanted to make a good impression.

He's holding your biggest dildo and you're worried about what impression you give him... pleaseeee.

Not now, can't you see I'm in a little bit of a predicament?

Drop the 'pre' and 'ment' part of that word and let's just go with the dic.

Hollis's lips twitched, laughter tickling the back of his throat at the bubble of hysteria from his animal's sense of humor.

Taylin's eyes narrowed on him. "Something funny?"

He shook his head, working to keep more heat from flooding his body and reaching his face to reveal itself. "My animal is trying to be *funny,* and failing."

A light of amusement appeared as Taylin waved the dildo in the air. "Over this? Or the fact I might be bigger?"

See what you've gotten me into.

Hollis glanced away, his gaze landed on the bed and everything that still lay on the covers. There were two more dildos. One had a knot at the base, the other was like the one Taylin held with the ability to inflate the knot when inserted. That one had a suction cup to stick to the shower wall. The other had an opening in it at the head that held a pocket for the synthetic alpha cum to be inserted into and warmed to simulate an alpha coming in Hollis's ass.

There was a twelve inch vibrator, ridged beauty, that had ten different speeds, which, if used right, could do a lot of the work when Hollis grew tired. That one required special placing against a head or footboard on the bed. There was a black fleshlight and alpha scented lubes along with nipple clamps that could vibrate. Amongst those was his favorite, a mouth that could suck and tongue his ass when it got too painful to fuck himself on the vibrator or dildos any longer.

There was no escaping or pretending about what he liked.

Taylin making jokes about himself and his size had to be good? Hollis wasn't sure if he was ready for this side of Taylin. Before, Hollis had struggled to keep his feelings tucked away, but playful Taylin was damn irresistible.

It didn't take a genius to know Hollis was now redder than a redhead who'd been out in the sun all day with no sunblock. Taylin came closer, his body heat and scent doing a number on Hollis. Only Taylin's gaze was on the bed.

Hollis watched him turn off the dildo, placing it down to reach for the mouth. Long, lean fingers stroked over it and pushed inside the parted lips, his groan was deep and guttural. His attention returned to Hollis, desire tightening his jaw and his liquid brown eyes glowing with his animal spirit.

"This. I want to see you use this," he growled.

Hollis panted at the images flashing through his mind at how he'd look to Taylin. Cock plumping, the scent of his arousal filling the room as the mouth sucked on his ass with *his alpha watching.*

His alpha!

No... he's not my alpha.

A wicked grin formed as Taylin's nose twitched, unaware of Hollis's uncertainty over whether this was just a one-off thing. "You like the idea of that."

Not a question, or one Hollis had to answer when his body spoke for him.

At the sudden banging on the door, both Hollis and Taylin jumped apart. They turned to the offending interruption at the same time.

"Fuck, dinner!" Taylin ground out. "I forgot, we're supposed to be meeting everyone to talk about what happened today."

Fuck dinner! I want to be *dinner.*

The next loud knock brought Hollis out of his trance. He dived to the bed, scooping up everything and threw it back inside the bag, frantic at thoughts of the others seeing what he liked.

One quick scan and Hollis cursed at Taylin's amused expression and the object he held out to him. "You missed one." His chuckle was pure filth before he walked towards the door.

"Wait, the room... smells of..."

Taylin's hand hovered over the door handle as he glanced back, one brow quirked up. "Sex?"

"Shut up," Hollis grunted, going to grab his suit jacket to head to the door. "That's not my sex smell."

Not even close, he finished under his breath, knocking Taylin's hand away from the door and opening it just enough to squeeze out into the corridor where Booker stood, wearing a thunderous expression.

"Dad's been in touch." His gaze moved between them and his nose wrinkled before he frowned. "Weren't you planning on coming to dinner?" Booker asked without preamble.

Taylin hissed through his teeth as he shut the door. "We were just unpacking."

He didn't look at Hollis as he continued on acting like there was nothing amiss. "Did Dad find someone to figure out if they'd want to sell the factory?"

Booker didn't look convinced by Taylin's casual tone. Hollis could tell with how many times he glanced between them. "No, he's working on it. But I need food, aren't you pair hungry?"

Taylin glanced at Hollis, his tongue running over white, even teeth. "I find I'm rather ravenous."

"Then why the fuck did I have to come get you both?" Booker grumbled, shaking his head as he headed off towards the elevator.

Hollis wanted to take back a bit of the control he'd left in the hotel room, knowing what was coming when Taylin threw a salacious grin his way when Booker turned away.

"We'll see just how hungry you are tomorrow," he whispered and then flounced off after Booker, his cock chafing against his damn boxer briefs.

When he got back, Monica was going to get a piece of his mind for encouraging him. This was the worst idea in the history of ideas. He would never be able to keep his desire for Taylin on the down low, not now.

It was going to be a goddamn nightmare trying to eat and pretend everything was normal when it wasn't

You came knowing this was going to happen.

Shut the hell up!

The laughter in his head grated on his last nerve as he picked up his pace and stomped down the hall, ignoring Booker's next quizzical look and Taylin's wide cheeky grin.

Worst idea ever!

Chapter Thirteen

Taylin

Every bit of tiredness he had felt earlier fled with the excitement that pulsed through him at all the possibilities of what lay ahead of them.

It took concerted effort to hold a conversation with those around them when Hollis sat opposite him, looking flushed, smelling tastier and more edible than the meal in front of him.

To Taylin, it was obvious Hollis was doing his utmost to avoid looking at him by the amount of time he spent staring at his food while he ate. Almost like he'd not seen food or eaten in a week. Taylin had decided, on the way down to dinner, he didn't care who noticed what was happening between him and Hollis. He'd waited too long for this, and he wasn't going to fuck it up by acting like nothing was going on—unless Hollis wanted that.

It wasn't like his brothers weren't aware of his attraction to Taylin, the ribbing he'd already endured would be nothing once they discovered what was going to happen. He was well aware his brothers could be relentless when they got it into their heads to torment each other. He'd done it a time or two himself, but it had been years since they'd all lived under the same roof, which would make him an easy target. Yeah, that wasn't something he wanted to think about and potentially spoil his mood.

To distract himself, he stared at the top of Hollis's glossy head. Admiring the way the lights above them highlighted the thick, silky locks, bringing forth an urge to reach over and touch them. Resisting carried with it a wave of pure want. It stole his ability to take a breath and replaced the hunger for food with something far more appetizing: Hollis. The attempted deep inhale was a mistake when Taylin's senses swam at the fruity aroma coming from Hollis towards him. Was it just him, or was Hollis's fruity scent increasing? Could the others smell how it was changing?

One quick glance around the table showed no one was paying any extra attention to Hollis, which didn't help when Taylin's animal spirit preened like a damn ballet dancer at their obvious connection to the pygmy loris.

"Do you think those omegas in the workshop get to go home?"

Frey's quiet question pulled Taylin from the growing sexual haze he was falling into and dumped a bucket of icy realism on him.

"What do you mean?" Booker asked before anyone else could, his features taut with worry as he shifted his large bulk in his seat, causing it to groan.

Glittering tear drops hung suspended off Frey's long lashes when he looked around the table that was tucked into the corner of the restaurant. They asked for it as it was the one that offered the most privacy for conversation.

"They were so..." His small nose wrinkled, and caused a tear to roll down his cheek, plopping onto his plate. "Lost."

Frey used the back of his tiny hand to dash at the next tear that fell. "That atmosphere was full of despair. Couldn't you smell it? I thought we'd talk about it. Why aren't we?" He hiccuped out a sob, his sorrowful eyes swallowing his face up, making it impossible to not feel his sadness. "How do they cope with it?"

Booker wordlessly laid an open palmed hand face up on the table, offering it to Frey.

Frey reached out, his tiny hand engulfed in Booker's meaty fist. Those around the table looked at the joined hands, most with speculation.

Taylin tucked away his questions about the magnitude of what Booker had just done to think about later.

"I don't know," he replied solemnly to the first question Frey asked. The weight of responsibility and the possibility they'd left those omegas to suffer cut deep, leaving Taylin at a loss for words.

"We're gonna fix it," Booker said with a fierceness that suggested anyone that tried to stop him would get removed in any way he saw fit. "Dad is working on it now. And we weren't talking about it because"—his gaze swept the busy dining room—"having this type of conversation where it can be overheard isn't how we do business. What we need to do is have a little patience."

His thumb stroked over the back of Frey's hand, looking solely at the little fox. "I promise you we'll go back and fix those shitheads." The growl he released was full of menace, and those at the tables closest to them cast wary glances in their direction.

Taylin shivered when memories of another time came unbidden, throwing him into his past and to the first time he had heard that sound.

Taylin sniveled and rubbed at his icy nose—it hadn't stopped running since he'd left the warm school to head back to hide in the alleyway three blocks from school—with the back of an even colder hand. Each step was a reminder of the beating he'd taken from his father and brothers four days earlier. They'd been real careful to keep his face unmarked, because none of them wanted to answer any questions.

Shame was real, it came in rejection and Taylin now knew the hard cruelty of it. There was no such thing as love without strings, not for him or his kind. The wind stole his quiet sob as he kept his head down, keeping his fast pace as close to walking as possible. It stopped folks from paying too much attention when he didn't need or want it. It was bad enough keeping it together at school, in front of the teachers and his friends while he tried to figure out how he was going to survive the next three years when the next three days, hours, minutes felt impossible.

His eyes stung as he fought the tears burning his nose and adding to his overall distress. A bone gnawing hunger competed with the cold and made his brain churn over every slight movement that came with being homeless. Destitute. Taylin hadn't understood what that word meant until his family had figured out his secret.

A secret that was an enormous bag of despair that weighed him down enough he felt his face was dragging on the asphalt. Divergent. It went hand in hand with destitute, or so it seemed to his family.

A lone tear ran unheeded down his icy skin at how he'd gotten thrown out of his childhood home like garbage. He choked back the next sob that worked to hold his throat in its tight grip, forcing him to struggle to swallow. More shivers racked his body as the icy wind blasted through the coat he wore that was no defense against the freezing conditions that had hit Hazardville three days earlier and took up residence like an unwanted homeless person—just like me.

Life on the streets, Taylin was figuring out fast, wasn't for the weak. Didn't matter that Hazardville had a high population of the affluent. On the streets, hidden in the shadows, were those who preyed on those less fortunate. Hiding in alleyways had already taught Taylin a valuable lesson. Being invisible was much better than becoming sucked into the seedy nightlife and selling his soul to survive. To become one of those he'd seen with vacant eyes selling themselves for the next hit to get through. He'd be damned if he'd let that happen.

I'd rather die!

His hands balled into fists inside his coat pockets at his conviction. It see-sawed in the dead of the night with every scream and cry that made his pulse thump hard, and his sleep deprived brain conjured macabre pictures that were hard to shut out.

He gave a furtive look about, checking no one was watching as he darted down the alleyway at the back of Hudson and Park. The vents blasting food smells at the back of the restaurants tortured his stomach, reminding him—like he'd need it—that the few meager scraps he'd salvaged from the cafeteria bin, when no one was looking, weren't nearly enough to keep his hunger at bay.

As he passed, he inhaled the warm, scented air which touched his exposed face. Taylin paused for a brief second to enjoy the smell of something spicy and allow the heat to warm him before he crouched behind the large dumpster pushed into the darkest part of the alley. The short winter days meant it was already gloomy at this time and in the next hour would be full dark. Until then, he'd use the dumpster to shield him from sight and from the worst of the cold.

He'd barely ducked down when he heard the sounds of muffled voices and boots scuffling over the concrete. There was the sound of flesh hitting flesh and a grunt before a voice jeered, "Stick it to him, Race,"

"Let's show him what happens to freaks," another male voice said with excitement.

"Hold the divergent fucker," came another voice, full of hatred.

There were other voices, all male, full of anger. Full of hate.

"Fight me one on one, you chicken shits. Let's see how you fair then." Although slurred in pain, the voice was one Taylin recognized.

Silas.

They're beating up Silas, holy shitballs.

Silas was a senior and a well-known divergent in Taylin's school. Silas was always polite, or had been to Taylin when they'd crossed paths. In fact, for a moment, Taylin had considered working up the courage to speak to Silas, to see if he knew anyone who could help. Silas's parents were of mixed origin. Taylin's father had talked about it, nothing nice though.

Lane Starling was an omega divergent who didn't shift, whereas Derick Starling was an alpha wolf who could shift into his animal half. Their fashion business promoted equality for all. And secretly, even before Taylin had figured out he was divergent, he liked what they supported.

Taylin would bet the few meager dollars he had that they'd never kick their son out. Yet Silas wasn't immune to life's crap either. The shock of that reality brought Taylin out of his hiding space, his fists raised to fight. He counted eight boys laying the boot in on Silas who was on the ground, no more than four feet from him.

It was hard to tell in the gloominess where Silas's head was, but the way they were booting at him, Taylin suspected Silas would die if Taylin didn't help.

His anger and frustration at his own situation roared to life, and he jumped at the nearest figure and started swinging, landing punches hard enough to zing up his arms.

"What the fuck!" the guy called out, staggering.

Taylin didn't pause, he just kept hitting, his fists crunching against bone. Wetness spread over his knuckles as his mind be-

came a blur. His animal spirit was right there with him, pushing him on to defend themselves and the man on the ground.

Blows rained down on Taylin from different directions, black spots formed in front of his eyes and he fought to stay conscious as his energy waned from the lack of food, and the cold. His anger was the only thing fueling him.

"Fucker, grab him," someone called out.

"Get his damn legs," a gravelly voice demanded.

His legs?

Taylin only then noticed he was not only punching but kicking too.

"Arghhhh... fuck..."

Endless sounds of cries and wet flesh being smacked resounded in Taylin's head. His heightened senses were in overdrive with the coppery smell of blood surrounding him. Some of his own, but not all.

His vision wavered at the blow that landed on his temple and his head fired back, hitting something solid, causing his legs to give way. The ground veered towards him as he listed and slid down—his nose wrinkled—the dumpster. He blinked, blinded by the wetness seeping down through his curls.

His sluggish system tried to keep him conscious when a roar so terrifying rent the air and Taylin's bladder took fright. Warm wetness soaked his pants and the scent of urine didn't quite get masked by blood and fear, adding to the overall shittiness of the situation. Taylin rubbed at slitted and puffy eyes with trembling hands, staring at the enormous bear that was standing upright, towering over everyone, growling in a way that suggested Taylin was about to breathe his last.

Hell and damnation!

Chapter Fourteen

Taylin

Taylin jerked at the hand touching his arm and turned to see Lennon staring at him with deep, pinched lines between his brows.

"Is everything okay?" he whispered, barely loud enough for Taylin to catch, his gaze moving quickly around the table.

With the past clinging on with damn greedy fingers, his nod came out as an erratic head bob. Taylin reached for his wineglass and took a sip to help calm his bounding pulse. That fateful night had given Taylin an insight into Booker and revealed the bear Booker hardly ever let out, and for good reason.

A shudder ran through him at how Booker's bear, when in a tear, was a sight to behold. He was one scary mother-fucker who took no prisoners. It was a lowering moment to remember his first encounter and being left sitting in his own piss. Taylin's official introduction to the Starling clan wasn't the most auspicious. Although that one act of bravery had changed Taylin's life for the better, despite how they'd all ended up getting patched up in the Emergency Room that night.

Taylin took another sip of wine at the painful memories of explaining the circumstances in which he'd found himself homeless, when they wanted to crowd back in. They worked to suck him to the dark places he'd long since tucked into the box labeled 'do not open under any circumstances'. It wasn't often they were able to creep out and blindside him, but today, seeing those alphas must have poked at the cage that guarded his past and opened the damn latch, setting them free. They had no place in the present, none. He'd dealt with them and moved on.

He had!

It took more effort than he liked to return his attention to Frey, who gave a watery chortle and dropped the fork he held—Taylin noticed he continued to clutch at Booker's fingers—to swipe at the tears tracking down his pale skin with his now free hand.

"It's so hard to think they don't have any choices." He didn't look away from Booker. "Just make sure to let me know when you are going to do some head smashing. I'll want to watch." The light in the little fox's eyes suggested he wasn't joking and gave Taylin pause to consider what he'd missed from the conversation.

Frey was the flirty one. The one who liked people to laugh. Whatever this side of him was, it differed from what they'd all previously seen and, judging by the interest in Booker's gaze, he liked this side of the flirty fox.

Hollis groaned loudly, nudging Frey's shoulder with care. "How can you look so cute and love violence?" Hollis shook his head, his lips curling up at the edges in apparent bemusement.

Frey's sad expression disappeared and his usual flirty grin returned, albeit his eyes continued to glisten with unshed tears. "There's something hot about watching an alpha kick ass." Frey glanced at the other PAs. "Don't you think so?" His interest returned to Booker, appearing not at all bothered about getting a response. "Big and fierce is…" he licked at his plump lips, "hot."

Booker coughed hard enough that the table shook as he tugged his hand out of Frey's grip so fast, Frey's hand landed with a thud on the table. Booker didn't appear to notice because he was rubbing both hands over his rather flushed face, then into his hair to shove it back off his face. The attention he then gave his plate was comical.

Glad of the distraction, Taylin's gaze narrowed on his brother, watching him closely. Booker seldom gave a lot away, but right now, he was clearly struggling with something. Taylin sucked his lower lip between his teeth to keep a grin in check when Booker picked his cutlery back up and stared at it like he didn't know what to do with what he was holding.

The amusement was short-lived when Booker brought the conversation to the plans for the next day, giving Taylin a sinking feeling in the pit of his stomach.

"What time are we planning to go to Brand Alliance's factory tomorrow? I considered suggesting we leave it, but as that would be disrespectful after they were good enough to adapt to our changing plans, twice, I think we should see what they can offer. They may be able to fulfill the brief while we work to purchase Design Detailing & Co. Both companies showed potential, and I don't want to discount one, despite the other company's products being of exceptional quality." Booker held up his hand when Frey's lips quivered. "Yes, I know how they obtained that standard of work! Threats and bullying, possibly more. Hopefully, those omegas, under our care, will flourish without threats. But that will take time with how I imagine those fuckers treated them, and we don't have leeway for that with the Spring collection right around the corner." He finished with a deep sigh, showing his displeasure at the awful situation.

Taylin didn't need to look at Hollis's expression to know he had tensed up. The white knuckled hold he had on his cutlery revealed he was not as relaxed as he had been before Booker mentioned the next day. Taylin didn't need to be a rocket scientist to figure which part of the conversation could cause his worry.

"They are expecting *you* at ten am." Taylin lifted the glass of wine he'd continued to hold and took another sip for something to do while he put his thoughts in order and give himself the moment he needed. "Hollis and I won't be coming with you tomorrow. You can give us the feedback on what you find when we return to Hazardville late next week."

"What? Hang on, what's next week got to do with anything? We'll be done tomorrow and flying home in the evening," Kodi stated in confusion. A light of interest appeared a second later when Taylin could literally see Kodi's mind working as he stared pointedly at Taylin. Then he shifted his attention to Hollis, who was now dabbing at his lips with the napkin, looking more flushed than earlier.

Feeling much like when he'd been a teenager and getting caught doing something he shouldn't, Taylin clenched his thighs together to resist shifting in his seat. "Something else has come up, so we won't be able to go with you. I'm sure y'all will manage without us."

They'd have to, there was no way on heaven and earth they'd be leaving their hotel room until Hollis was past his heat and the way he smelled to Taylin, they were already cutting it close to get some privacy.

Booker jabbed his finger across the table at Taylin. "Hey, this was your damn idea and after the last place, I'd be damned if you're not coming!" Booker bristled, anger pouring off him.

Taylin refused to be intimidated, even when Rue and Kodi grinned and relaxed back in their seats, looking as if they were preparing to watch a show.

He should have known better than to have this conversation in the busy hotel restaurant, and Taylin mentally kicked himself for his lapse in judgment. His brothers could be loud and obnoxious when they didn't get their own way. He suspected that Kodi and Rue would egg Booker on if he wasn't careful. "We can't come—"

"What he means is, it's impossible for us to attend because," Hollis's gaze moved to Taylin, "I'll be dealing with my heat."

His declaration had as much impact as a sudden earthquake, stunning everyone into immobility where they sat wearing mirrored, shocked expressions.

"You are?" Lennon squealed, the first to recover.

"Holy fuck," muttered a wide eyed Frey.

"What!" Booker barked.

"Well, I never. The quiet ones are always the ones to watch," laughed Kodi.

Taylin held up his hand to stop any more comments, seeing they were attracting unwanted attention by how the level of noise dropped on the tables closest to them. "I think it's time we took our leave. I'll message when I need the plane to return for us."

Up and moving quickly to prevent anyone from continuing the conversation, Taylin was guiding a more than willing Hollis towards the exit. Taylin made a mental note to contact room service and put in requests for meals to be delivered and left outside the room. From past experience, he knew they were both going to need all their strength.

Thinking along those lines got his animal's attention, and a restlessness came with the anticipation of what would happen when they returned to their hotel room.

They'd barely taken more than a few steps when Rue's voice carried to Taylin, "I hope you aren't gonna charge the company for the use of the hotel for these *extra curricular activities.*"

Rue's grin was wide and cheekier than Taylin had ever seen it when he pivoted on his heel and gave his brother a death stare. “Screw you,” Taylin said politely, although his hard stare was anything but and threatened retribution when he got home.

Ignoring the small gasps of other patrons eating, Taylin placed a hand at the base of Hollis’s rigid spine to escort a scarlet cheeked Hollis from the restaurant.

“Ignore him,” he whispered in his ear, “he was just being a dick.”

It was impossible to get a read on Hollis when Taylin witnessed the professional mask slip into place. He silently cursed his ass of a brother as they walked soundlessly through the busy hotel reception area to the bank of elevators, where several people waited.

They entered behind everyone else, but Hollis traveled towards the back of the elevator, turned and kept his gaze forward. Following, Taylin returned his hand to the base of Hollis’s back, needing the contact like he needed air to breathe when the doors closed and he got a confined hit of Hollis’s scent. Taylin did his best to stop the strangled groan from escaping while he worked to breathe through his mouth.

It was far too easy to distinguish Hollis’s sweetness from everyone else. Over dinner, his normal aroma—one Taylin was very familiar with—had definitely become fruitier. In the small space, the change was very obvious, as was just how potent it was.

Intoxicating.

It was as if Hollis had gone for a swim in a pool of the sweetest, juiciest fruits. It made it impossible for Taylin to think logically over the lusty fog that it caused, even when he breathed through his mouth. Each passing second felt like an eternity as his body thrummed, his ability to think beyond the man he was touching becoming nonexistent.

Formidable need, the kind Taylin hadn't experienced before, adjusted his senses to home in solely on Hollis. The world ceased to exist outside of the captivating emotions streaming through him. His animal side paced, snarled, and clawed at his mind.

There had always been a separateness between him and his animal spirit. This was a first where they were in tune with each other on every level. It gave Taylin a unique perspective on the world. His field of vision increased beyond one-hundred-eighty degrees. His sense of smell became more sensitive, along with his hearing.

Acutely, he heard the fast strum of Hollis's heartbeat. Scented his... *mate.*

At the recognition, a sizzle of sharp desire jumped from cell to cell within him. Frantic anticipation came with the knowledge Taylin would taste, touch and explore every inch of the man—his mate—pressing closer to him. Consumed by thoughts of discovering how Hollis would sound, each whimper, moan, groan of desire, Taylin heard none of the conversations of those standing next to them.

His clothes felt restrictive and Taylin dropped a casual hand over his throbbing shaft, readjusting himself, getting little to no relief given how snug his trousers were.

Hollis's chin dropped and Taylin felt the weight of his gaze on the hand Taylin had pressed to his groin. Tension crackled in the surrounding air, lifting the tiny hairs on Taylin's skin when the doors opened and two women strolled out, laughing. When the doors shut, Hollis made a whining sound, then stepped back into Taylin's body. It dislodged his hand but Taylin didn't complain when Hollis's move brought his body flush against Taylins' when he widened his stance.

The height difference meant Hollis's ass pushed against the top of Taylin's thighs. To aid a closer connection, Taylin moved his hands under Hollis's suit jacket to place them on his hips, bringing the little omega closer. Next, Taylin effortlessly lifted him up off the ground so Hollis could rub his bountiful ass against Taylin's cock.

"Arghhh," Hollis gasped, flexing his hips in a rolling motion, sliding up and down the clothed cock behind him as best he could while dangling in mid-air. Hollis grabbed for Taylin, laying his hands over his and gripping hold. Silky hair brushed the side of Taylin's cheek as Hollis laid his head on his shoulder. Barely a beat passed before Hollis buried his face into Taylin's neck, his lips parting to suck at the spot right under his jawline, where his pulse beat.

Hot pants ghosted over Taylin's neck as two tongues emerged and ran over the fast beating pulse, adding to the sensory overload. The closeness Taylin had craved for so long morphed into a voracious monster. Taylin gasped right along with Hollis as the pygmy loris tongues moved in differing motions over his throat. One flicking over the skin while the other licked a path up to his earlobe.

Taylin's grip tightened, his biceps bulging with the effort to maintain their current position in the confined space. He worked hard to resist his baser instincts when a part of his brain tossed at him the reality that they had an audience mere inches away, apparently unaware they were putting on a show.

No sooner had the thought floated through his head than there was a loud gasp that didn't come from him or Hollis. Did he care... *no.*

The issue was, he'd been with other omegas in the past when they'd gone through their heat, and never felt an incomprehensible desire to rut. He'd heard other alphas explain the maniacal need. Being divergent, Taylin had believed that was the reason he'd never experienced that kind of driving passion.

It was a mind fuck to discover this in an elevator. He wasn't different, he'd just never met the one—until now—to bring out his full animal needs.

Mate.

Hyperventilating, his chest erratically rising and falling, he lowered a mewling Hollis to the floor, hating the loss of close contact. He worked hard to focus and breathe while getting his brain to figure out how much longer till they got out of the box. It was impossible to talk, to act like a civil human when Hollis gyrated his ass on Taylin's thigh. It became a battle. A war of resistance.

Keep it tofuckinggether.

Only four floors.

Hot and ridiculous smelling skin tantalized and provoked his animal.

Bollocks!

Fuckity fucking bollocks!

Stop pushing, we're in public, he demanded of his animal as his jaw ached. A feeling so deep-rooted to bite caused pain to ripple through Taylin at holding back his innate need to claim the man currently wriggling impatiently against him.

"Hollis," he snarled through the pain.

Sweat beaded on Taylin's skin as he fought himself and his animal. His shirt clung to his skin, and he prayed like a motherfucker they'd reach their floor before he did something utterly out of character. Ripping all of Hollis's clothes from his body and mounting him in front of an audience sure as hell would not go down well.

Come on!

Please, get us the fuck there already.

The doors opened once more and the last two people got out, giving Taylin a look of disgust. He didn't care when it gave him a moment of relief, right until the door went to shut. Instead of closing, a large hand shot through the gap, stopping it from shutting, and an inhuman growl followed. Taylin, fast as lightning, pushed Hollis behind him and matched the growl with one of his own when a huge alpha appeared.

Easily as big as Booker, Taylin didn't think twice and bared his teeth, snarling, "He's mine!"

Hollis pressed against his back, his hands tearing at Taylin's shirt. "Need you," he whimpered, appearing unaware of how serious the situation was.

The air became charged with alpha aggression. The posturing man wasn't going to listen to reason as he eyed up Taylin. How could he when then the sound's Hollis was making were as delicious as his potent pheromones.

"He's mine," Taylin reiterated, snarling, ready to fight to the death to keep the alpha from touching Hollis. Only Hollis was too busy trying to distract him with roving hands.

"My love..." Taylin untangled himself, "we got a situation..." and stepped away from Hollis.

"Don't leave me!"

"I'm not my love," he explained in exasperation, not once taking his eyes from the red faced, foaming alpha who was craning his neck to get a better look at Hollis.

"Get out of my way," the guy snarled, stretching to his full height.

Taylin didn't give the alpha the chance to do or say more and came up on the balls of his feet, both fists raising. He leapt forward and double punched the enormous chest, using all his strength to propel the guy into the hallway. He thanked Booker for teaching him how to do that when the guy landed with a thud that Taylin felt through the soles of his shoes. Back in the elevator and hitting the button to close the door, the man's screams got blocked when the elevator moved.

Taylin snarled in satisfaction, swinging around to check on Hollis. He grunted at the impact of a leaping Hollis hitting his chest. Taylin instinctively cupped Hollis's ass to hold on to him, while adjusting his stance to stop from toppling over. Hollis's legs encased his waist as arms slid around his neck before fingers dove into his curls and fisted tightly enough to make his eyes water.

With no time to take a breath, Hollis slammed his mouth against Taylin's.

"Kiss me!" Hollis demanded against his lips.

Chapter Fifteen

Hollis

Throughout the meal, Hollis did his best to present the professional he was.

Really?

I did!

It was pointless to argue with his animal half when his hormones had shifted around inside him to create a heady mix of want and need. One more powerful than he'd expected. It hit harder and faster than an indie racing car. Hollis had fought himself—he had—then done the only sensible thing and given in, telling everyone at the table what was going to happen.

Who knew what would be in the PA group chat when his body stopped playing with him—did he care? Part of the reason he'd lingered too long in the restaurant was just that and as speedily as they'd left, he was now in trouble. He should have prompted an earlier conversation with the others about what was going to happen.

What is happening right now, his animal pointed out in a snarky way that riled Hollis up further. His skin flamed with the need to be naked. To have Taylin's large body against his without any barriers.

In his current state, Hollis directed all the roiling passions at the man who'd violently defended him against the unwanted attentions of another alpha. Through the tunnel vision of lust, a part of Hollis understood how dicey things could have gotten. Despite that, another part hadn't contemplated a different outcome, even with the seriousness of the situation.

Witnessing Taylin acting all aggressive over him... should he have gotten pissed at that?

Good luck with that. Your hunger is my hunger, his animal came back with, pushing all of Hollis's buttons with images, flooding his mind with them as he devoured the mouth crushing his. An image of biting at Taylin's throat while being impaled on his cock, his knot stretching him until all he could feel was the burn, made him shudder and rock against Taylin's body wildly.

Was he gasping into Taylin's mouth? It sure as hell felt like it as he fought his baser instincts while his tongues delved inside Taylin's parted lips. One wrapped around it, while the over teased at where the taste buds were eliciting a guttural moan which vibrated through both men.

Had anyone ever defended him so animalistically? If they had, Hollis had no recollection of it, and it fed his inner desire. A fierce and commanding Taylin—something Hollis had never witnessed before and never thought Taylin capable of—was wholly different.

Taylin's aggressive energy fueled the insatiable side of Hollis that his heat brought on. Gone was the man who thought too much and worried about professional boundaries. Taylin's behavior tore away the last vestiges of Hollis's resistance. His attraction to Taylin from the beginning paled into insignificance. The revelation of what hid underneath that calm exterior scorched a path directly to Hollis's soul.

He understood there was no going back now, that Taylin was his. It was a moot point—how could it be anything else when Hollis was grinding on a rock hard cock and sucking and playing with Taylin's tongue like it was his favorite strawberry lollipop?

Hunger drove Hollis to deepen the kiss, demanding more from Taylin. His taste was more of an explosion of exotic flavors that drove the craving higher. He clawed at Taylin's clothes blindly, to get to the warm, fragrant skin beneath. His hips gyrated in a sexy rhythm as his slick scented the air. The feel of stickiness at the back of his trousers sent out a signal of his neediness *for his alpha.*

He groaned in dismay when hot, erratic breaths touched his face as the ripe tasting lips disappeared. Ripples of desire that charged thousands of cells and made his body hum, lessened.

In a daze, he groaned in frustration when Taylin evaded him. "Don't stop," he begged, freeing his hands from the torn shirt to clasp Taylin's head and forcibly bring his mouth back to where it belonged.

"We... need... out... of the lift," Taylin wheezed breathlessly, staggering as he dodged Hollis's wet, hungry kisses.

There were voices coming through the fog clouding everything, but Hollis didn't care about them. He wanted *his alpha*. Needed him to help with the wildness running through him that only the enormous cock pulsing against his ass would assuage. "Fuck me," he demanded against Taylin's throat, where he trailed kisses in the absence of Taylin's mouth.

Hollis buried his face into the musky skin and bit hard enough to get a curse and a full body shudder. The cock under his ass hardened and pushed up.

Oh yeah!

Hollis ground down, his thighs squeezing tightly and angled his ass to rub on the head of the pulsing shaft under too many layers.

Taylin cursed loudly, or so Hollis thought, but he was enjoying himself. His teeth sinking deeper into the flesh, as desperate as his animal to taste Taylin's life force.

At the odd jostling that lifted his hips up and down, Hollis's lips quirked up. "Yes... more... naked... need to be naked," he demanded, unable to focus on anything other than how his ass ached to be filled. For Taylin's thick shaft to slide deep inside him... fill him until Taylin sated the wild cravings.

Nothing else would do, not even his toys, now he had Taylin's scent in his nose. There was jostling and more noise, none of it made any sense.

A feeling of falling got his eyes to open as he landed and bounced on something soft... *a bed.*

Yes!

"Nooooo," he cried when he got some of his brain cells to work and noticed Taylin heading back for the door. His nose wrinkled in distress while his ears pounded with the rate of his heartbeat.

Go get him, his animal stated, none too happily.

Hollis didn't need his animal side to encourage him. He scrambled off the bed like a heat-seeking missile locked on his target, only with an uncoordinated body.

Taylin stopped at the open door then slammed it shut, but Hollis's heat made it impossible to compute why he wasn't naked and giving Hollis what he desired.

"Need you," Hollis sobbed in desperation as he grabbed Taylin's shredded jacket and yanked it off.

When Taylin swung around, his chest heaving, what was left of his shirt whipped at Hollis's face. Their gazes locked and the air between them buzzed with the fierceness of their mutual desire. Hollis felt it right down to his bone, to his heart, connecting him—connecting them. The rawness of desire was too much to resist, so he didn't. He launched himself at Taylin, only to find air where Taylin had stood.

Taylin's hands came up to ward him off as he backed away. "Fuck, you're killing me," he rasped. "Gotta lock the door before I lose myself in you. Please, I need to keep you safe."

At the frantic beat of his own thudding heart, the words came mashed together. At a resounding clicking sound, Taylin returned his attention to Hollis. Trembling hands tugged at what remained of his shirt, throwing it on the floor where the jacket lay.

Yes!

Naked was what Hollis wanted.

Hollis mindlessly tore at his own clothes, his hands uncoordinated, his brain running faster than a cheetah at its top speed. Some part of him registered that Taylin's actions were about keeping him safe, which spread a warmth through him. It was wholly different from that of his heat, and it made his chest swell with something he wasn't in the right mind to consider.

Later, worry about it later.

The time for logic was gone—his animal was right—when a naked and fully aroused Taylin was stalking him. His eyes blazed with the beast inside he couldn't transform into, but it was there, showing Hollis's animal he wanted them. Hollis' animal reacted and used his own method to attract its mate; he whistled.

The musical sound startled Taylin into immobility. His head titled to the left, and then he snarled, a sound that sent shivers of longing through Hollis and straight to his ass.

Next thing, Taylin came at Hollis so fast he didn't have a chance to blink before Taylin had his arms around him. Full body contact came with a low moan that vibrated through both men when Taylin effortlessly lifted Hollis's naked body into the air so their mouths became aligned. Taylin kissed him with a passion so breathtaking, Hollis sank into the headiness of it without a thought about his need to breathe. It addled his already confused brain when his lungs screamed for air and he found they were back on the bed.

He had wrapped his thighs around Taylin and cradled him against his pelvis, rocking up to get as much friction on his throbbing shaft. Firm, warm flesh rubbed against his, stimulating his overheated body. The scents in the room were powerful enough that Hollis's animal pushed him to shift.

I need Taylin.

Give me a minute, he snapped sulkily, *you always get to have all the fun times. I want to play.*

Hollis fought his animal and the sulky tone, only his animal wasn't listening and before Hollis could stop him, the shift was upon them.

"Holy shit," Taylin exclaimed, rolling immediately onto his back. Wide eyed, he stared at Hollis. A second passed before he reached out to run a finger gently over the top of his pygmy loris's head. "Fuck, I knew you'd be beautiful, Hollis."

The reverence they could hear was all the invitation his animal needed to crawl up on top of Taylin and for him to whistle again, presenting itself in a submissive pose on his chest.

Everything else ceased to matter in that moment when Taylin's growls rumbled with a possessiveness that Hollis's animal fawned over.

Time passed as Hollis receded, knowing his animal wanted the time to acquaint itself with Taylin.

Our mate.

In his mind, he chuckled at the assertion. Hollis's awareness in his animal form varied depending on his animal's mood. Right now, he was helping Hollis control the wild urges while in his animal form. Hollis had never shifted when he was in heat before, so this was new to him.

He's our mate, everything is different this time.

Hollis was sure his animal was right, but he worried his reaction was all because of his body's soup of pheromones.

Stop being so stupid! Smell him. Taste him.

Before he could argue that he could do none of those things in his animal form, he shifted once more with no warning, finding himself sat astride Taylin's large body. Golden, hairless skin had a thin layer of sweat covering it. It glistened in the low lights above the bed, highlighting all the dips and curves of Taylin's musculature.

"Beautiful," Hollis whimpered as he came forward, his desperation returning in a violent rush of endorphins. His hands slid over the silky feeling skin, his body gliding down Taylin's. The movement caused his breath to arrest in his chest when his slick ass moved down the hard shaft under him. His ass clenched and the slick coming from him coated the cock he sat on top of. There was no thought to stop himself rocking back and forth to elevate the molten fire singing through his veins.

Taylin bucked beneath him, thrusting up, adding friction causing them both to release throaty groans.

"More," Hollis whimpered when he got his breath back. "Want you inside me. Want to feel your knot."

Beneath his ass, the cock swelled impossibly bigger, branding Hollis's ass. He rocked, groaned and mewled, begging for more. The ache deep inside him was impossible to think past it. To give him time to get with the programme of how to make it happen when all his senses were being bombarded at once. At home, with his toys, he could prepare.

Here and now, with the cock beneath him, which teased him mercilessly, he had no presence of mind.

"In me," he begged. "In, me, now." The words came from his desire. He rose and slick dripped from him as he reached between his legs and groaned at the slippery, pulsing hardness.

Taylin's groan sounded painful as it rent the air and his hands took hold of Hollis in a punishing grip. He reveled at it. Losing control was what he and his animal wanted. They pursued Taylin, wanting him to be as mindless as them.

The sounds of their rapid breathing didn't quite mask the squelching noise as Hollis's ass painted the head of Taylin's cock, which throbbed in time to Hollis's own heartbeat, fast and wild. Time and time again, he used his aching hole and circled his hips so the head of Taylin's dick opened his ass.

"Fuck, that's hot," Taylin rasped. Nerve endings woke to the stimulation, but it was Taylin's words that added power to the desire to sink down and feel the hot, hard cock split him open.

Dark, deep pools of desire held Hollis's gaze. His desire was evident as his ass opened, taking the head of Taylin's cock. The slick made his ass yield and his muscles burn in delight as Hollis squeezed, producing more slick.

"Motherfucker," Taylin ground out, coming up off the bed, his cock sinking deeper, rubbing against the nerves and driving Hollis wild for more.

Hollis's brain didn't compute that it should maybe wait with how thick and long Taylin's cock was. Fuck no, he reached back and held onto his ass cheeks, stretching himself wide and, in a fluid move, slid down until his ass hit Taylin's groin.

"Fucker... what... oh fuck... don't fucking move," Taylin cried out as if in pain. His eyes rolled back as the grip on Hollis increased. He suspected there'd be bruises and his animal fawned at the idea once more.

"More... need you to move," Hollis growled, uncaring of how harsh Taylin's hold was, or how his ass was adjusting to the wonderful burn and stretch of his muscles. His toys had never filled him so full.

The air hissed through his teeth when Taylin ignored his demand. Never one to wait, his animal side forced the matter. His teeth became sharper as he surged forward and his mouth opened to latch on Taylin's throat.

They moaned together, Taylin pushing into the scrape of teeth and that was all the invitation they needed. He struck true and at the first sip of blood touching his tongues, Hollis lost it.

It was surreal how everything faded away and his body quaked, and sparks lit behind his eyelids in an array of fireworks that burst with beauty as his eyelids drifted shut. Nothing he'd felt or seen was more beautiful than Taylin taking up residence in his soul. He nestled right in, Hollis could feel his presence right along with his animals.

Tears ran unheeded down his cheeks, unnoticed as the potent desire followed quickly in its wake to assault Hollis's senses. Violent shivers came in the aftermath and Hollis swallowed deep to assuage the hunger.

"Yes... my sweet pygmy loris... claim me... I'm yours," Taylin moaned, driving his desire higher.

Hollis's ass contracted as he rose to help alleviate the ache that increased tenfold with the taste of Taylin. His fingers fisted in Taylin's curls, dragging him closer to slam back down on the hard shaft. The feel of it stroking deep drove him on to repeat the move, stealing his sanity with how he couldn't feel Taylin deep enough.

"Deeper," he growled breathlessly. "Need you deeper."

In response, Taylin's hands went under his ass, holding him as he came up.

Before Hollis could complain at Taylin's cock sliding from his body, he landed on the mattress. Taylin placed his legs on his shoulders, and he sank back into Hollis. Taylin came forward, his cock brushing all the right places as his arms supported him and caged Hollis in. A light of wickedness was the only warning as Taylin powered into him with a force that made the bed creak.

"Yes," Hollis moaned, "yes... deeper. Need it."

His cock bobbed in time to his pulse. Every forward thrust caused Taylin's stomach muscles to graze sensually against the head of Hollis's weeping cock.

"Yes... gods... more. Want your mouth on me," he gasped, knowing it was impossible, but his logical mind wasn't in charge.

He moaned in complaint when Taylin changed position, his eyelids too heavy to lift. They struggled to get with the programme and do what he wanted when he heard noise and Taylin hips stilled.

"Ohhhhhhh," Hollis moaned, when his cock got sucked into the fleshlight and a moment later, Taylin grasped the back of one of Hollis's legs while the other took hold of the fleshlight.

Then Hollis's world became a sensory display of pleasure that didn't miss one cell in his body. The passion skipped about causing utter chaos until Hollis no longer had a thought beyond the need to come.

"Wanna come," he whined mindlessly, his body on the brink but somehow unable to dive off the platform into the abyss of pleasure waiting for him.

"I'll give you everything you want, I swear," Taylin growled harshly. Skin slapping loudly came with desperate panting as sweat gathered on Hollis's skin. The deep seated ache in his ass grew until there was only that. He clenched down and thrust up when Taylin slammed deep. Before he could register the powerful pull on his sac and the surge of gut wrenching need pulsing down his cock, Taylin claimed his mouth.

He bit at the two tongues winding around his. Blood, his own, filled Hollis's mouth and Taylin's knot expanded, sealing them together as cum pumped deep in his ass. It seared and burned along with the stretch of the knot.

Unbelievable, mind-altering pleasure came when the knot locked them together. Hollis, unaware of his actions, tore the fleshlight from his cock at the first spurt of cum tearing from him. Cum coated him and Taylin with his scent.

His primal side needed to mark his mate while Taylin's knot made them one.

Made them whole—

Ours, his animal interjected as Taylin's cum continued to pump deep in Hollis's ass, his cock giving up its last valiant spurts.

Ours!

Chapter Sixteen

Delicious & Vicious Chat

Frey: *You'll never believe what's happened. Hollis has come away knowing he's going to go into a heat! Why would sensible Hollis do that?I mean that's something I'd do, but Hollis*

Ziggy: *What… wait… what the heck am I missing? Hollis is having his heat. Now?*

Bowie: *What Ziggy said. I was snoozing because the shit who's my boss decided we needed to work late! Am I dreaming this or did you really say Hollis is having a heat in work time?*

Wilder: *If you're dreaming Bowie, then so am I, cause there's no way Hollis would be so… I don't know what the word is!*

Lennon: *Daring! But Frey's telling the truth. You should have seen the brothers' reactions. Rue looked like a guppie. I'm gonna admit the thoughts of Hollis and Taylin right now getting their grove on in this hotel, I'm a little jealous. I can't remember the last time I had an alpha to… well… you know.*

Wilder: *I feel you Lennon. I went to one of those places once, to hire an alpha, he was okay but my raccoon wouldn't let me step fully into the room. I've never driven home so fast in my life, terrified I'd have an accident and some alpha would find me and I'd be too far out of control to say no. I didn't speak to my animal for a* *month after that. But I gotta say, at least one of us is happy with their choice of Starling brother.*

Ziggy: *We can come back to that Wilder, as I'm sure we are all in the same boat with our choice of brother. So Frey, how did y'all find out?*

Frey: *Booker isn't as bad as I first thought.*

Ziggy: *You hated him only days ago! And you never answered my question.*

Monty: *He announced it at dinner, like it was nothing important. Much like he would when he's asking whose turn it is to make cake. I swear I nearly swallowed my tongue at his boldness. I wish I could be more like that.*

Bowie: *Huh! Frey, what Ziggy said. Wasn't it you that was calling him out for everything exactly five days ago when he wouldn't let you go to the hairdressers before your trip away?*

Lennon: *They had a moment tonight……*

Isley: *Wait, what am I missing? Let me catch up, my Starling brother is trying to work me into an early grave!*

Ziggy: *Can we go back to Hollis?*

Frey: *Shut up Lennon, we didn't have a moment. He was being nice after the awfulness of the visit to the factory, is all.*

Isley: *I'm lost. What are we talking about?*

***Bowie:** Me too.*

***Frey:** Blame Lennon. To recap, Taylin announced at the dinner table that he wasn't coming to work tomorrow, and this pissed off Booker. Not hard as we know. Anyway, Hollis then added his two cents worth when Booker got all growly at Taylin not following his plans by saying Hollis and he wouldn't be available because they were going to be getting it on because of Hollis's heat. I must say I noticed Hollis's change of scent, but I was too upset to notice why until after they dropped the bombshell.*

***Lennon:** It wasn't quite like that, but near as, I suppose. It's not like we didn't know that Hollis was pretending not to be interested in Taylin. He's good but not that good at hiding how he looks at Taylin when he thinks no one is watching him.*

Ziggy: *I didn't know. I don't suppose that matters right now when I've a feeling this is going to piss off a few of the brothers when Hollis has a casting vote on things related to the business. I'm sure they aren't gonna like that Taylin and Hollis are getting naked, hot and sweaty. Big sigh! I'm with Wilder, I'm a little jealous, my ex moved on faster than a slab of hot butter on a grill.*

Frey: *Alpha's can be such pigs, so sorry Ziggy. How do we know this is going to be more than a one off?*

Bowie: *Don't forget Beta's can be the same! And please, when did you ever see Hollis do anything without careful consideration? This means something serious to him, I'd swear it on all of my secret cake recipes!*

Wilder: *Wow, your cake recipes, that's some confidence. Do you have some insight we don't?*

Bowie: *Nah. I'm just very observant.*

Frey: *We all know how observant you are of a certain brother.*

Ziggy: *Leave Bowie alone Frey, you're just as bad, even though you flirt with all the brothers.*

Isley: *I like you Ziggy*

Bowie: *Me too*

Frey: *Getting back to the subject. Do you think Taylin will be a sex machine? I mean, I've seen Hollis's sex drawer with all his toys. The man is a size whore for sure. I've never noticed what Taylin was packing. Anyone else notice?*

Ziggy: *And on that note I'm out.*

Bowie: *You had to go there, Frey! I'm off to bed too.*

Frey: *I was only concerned for Hollis. No one wants to be disappointed in the bedroom… or any room, for that matter.*

Monty: *Night Frey, see you in the morning when I hope you'll bring your best behavior with you to breakfast.*

Frey: *You guys are no fun…*

Isley: *We are, we just don't always think with our dicks. And you seem to have forgotten Hollis can see this conversation…*

Frey: *Sorry Hollis*

Chapter Seventeen

Alphaholes Chat

Booker: *You guys, did Tay mention his plans for the weekend?*

Silas: *You're away working, that's his plans. What am I missing?*

Jupiter: *Something evidently by the cryptic question if Tay is not working. Get with the program, Silas.*

Silas: *If you are chatting on here I'd say you've lost your program!*

Booker: *Give over you pair. Tay isn't working unless you figure him getting naked and working Hollis into the mattress or any flat surface he can find as work?*

Kari: *Wow… have I missed a conversation or something? I thought he was still batting zero with Hollis?*

Kodi: *Yeah. That is not what's going down right now. You could have knocked me over with a fucking feather the way Hollis announced in front of everyone our bro was gonna help him through his heat! And we weren't the only shocked ones, his team were none the wiser by the way they went silent after Hollis and Tay left.*

Rue: *I wasn't that surprised!*

Laken: *I'm not surprised either. Those two have been circling each other for years. It's about time they did something about it. Although the timing leaves a lot to be desired. At least there is an upside… Tay will stop nagging us for information about Hollis, hopefully!*

Silas: *Laken's right, the timing fucking sucks. How is this going to affect the business? It's gonna, I'm telling you. That damn casting vote if it's needed will be… fuck knows, but something is gonna have to be said!*

Laken: *Silas, you are saying something. Have you forgotten Tay can see your concerns in black and fucking white? What about Tay's happiness, shouldn't that come first? You want him happy, right?*

Silas: *Of course I do! He's my brother, was there to save my fucking ass when it counted. It's just… fuck with all these* *recent changes, we haven't had time to adapt. Then we have the damn press conference next week. I'd hate for them to target Tay if anyone got wind of Hollis's new role in the company and that Tay, and he were getting down and dirty*

Booker: *Is that what's playing on your mind? The press conference to announce you're the new head of Starling Enterprises?*

Silas: *Yeah… I suppose… fuck! And let's not confuse the issue, I'm not the head of the company and neither do I want to be. Replacing Dad as the face, I fucking don't want that either because…*

Kodi: *We got you covered, you don't need to say it. Fuck those divergent haters!*

Kari: *Exactly that! And we have your back, big bro. We're all gonna be there showing a unified front. Let the haters* *hate and stick their crazy ideas where the sun don't fucking shine. It won't stop us from loving and supporting each other. Never has.*

Kodi: *Well put, little bro.*

Kari: *There's fucking three minutes between us and do I need to remind you I'm three inches taller than you.*

Jupiter: *Boy's behave. You Alphaholes have gotten nothing to worry about, they'll all be looking at me.*

Silas: *dickwad!*

Jupiter: *Made you laugh though, didn't I? We all got you covered. So, what's this about Tay? Come on, dish all the deets.*

Booker: *What deets, you perv! They're in the hotel room as we type doing… whatever!*

Jupiter: *You jealous?*

Booker: *Fuck you and with that good night!*

Jupiter: *Booker, sometimes I worry about you. Where's your fun side?*

Silas: *Behave, Jup. We aren't all like you, who have to be the center of attention, despite what attention you get!*

Chapter Eighteen

Taylin

Sex. The room reeked of it and although Taylin was exhausted after the last three days, his cock twitched as he roamed away from the bed. The smell they'd produced together was powerful and enough to make him wonder if the extra precautions the hotel took might not be good enough. Not that any alpha besides the one at the lift had tried to get into the room. Hollis's insatiable need had been Taylin's own undoing. He'd used every ounce of his willpower to make sure the door got safely locked.

The tiny pygmy loris was a damn sex machine, not that Taylin was complaining. He just hadn't had so much sex in a decade. His cock was raw with how often he'd had his cock inside Hollis. They had used every surface in the room, including the walls.

Would he be the same when he wasn't having his heat?

God, Taylin hoped he'd find out. They hadn't talked about what came next, and a sliver of doubt that this could be a one time thing crept past his contentment. In the bathroom, he filled the sink to occupy his mind with anything that wasn't an actual thought. Picking up the body wash off the shelf, he uncapped it and gave it a quick sniff before pouring a liberal amount into the warm water.

Hollis was out cold and had been since after the last round of sex. It was the need to take care of Hollis that drove an exhausted Taylin from the cum stained sheets. His gaze caught his own reflection in the mirror. Besides the dark circles under his eyes and the possibility he'd lost a pound or two, Taylin looked the same. Yet, he wasn't. His gaze drifted to the bite mark on his neck, his fingers traced the edges of the healed, slightly raised skin. Taylin could easily remember the euphoric feelings crashing through him like a bulldozer in a forest, uncaring what path it took or what it demolished. Those tiny teeth had wrecked him. He'd come so hard, filling Hollis with his seed until his balls throbbed at the force.

His heart thumped hard enough to make his ears pound at how he'd wanted desperately to bite Hollis in return, yet he'd held back. A part of him wanted to know for sure that it wasn't Hollis's heat that made him want to mate. The command a heat held over an omega was strong. But was it strong enough to make them want to mate without consequence?

Taylin had never felt the urge to bite. Rut, yes, but never to bite. To taste the rich blood that flowed through Hollis's veins. He'd nipped at Hollis's tongues, driven by the wildness of his animal pushing at him.

It wasn't just me!

Are you sure?

Give over, you lapped at his tongue with a desperation unmatched by anything you've eaten or drank in your whole life. I would know.

Taylin had no comeback when his animal side spoke the truth.

It was as lowering as when Taylin had needed to use the bag of sex toys to keep Hollis satisfied, giving his body a chance to recover. In the beginning, Taylin had used the fleshlight more to give Hollis what Taylin wasn't flexible enough to give him. After a sweaty round four, with legs shaking through the sheer amount of energy he'd expelled and balls that felt like they'd shrunk to peanuts by the time Hollis had wrung them dry, he'd known that sex toys were necessary.

His mind was a blur with how many things they'd done, with and without toys. His cock and knot were indeed bigger than Hollis's toy, which was a double-edged sword. Hollis, it turned out, wasn't as happy to have the dildo when it didn't stretch him the same way Taylin could.

A noise came from the other room and Taylin realized he had been standing staring at himself with one hand in the sink, the other rubbing at his neck.

He shook his head and reached for a washcloth that sat on the counter next to the marble skink and tried not to think about how his body ached from his head to his pinky toes.

Walking from the sink to the heated towel rail, he noted he was walking like one of Silas's cowboys who managed his ranch after being in the saddle all day. Three days would do that to a person, or so he'd found out.

He strolled back into the bedroom, clutching the towel and the soapy washcloth, only to get assailed by the strength of their combined scent once more. Neither of them had showered since Saturday night. They'd eaten what Taylin had ordered after the first twenty-four hours when he'd run out of steam. He'd wanted to take care of all Hollis's needs, despite him only being interested in eating Taylin's cock at that point, wanting it hard and serviceable.

He chuckled, wondering if Hollis would recall his behavior.

Mind bending. Utterly mind bending that Hollis was so different. An experience so life altering now Taylin had some breathing room to think about it and acknowledge Hollis was indeed his mate. Taylin was old-fashioned enough to want to take Hollis home to meet his dad's officially before letting the raging hormones take over.

Too late for that.

He dropped the towel on the bed and stared at the man lying on his stomach, one arm thrown above his head and the other buried under the pillow Taylin had been lying on.

Was he using it because Taylin had lain on it?

The romantic part of his soul loved the idea, even as the practical side said it was just the closest to his hand.

The mark on his neck tingled when Hollis made a muffled noise, between a soft snore and a contented sigh, his ass catching Taylin's gaze as it flexed, then relaxed.

Fuck!

Taylin eyed his own stirring cock with disbelieve.

He needs to rest! I need to rest!

He shook his head once more, his lips twitching as he placed a knee on the bed to get close enough to reach the drying cum and slick coating Hollis's ass and the back of his thighs.

An unbidden thought got him pausing. Would Hollis regret what they'd done? Would he even remember?

While he stared at the sleeping man, he could find no answer.

His gaze shifted away, needing a moment to contain the need to wake Hollis and demand answers. Torn clothes, dirty plates, half the bedding littering the floor. All that was easier to think about. One of the rugs was in a heap, furniture had moved or looked like it had cum and slick stains on it.

His eyes widened at how nothing was untouched.

Taylin returned his attention to the man on the bed and flushed, worrying how he'd feel to wake to the mess. His dark hair resembled a bird's nest, pretty much like Taylin's after the amount of times Hollis had tugged on it.

He was gorgeous. A feast for the eyes, one Taylin never wanted to look away from. He came closer to gently wash away the flaking cum on Hollis's skin. Once happy, he dried the skin, only occasionally getting a twitch in response from

Hollis, who didn't once open his eyes as his chest rose and fell rhythmically.

Taylin returned to the bathroom four more times as he silently bathed Hollis, rolling him carefully and changing the sheet under him after finding replacements in the closet. The hotel really had thought of everything. When the scent of sex lessened, Taylin felt satisfied he'd done enough and retrieved a fresh cover to place over Hollis before returning to the bathroom to shower.

Tiredness swept through him as he stepped under the steamy water. Heat soaked through his weariness, but he didn't have enough energy left to do more than give himself a perfunctory wash.

Out of the shower, he ran the towel over his wet skin before giving his curls a quick rub as he gave a jaw cracking yawn. What little energy he had when he returned to the bed, he used to pull Hollis on top of him after he lay down.

Hollis curled up on him, groaning and shoving his face into Taylin's neck, snuffling around until he settled right over where he'd bitten Taylin.

A smile tugged at his lips. "Sleep, my love, sleep," he murmured sleepily as the tiredness swept over him and his eyes drifted shut.

Lights flashed above him and directly into his eyes, making Taylin struggle to escape the following burning sensation.

"Stop," he whined, finding he had no energy to do more when his body hurt everywhere.

"It's alright, they're just examining you to see what injuries you have," the sweetest voice said as a gentle hand stroked the side of his painful cheek.

It hurt too much to open his eyes, however Taylin suspected by the smell of antiseptic he was in the hospital.

As it sank in, he jerked up, aware he had no money for medical care. His thoughts were all jumbled together when he saw Silas on a gurney next to him. A giant of a guy hovered at the side of his bed wearing what looked like a hospital gown, though he wasn't sporting any obvious injury Taylin could see.

A tiny man stood, dressed in a suit that Taylin thought by the cut and style was worth more than his father earned in a month, next to a guy in a set of scrubs, and gave him a bright smile. "It's alright, we're going to take care of you."

"I don't have any money," Taylin blurted out in a panic ridden state, causing his body to ache from every punch and kick those boys had landed before...

His gaze darted around the room, searching for the bear he recalled before passing out. How had he escaped the bear? The sound of alarms going off made the situation worse as Taylin scrambled to get off the bed, caught in the wires attached to him. His gaze roamed wildly as he searched for his things, terrified the bear was somewhere close.

"Calm down, Taylin." It was said with a calm authority that Taylin wanted to immediately do as he was told. "Please child, you have nothing to be frightened of in here. If you give me your parents' number, I'll ring them to let them know that you're safe and to tell them how grateful we are that you stepped in to help our son, Silas, from those dreadful bullies. They'll be so proud of you. I'm just so sorry you got hurt in doing so."

Heart beating so hard his ears rang, Taylin shook his head. "It's fine... honest... just let me have my stuff back..."

He didn't know the other man or the doctor—he had to be one as he wore a look of authority that suggested he knew what he was doing—but the expressions they wore suggested they would not do that.

"He can't go home. They kicked him out," said the big guy standing next to Silas.

Silas gave the big guy a hard knock to his ribs with his elbow, causing him to wince and rub at his side.

Taylin cringed at how these guys knew about his personal circumstances when he had done his best to keep a low profile at school. He could only guess it came from his older brother, who was in Silas's year at school.

Desperation crawled through him and he decided enough was enough and jumped off the gurney, only regretting it when the full extent of his injuries sang a painful tune, causing his legs to give out.

The doctor was the fastest to catch him, and Taylin released a painful moan at the feel of the arms tightening around his bruised ribs.

As the doctor helped him back onto the gurney, Taylin tried hard not to cry.

"Is this true?"

Silas's dad stared at him once the doctor stepped back. Something distinctly honest about the openness of his expression forced Taylin to swallow back his denial. He wet his lips, getting a taste of coppery blood, seeing there was nothing for it but to tell the truth.

"Yes," he replied, holding the man's gaze, feeling unable to break it when he thought it was the only thing tethering him in place right then.

"Then you're coming home with us." He turned to the stunned-looking doctor. "Give him a thorough check, and then we can talk about a treatment plan. I'll need one for Silas and Booker."

"I'll be fine. I need to head home before I miss my curfew," Booker muttered, a deep red flush spreading over his cheeks when Silas's dad gave him a look that could rival any alpha, which clearly Booker was, and Silas's dad was not.

"You'll do as you're told, young man. I'll explain everything to your parents." His gaze moved between them, his eyes glistened with tears. "There is no way I can ever repay you for saving my boy tonight, but I'll try."

The words ran through Taylin's mind and a sob brought him from his slumber at the feel of a hand touching his wet cheek. Taylin blinked into the inky darkness and worked to suck back the next sob as his mind woke to the reality the hand touching him was Hollis's.

A gentle caress came first as the hand slid down his cheek until it rested against his neck, cupping it with a tenderness that made Taylin's chest constrict.

"What's wrong?" There was a strain in Hollis's voice to suggest a concern that the hand didn't convey.

Had he been talking in his sleep? It happened when he was stressed. Tired. Over-stimulated. And he was certainly all three. He was also unsure how long he'd slept for.

Taylin placed his hand hesitantly over Hollis's, inhaling deeply his sweet scent. Somehow, that helped to settle his bounding pulse the past had caused.

"Dreaming," he answered, unsure whether Hollis would be interested in his sordid history or if he could share some of his most painful memories.

They'd had amazing sex and Hollis had claimed him, but what did they really know about each other?

He heaved a deep sigh of displeasure at how ass about face he'd done this relationship thing with Hollis.

"Did... did I do something wrong?"

In a flash, Taylin rolled to switch the lamp on, one he had no memory of switching it off in the first place. He took a deep, steadying breath before he turned back to see the tension in the stiff posture and deep lines etched into Hollis's forehead.

"You've done nothing wrong. I... I was dreaming and... it's hard to sometimes remember how I came to be so lucky to have met Popi, despite the circumstances."

Hollis came closer and encouraged Taylin to lay back against the head of the bed, before he moved to curl up on his lap. Tentative fingers roamed down Taylin's chest, stroking with a tenderness that once more brought tears to Taylin's eyes.

"Do you want to talk about it?"

He only talked about what happened with his brothers and Dads. Up to now, it felt far too personal to share beyond them. Who wanted to admit their family tossed them aside?

"You don't have to," Hollis said after a few seconds of silence while Taylin considered how to start.

Hollis tucked his head under Taylin's chin, somehow making it easier to talk. The hand on his chest never stopped moving, gentle strokes that relaxed his body.

"What would you like to know?" he whispered hoarsely, being brave.

Chapter Nineteen

Hollis

The question came with a shuddery breath that touched the top of Hollis's hair. He kept his touch light but pressed closer, wanting to protect Taylin, though he wasn't sure what from. Whatever it was, it was powerful enough to evoke mournful sobbing so strong that it had woken him and made his heart bleed.

Grief. Heart-wrenching loss. It was the only way he could describe it. The kind that tore at one's heart. The kind that a person may possibly never recover from, or not fully.

None of the Starling brothers talked about their past, especially how Booker, Rue, Laken, Jupiter or Taylin had become a part of Lane and Derick's family.

What they had done—or what he imagined by how sore his ass was—had created a deep connection Hollis felt in every fiber of his body, and it pushed him to ask. To know this man on a level he'd feared in the past.

There was no escaping the fact Taylin was now there, inside him. Hollis could sense how Taylin's blood removed the barriers he'd erected to protect himself. What he'd denied to stop the yearning.

Hollis had heard some gossip, but who hadn't when the family was so much in the public eye.

Taylin and Booker had become part of the Starling family first. Beyond that, Hollis had minded his own business. After the last few days of getting to know Taylin, to dig beneath the exterior, Hollis felt like he used a barricade to construct the lie of the laid back and easygoing man he presented to the world. There was so much more to this man and Hollis was ready to explore what that would mean to him—to them.

"How did you meet Lane and Derick?" He kept his tone light, speaking low, matching Taylin's going with the first question that popped into his head.

The chest Hollis lay pressed against revealed how hard Taylin's heart beat. It bumped hard enough for Hollis to feel it deep inside him, like it was his own. He let the silence lengthen, unsure if he should say more. He pretended he didn't need to know, even when it wasn't the truth. It was important, more so now he and his animal had decided Taylin was theirs. That he'd bitten Taylin. Marked him, permanently. Irrevocably.

Before he could utter a word, Taylin pressed his face into Hollis's hair in a move that touched Hollis's soul with its show of vulnerability.

"I think I knew when I was about ten, maybe eleven, I was divergent. It wasn't one thing, just a lot of trivial things that made me different from my family, my siblings."

His lips brushed Hollis's hair, his breath warming Hollis's scalp as he explained, Hollis listening intently to the quiet words.

"At first, I didn't worry if I couldn't feel my animal rippling under my skin. Or I didn't have the same heightened senses my brothers had at my age. Even the lack of excess hair on my body didn't really bother me. Then one day, I came home from school and heard my brother and father discussing a divergent that worked with Father and how he'd gotten a promotion over him and considered should have been his. The hate and anger were staggering to the boy I was. I was naïve at first, believing that he was just mad at missing out." Taylin's body rippled under Hollis, and he made a concerted effort not to tense when he sensed the inner turmoil rolling off Taylin.

Hollis's gut recoiled in apprehension at the possibility of what was coming.

"In the following months, the vitriol continued, only the target of his hate went beyond his colleague. It was anyone successful that was divergent. Then my brother came home having been involved in a fight with another boy who was like me. My father was so happy my brother had given the boy a bloody beating. Even Mom seemed to approve. The reality of what it meant to them became this weight of dread that hung around my neck as each day passed and I worried how long I could hold on to my secret."

Hollis tried and failed to imagine how hard that must have been. His family was supportive of divergents and had met Lane and Derick at several functions. They were proud Hollis worked for a company that wanted to highlight how much it didn't matter about individual differences. For them, they encouraged others to embrace who they were without fear. The sickening dread increased at how this wasn't the case for Taylin and Hollis's heart broke for the boy who had to hide because of hate.

When Taylin lapsed into silence, Hollis waited, holding him closer, softly caressing down the skin he could reach.

When time drifted along, and Taylin's heartbeat slowed, Hollis finally murmured, "What happened?"

There was a second's pause. "Father wanted to go for a run on a full moon when I was fourteen... he expected me to be able to shift with them as I'd reached an age my brothers had all gone through their shift..."

The shudders that followed left Hollis dry mouthed when he thought about Taylin reliving that night, when his heart rate picked up like he was running from a monster. "You don't have to tell me."

Taylin moved and Hollis lifted his head off his chest to see dark, glistening eyes that held pain. Pain that cut deep at Hollis's soul.

"No, I do." Taylin didn't look away, but the way he stared at Hollis suggested he wasn't seeing him, but the past. He licked his lips. "I knew it would happen, that they'd find out the truth. A part of me hoped that because I was family, they'd see past the difference." He blinked so slowly it was as if he was going in slow motion. "I was wrong."

The air in the room disappeared at the despair that came in those three words. Taylin rubbed absently at his side where there were scars that looked like claw marks, and Hollis's blood ran cold at how they'd possibly gotten there. "The beating they gave me was bad enough I couldn't stand straight for days afterwards. It was bad..."

Hollis sucked in a sharp breath at how flat the words came out.

"It was bad," Taylin repeated with more force. "But not as bad as being clawed, spat on, pissed and shit on before they left me in the middle of a wooded area with nothing but the clothes they'd defecated on and told not to bother coming back. That I no longer existed to them."

Tears burned and blurred Hollis's vision as the sobs tore from his throat at how a child would have felt to be violated in such a way. Contempt left a taste so bitter in Hollis's mouth he wasn't sure he'd ever get rid of it. Contempt for Taylin's family—though that term didn't fit what they were to this beautiful man—and the degradation they put him through.

"I'm so sorry," Hollis said through his tears as he shifted to straddle Taylin's lap and cup his pale cheeks.

The man's vacant expression scared Hollis as he came forward and pressed their mouths together, desperate to bring Taylin back to him and away from his past. Hollis tasted the saltiness of their tears as he murmured, "Hold on to me. I'm here, see me. Feel me."

At first, the choked words didn't seem to penetrate, then tension slowly released from Taylin's large body. His mouth went pliant, and his lips parted as hands slid around Hollis's middle, tugging him closer.

Going with it, needing the contact as much as Taylin, Hollis swallowed the sigh Taylin released as he trembled against him. Hollis kissed him softly. The urgency of his heat was long gone and now he wanted to show Taylin the affection he would have lacked.

Hollis took his time to explore the contours of Taylin's mouth. To convey how much he wanted to treasure the moment between them. Honor the gift of trust Taylin had bestowed by sharing something so painful. So personal. Hollis, on so many levels, wasn't able to fully comprehend how one survived such a betrayal, yet Taylin had.

Soft pants brushed against his skin as his mouth trailed down Taylin's stubbly skin, down his throat to where Hollis had laid claim to this man. He teased the healed flesh, running his tongues over the skin that tasted of not only Taylin, but of himself, too.

Ours.

Yes.

The reply, this time, was done with full cognizance as Taylin trembled, his cock hardening under Hollis, but he ignored it. This wasn't about sex, this was all about appreciating his mate.

"Kiss me," Taylin murmured, a hand gently stroking Hollis's cheek. "I need you to kiss me again to stop... to stop the thoughts."

Happy to do just that, Hollis moved, his gaze lingering on Taylin as he inched closer, their lips barely touching. He knew that Taylin had stared once or twice at his mouth when his tongues both came out. He brought them both out and licked at both corners of Taylin's lips in a tiny caress.

Taylin's lips parted on a moan that sent a shiver of longing through Hollis. Taylin's eyes hooded with desire and a heady feeling came at seeing the sadness and pain fade. He teased the upper and lower lip at the same time, getting rewarded with a body shudder.

"Like that?" Hollis asked, knowing the answer from the cock spreading his ass cheeks as it grew harder.

"I never knew you were such a tease." The rasped reply sent Hollis's blood pressure to sore when it came with a wicked glint in pools of decadent chocolate. The hands at his waist slipped down, fingers sliding sensuously over his buttocks as they roamed freely, eliciting a moan of delight. "I've imagined you using those tongues..."

How had the tables turned on him so fast? "Where?" he asked breathlessly.

"On every inch of my skin." Taylin tapped his lips. "Starting here." The sexy grin that fried Hollis's brain cells appeared. "So, what are you waiting for?"

Twenty

Alphaholes Chat

Booker: *How many damn days does a heat last for? Has anyone had any contact with Tay? Dad, anything?*

Dad: *What are you asking me?*

Silas: *Isn't that obvious, Dad? He's asking if you have heard from Tay. He's probably thinking that Tay wouldn't have the balls to reach out to us after taking five days* *to get… off. All I'm gonna say is he better get his ass back here for tomorrow's press conference or I'll kick his fucking ass so hard he won't know which way to sit.*

Dad: *Son, you are clearly not getting enough sex if you are so interested in Taylin's activity in the bedroom. Booker, Why? I'm not in charge, you guys are, or have you already forgotten this?*

Taylin has never let you down Silas, you know this, he'll be here for you.

Booker: *Are you doing this on purpose, Dad? Of course we haven't forgotten. Although maybe Tay has! I knew this was a bad idea for all of us to work together. Tay's supposed to be here working. Instead, he's doing… whatever with Hollis, someone who should also be here doing their job. Only he's boning one of the bosses, which isn't very professional* *if you ask me! I've deadlines to meet and I need to discuss progressing buying the accessories for the spring show.*

Jupiter: *Jealous big bro? You folks need to get a life… just sayin'*

Booker: *Don't you start on me, Jup. I'm in no mood for you. And I'd say you've got your own PA issues. I saw Wilder crying in the passageway earlier. I wonder who caused that?*

Dad: *Do I need to send Popi into the office to sort you all out?*

Silas: *Please don't do that!*

Booker: *I'm sorry, don't send Popi. I can't bear to see his disappointed stare.*

Jupiter: *I second that.*

Dad: *Then stop behaving like a bunch of idiots.*

Booker: *Any update on the purchase of Design Detailing & Co?*

Dad: *Nice dodge Booker... Yes, it's why I came into the group chat in the first place, to update you all. As discussed, we've used the side corporation we established when there is a possibility of backlash because of divergent haters.*

The greedy fuckers snatched up the deal, and it's with the lawyers who are going to iron out the details. Make the deal air-tight in case of any backlash in the future. They're eager to get things progressed, now Booker has explained that Starling Enterprises isn't interested in buying from them. The potential rebound on those omegas is what I'm working on minimizing right now.

Silas: *Thanks for dealing with this Dad. I know you wanted to step away…*

Dad: *This is important to me and your popi. He understands there are some circumstances that retirement takes second place to. We would never turn our backs on something this important. It's not an issue as far as we are concerned. As long as y'all remember that this will not be a way to get me to step in. It made us realize that we should have put in place something to prepare y'all for dealing with this kind of issue in the first place. Because unfortunately, it won't be the last time you'll face this.*

***Booker:** Fuck!*

***Jupiter:** What a fucking depressing thought.*

***Rue:** That! Ten fucking fold after having it shoved in our faces. The alpha ass wipes deserve a kicking!*

***Dad:** Although I get the sentiment, violence should not beget violence. It solves nothing, despite how good it might feel at the time.*

***Booker:** Pot and kettle Dad.*

Dad: *Your situation was different Booker…* ***very, very*** *different.*

Silas: *I love you, Dad.*

Dad: *I love you, too. All of you. I'm proud of the men you are and there is nothing I wouldn't do to ensure you are protected. Nothing. And that will never change.*

Chapter Twenty-One

Taylin

Something had changed between them, and Taylin felt almost like he was holding his breath waiting for that moment when a person trusts another to free fall, hoping like hell they'll catch them.

Hollis had slept on the plane and was now staring out the window as the driver, who'd waited for them, took them to Hollis's place. Indecision was Taylin's best friend and second guessing himself after sharing some of his past wouldn't let him break the silence. It crackled with tension. It was very real judging by the large knot of anxiety weighing heavy in his stomach.

Hollis's profile gave little away in the dim interior of the car. *Was he regretting his decision to bite me?*

Humans! Why do you fuss?

Taylin chose to block his animal and wordlessly sit and fret until the car pulled up outside a smart townhouse.

They both remained still for a few seconds, then Hollis glanced at him when the driver got out of the car. The light illuminated his beautiful face. One that Taylin could stare at for hours, only that couldn't happen unless he manned up and asked for what he wanted.

The noise from outside the car said he was running out of time when the driver shut the trunk, clearly having retrieved Hollis's bags.

"You must be tired," Taylin muttered when nothing else came to him and, conscious that with the door open, the driver could hear them.

Save me! What are you doing?

Again he blocked out the animal, which was getting on his last nerve, and gave Hollis an overbright smile when Hollis nodded.

"Been… a busy few days."

Busy?

What was that supposed to mean?

"I'm sure you need sleep, too. There'll be a lot to catch up on for work… and the press conference tomorrow. We'll need to prepare… so I'll see you tomorrow." Hollis leaned in and brushed his lips over Taylin's in a kiss that was nowhere near enough to satisfy him. Then he was out of the car, the door shutting behind him before Taylin could say more or figure out how he was now alone and feeling like his heart was walking up to the house.

He watched in utter bewilderment when Hollis not once looked back when he reached the entryway and two seconds later, a light came on and he disappeared inside the house. The door closing felt... *final.*

Taylin sank back into the leather seat and shut watery eyes, working on breathing past the continued 'heart ripping out of his chest' feeling.

Yikes a fucking do-do!

The engine purred with life and moved smoothly away. Taylin's eyes darted open. He rubbed at his bristly jaw, cracking a yawn, and searched for something to distract himself.

Work!

Think about work...

He labored to recall exactly what in his calendar he'd missed over the past four days besides the obvious reason for being away.

Seconds bled into minutes before he sighed dejectedly at coming up blank.

His brain was a roller deck where he could flick through it and find the information he needed. Why was none of it there like it would normally be? The man who'd just left him wasn't answer enough, so what had changed?

Why does work matter now? Stop being a dick.

The blocking of his wolf spirit's snippy voice was becoming a full-time job.

His thoughts didn't venture far.

How had Hollis made quick work of rearranging his brain so that nothing made any sense except for him? Taylin rubbed at the center of his chest. At the sensation that came from... Hollis leaving him.

You never asked him to say.

Was this part of the mating bite?

If it was, he royally screwed himself.

Taylin pressed his forehead to the cool glass of the window and stared out at the darkened streets, acknowledging the truth. Hollis was his heart. The throbbing pain hadn't been there while he was in Hollis's presence. The fucker came right after Hollis shut his front door, *leaving him.*

Work... they both needed it to be a priority after their time together. They should get back to that and some form of normalcy. Then why was being sensible the last thing Taylin wanted to be?

He wanted to blame Hollis, but he wasn't that man. He was equally complicit by not talking about it, which left him now feeling like shit.

Mating... was causing his senses to swim hard against the currents and left him splashing around, unable to see what was important. One small bite changed everything, and he couldn't fool himself that it was just sex.

Taylin stared blindly at the buildings they passed as he failed to convince himself that his world hadn't altered, and he wasn't clueless of where to go from here. Dating followed rules, they were easy to navigate. He ran his fingertips over the ridged flesh, getting prickles—that if he closed his eyes—ran straight to the organ pumping blood around his body.

Was it possible to go back to the way things were before those teeth had sunk into his flesh?

What kind of stupid question is that? What you should ask yourself is why you didn't give him a true bite?

Do we need to have this conversation again?

His wolf spirit snarled, and Taylin grunted back in frustration.

"Is everything okay, sir?" The driver's voice interrupted him as he was about to continue the fight with his animal.

Taylin met the driver's gaze in the rearview mirror, and he offered a reassuring smile. "Yes, thank you. Just tired." He was. His body ached in unusual places, if he discounted his heart.

He'd possibly had ten hours of sleep in the last five days, and some of those had been on the floor. Was that the real reason he'd not stated his case for staying with Hollis? Was it?

They did both need rest.

Couldn't they have rested—slept together?

Taylin—*alone*—decided he had made an epic error of judgment. Fucking monumental, truth be told.

Get the driver to go back.

Please, Hollis didn't ask us to stay at his place, did he? Taylin pointed out, only he wasn't sure if it was to his wolf side or himself. Although it wasn't like he could forget he was alone when the seat next to him remained empty.

Had opening up changed how Hollis saw him? It was hard to think differently and it came with the negative that his old family was fucking with his life once more. Was that why Hollis hadn't asked him to stay now the heat was over?

Memories of the sweetness Hollis displayed post heat made his nose burn and disproved the negative thoughts that had no place telling him differently. Taylin held on tight to that and how Hollis had displayed affection both before and after they'd talked. When they lay sated, Hollis had shifted and curled up on Taylin's chest, nestling his face into Taylin's neck, where he'd fallen asleep. The beautiful whistling the pygmy loris had done and Hollis's explanation around how it was to attract their mate increased the ache of loneliness.

His animal had trusted him to keep him safe. Shown their affection. Then why had Hollis insisted that they should part ways?

They were mates—that beautiful man was his—*forever.*

Fuck! Why didn't I push to stay?

Because you're an ass.

Taylin hated that his wolf side was probably right.

No, I'm most definitely right.

Shut up!

Reaching for his cell phone, he considered his next move. They'd see each other at a very public event, the press conference, the following morning. There would be no privacy to talk about personal stuff with everyone there.

Why couldn't I be more like Jupiter, Rue, or Laken? They didn't appear to shy away from shit like this.

Taylin didn't lie to himself and pretend that the feelings of vulnerability after exposing his weak spot had left him raw. Another groan of frustration came out just as the car came to a smooth halt. Was it foolish to ask the driver to turn around and go back?

While he hesitated, out the window Taylin witnessed the front door burst open to reveal Booker, who vied to get outside at the same time as Silas, who pushed from behind.

"Fuck it!" he groaned in distress. His shoulders slumped at leaving it too late and the reality of what was coming his way.

Both men wore similar expressions... pissed.

Taylin blew out a breath and tucked his cell phone back into his jacket pocket, reaching for the door with equal measures of guilt and resignation. He had purposely avoided reading the forty odd messages in the Alphahole group chat because he wasn't foolish enough to know his brothers would have had plenty to say about what had gone on.

He stepped out of the car, standing to his full height, meeting his brothers' stares, showing none of his feelings.

"A welcoming committee, how nice," he said sarcastically, going to retrieve his bags from the driver, who had gone to the trunk.

"Where the fuck have you been?" Booker's angry growl added to the overall pissed impression Taylin had.

"You know where I was," Taylin pointed out simply, not rising to the bait to have an argument outside, in front of an audience.

"Do you know how stressful it's been thinking you wouldn't be back for the press conference tomorrow?" Silas's quiet demand impacted hard. "You could have at least answered my messages to let me know you'd be here."

Taylin bristled at the accusation.

He took a deep breath, released it, then took another when he gave the driver a nod of thanks.

He met Silas's angry glare with one of his own, having learned that in this family, backing down was never a good option when he wasn't in the wrong. "When have I ever let you down?"

The lights spilling from the house revealed Silas going pale at his retort, and rightly so. Taylin had aimed his dart with accuracy to deflate the balloon of hot air that was his brother's temper. He could understand Silas's fear about the following day, but taking a pot shot at him would not work for Taylin, not when he was already feeling vulnerable.

Silas's lips firmed into a tight line and Taylin waited his brother out. Silas was a hothead, and it was the reason they'd first met in that dark alley all those years ago.

"You could have given us some clue to when you'd be back," Booker replied, instead of Silas. Booker was always Silas's biggest supporter.

Taylin stepped up to Booker, showing no signs of being intimidated. They'd lived together too long for that. Although Taylin was a few inches shorter, he held Booker's stormy expression. "Are you mated?"

"What?" Booker's brows drew together. "What kind of question is that?"

"The only kind when you have no fucking idea what it feels like to bond irrevocably with someone." Taylin tugged at the neck of his shirt, getting gasps from both brothers. "Hollis is my mate. He claimed me. So give me a fucking moment to enjoy it." Taylin pushed past a stunned-looking Booker and moved around Silas to the open door, only to be met by an audience.

The rest of his brothers stood inside the entryway, each wearing varying degrees of speculation. "Great, another damn welcoming committee. Anyone else wanna have a go?"

Head shakes and muttered negatives gave Taylin no outlet for his frustration, which was growing by the moment. Even Jupiter, who could never resist poking at someone, remained unnaturally quiet.

Taylin had no one to blame, he really should have opened up the messages to see what kind of shit storm he'd created. "Where are Popi and Dad?"

"In the sunroom," Kodi supplied, before he bit his lower lip as if to stop the humor that was dancing in his eyes from morphing into laughter.

Taylin dumped his bags at the bottom of the stairs and stomped down the hallway toward the sunroom, with his brothers right on his heels. He didn't waste any energy sighing, it was pointless. If he was going to have to answer for his actions, then he'd only be doing it once.

Popi glanced up from his newspaper as Taylin stepped into the room. The lamps in the corner of the room cast a warm, welcoming glow that matched the sweet smile Popi gave him. "You're home."

Dad's expression was harder to read as he placed a book, a crime thriller by the dust jacket, down on his lap. He swept his eyes over Taylin and, judging by the narrowing of his eyes when he reached the neck of Taylin's open shirt, missed nothing. "Taylin."

"Dad." Taylin nodded at the man who he'd always measured his actions against. Then Taylin went to Popi and kissed the cheek he had raised.

"Popi," he murmured shakily as emotions came to the surface so fast he couldn't contain them, "I'm mated."

Taylin promptly burst out crying. He couldn't say exactly why, and he had no control over his reactions when Popi tugged him onto the large comfy sofa next to him and encouraged him to rest his head on his shoulder.

As soon as he had, Popi gently stroked his hair. "It's alright, my beautiful boy. Let it out," he crooned. "Hollis is a lucky man, as are you."

"Shit, if this is what mating does for you, you can keep it," Silas muttered.

To Taylin's blurry eyes, Silas's wide eyes, filled with alarm and disquiet, made him look like he'd rather face a firing squad than find his mate.

"Behave, Silas," Popi rebuked gently but firmly. "Until you experience it, and you will, you cannot judge how special the feeling is. This kind of connection to another is like no other. Your life force becomes strengthened. Everything becomes brighter, bolder, in ways that make the world around you shift and change for the better."

A hushed silence fell as Taylin dragged in a ragged breath while working to stop crying, somehow feeling vindicated for the sudden outburst of emotions.

Popi's comment put Taylin's outburst into perspective and explained why leaving Hollis was so hard. He wasn't a wuss at all.

Releasing a shuddery breath, Taylin swiped at the dampness clinging to his cheeks and looked at Dad. A tension at the back of his neck grew at the apprehension he was stuck feeling, making him so out of sorts.

"How did you cope with being separated from Popi? Leaving him behind for days, weeks, *fuck,* months at a time?" he asked, uncaring what his brothers thought of his question.

Minutes without Hollis were proving difficult and he needed to know how to deal with it, otherwise moments like this could become a common occurrence. Ugh!

Dad's powerful shoulders rose as he turned his attention to Popi, his gaze softening. "I never did. Your Popi is my world."

The simple answer left Taylin slumping against Popi, pouting before he could stop himself. He'd hate himself for pouting later, when he had spent years training himself to stop that one act, having gotten mercilessly ribbed for it by his brothers.

"You're fucking pouting." Laken was the first to point it out as he lounged against the far wall, his arms crossed over his chest.

"I've every right to pout," Taylin defended himself, jabbing a finger at his chest, "it feels like I've a brick pressing against my damn heart."

"Yep, totally not doing that shit," Silas said, then blushed when Popi gave him a hard stare. "Sorry, but no way do I want to be ruled by some mushy feelings in that way." He glanced at the other men as if seeking assurance he wasn't alone.

Taylin didn't miss how all his brothers agreed with Silas, nodding and looking more than a little uncomfortable at the same time. It was comical, sort of, when Taylin was the one dealing with his raw emotions at being parted from Hollis.

"You won't have a say," Popi announced, sounding pleased at the prospect.

At the following fatalist sounds coming from his brothers and the possibility of not being alone with how he felt, a cheeky grin appeared on Taylin's face.

Dad gave them all a look that Taylin couldn't interpret. "Fate doesn't listen to reason, boys. Mark my words."

The smile he aimed at Popi gave Taylin the impression it was time to change the conversation before things got out of hand and they were all witness to something Taylin, for one, didn't want to see.

"Is there anything I need to know or read before tomorrow?" he asked, to avoid watching his dad's make out.

"Now you want to talk about business when we were just getting to the ribbing part of the evening's entertainment?" Jupiter's smile was pure mischief.

Taylin stuck up his middle finger then looked at Silas when he spoke.

"The press statement is in your inbox, so if you haven't read it, you need to. We've all got our bit to say about supporting me as the figurehead." Silas looked relieved to be talking about something else even when he grimaced at calling himself the 'figurehead'.

"I can do that." He looked directly at Booker. "Catch me up on what happened last Sunday."

"If you'd—"

"Booker," Popi said in a tone that suggested he'd be very unhappy if Booker continued with whatever he was planning to say to piss off Taylin.

Taylin shot Booker a 'fuck you' grin at Popi intervening and got a warning look back.

"The second visit was a ton better than the first, and though the level of detail to the pieces wasn't as exceptional as the first, the quality was excellent..."

Chapter Twenty-Two

Delicious & Vicious Chat

Hollis: *I don't even know where to start…*

Frey: *With all the juiciness. Was Taylin packing?*

Ziggy: *Did anyone ever tell you that you have a potty mouth and a one track mind?*

Frey: *Of course they have. It's why y'all love me.*

Hollis: *I'm not loving you right now. Did you have to tell everyone about what happened?*

Frey: *You never said not to. And in my own defense, you announced it to the table and half the restaurant.*

Lennon: *Boss, I have to agree with Frey on this……you did kind of 'drop it like it's hard'.*

Ziggy: *Nice lyrics drop Lennon.*

Lennon: *I thought so too. It seemed to fit the occasion.*

Hollis: *Shall we just address this now so we can move on?*

Bowie: *Do you need to address it? I mean, it's no one's business how you deal with your heat.*

Wilder: *Suck up Bowie, and I think we need the deets. It's only fair when the rest of us had to work knowing what Hollis was up to… I have a very vivid imagination…*

Hollis: *Really Wilder, you had to go there too?*

Frey: *Have you got steam coming out of your ears? I bet you have Hollis… or is it coming out of other parts with how long it took you to get over your heat? How many days was it… five!*

Hollis: *I bet other bosses don't have to deal with this kind of… of…*

Frey: *Support?*

Ziggy: *Not sure that was where he was going with that. We just want you to know we got your back, is all.*

Wilder: *We do, honest. We're just having a little bit of fun 'cause we aren't having the same fun with our Starling brothers!*

Hollis: *Wilder, we'll talk about that in person and not here, okay? I'm sorry I missed your first call.*

Wilder: *It's alright, Ziggy talked me off the ledge of Jupiter's insanity.*

Ziggy: *You're welcome, but next time can we forgo the baby rocking chair and onesie?*

Bowie: *He got to you too, Ziggy? You have to watch our wily raccoon, he can get you to do stuff with little to no effort, somehow.*

Wilder: *It's a talent.*

Hollis: *Shall we get back to the subject of me and Taylin… so there are no surprises at the press conference in an hour… Taylin and I mated—*

Lennon: *Holy gods!*

Frey: *YOU WHAT!*

Ziggy: *Shitballs! I never expected that.*

Bowie: *He didn't force you, did he?*

Wilder: *I think I've blacked out and come to an alternate universe… I read that right?*

Isley: *What have I missed? Laken is in a very strange mood this morning and driving me nuts with triple checking details that he signed off on already.*

Monty: *I need to catch up too, are we talking about Taylin and the weekend?*

Hollis: *I've enough to do, so go back and read the thread! In brief, and please don't* *ping me with ten comments while I'm explaining, or I'll stop…*

Hollis: *Taylin and I are mates. I bit him. The end.*

Chapter Twenty-Three

Hollis

He was hyperventilating and so far nothing had worked to stop his heart racing or the dancing spots in front of his eyes.

Taylin and I are mates. I bit him. The end. Hollis re-read the words several times, knowing that those words didn't even come close to the magnitude of what happened after his teeth sank into Taylin's flesh.

Everything inside the hotel room had been easy, with the world locked out. In the light of day and even in the dead of night, there was no escaping what he'd brought on himself. He couldn't say that he was driven by lust. By his heat. A part of him, from the moment he'd laid eyes on Taylin, had wanted to do what he'd done. Had wanted to be brave enough to let it happen. Those years of quiet yearning, there was no ignoring them. How could he when he had slept for shit and his animal, who was in a foul mood, was tormenting him by forcing him to acknowledge it.

He dropped his cell phone on the desk and got up to roam his office. Excitement and trepidation warred with each other about the up-and-coming press conference. In less than an hour he would see Taylin—*but not touch.*

He thrust his hands into the pockets of his slacks, balling them into fists at how they'd need to stay right there, out of temptation's way.

Hollis took a deep breath, released it, then another, his mind going over everything he had read in the email from Silas. It was easier to think about memorizing it when left with too much time on his hands. He had arrived three hours before anyone else to catch up, or that's what he'd told himself when driven out of his house because he needed to be some place that was closer to Taylin.

Emails dealt with and preparations done for the press conference, Hollis had bitten the bullet and opened the group chat on his cell phone. A huge mistake with how angsty he was feeling. Frey hadn't been wrong, there was steam coming out of his ears from the discussions about him, especially when it came with the graphic details inside Hollis's head of what he and Taylin had done. Why had he expected any different?

Using the group chat to have the 'I'm mated' conversation... what was that about? Possibly because his brain remained addled after finding himself stupidly tongue tied and leaving little room for Taylin to ask to come in with him last night.

Fatal mistake... or that's how his body had interpreted it. He'd been in fight-or-flight mode since he'd gotten out of the damn car, acting like he didn't have a care in the world. This was why he was in his animal's bad books. What little time they'd spent sleeping with Taylin, his other half had enjoyed finding just the right place to sleep *on Taylin*.

You're a dumbass.

He couldn't argue. They'd both missed him, horribly. The discomfort that lived inside Hollis wasn't shifting. He had no answer to whether it was simply from the new attachment or something else was wrong with him. He bore no bite mark from Taylin. Yes, he'd nipped Hollis's tongue so technically they'd exchanged blood. Was that small amount enough to cause the ache?

He's our mate.

Like I need you to explain that to me, Hollis replied snappily, rubbing at his temples, hoping it would ease the throbbing or diminish the spots disrupting his vision.

Am I getting sick?

You're not sick. Stop being silly.

How is that being silly? How?

Silence. It was a great big chasm in his mind.

Now you chose to be quiet? Why couldn't you have done that at three o'clock this morning?

Once more, nothing and it was irking Hollis enough he had to resist stamping his foot, something he hadn't done in years and showed the level of frustration he was battling with. *Fine. Don't talk, but don't think when we get Taylin alone, I'm gonna let you out.*

His animal had the audacity to laugh, grating right on Hollis's last nerve.

The brisk knock on his door prevented his foot stamp as he swung around and called out, "Come in," hoping against hope it might be Taylin.

His expression fell when Monica sailed into the room dressed all in black. Smokey eyeshadow gave her a dramatic look, very much resembling the bat she was.

"How to make a bat feel welcome," she chastised, shutting the door behind her.

When she faced Hollis, her gaze traveled over him and shook her head. "I'm not sure if I should be offended or not by the look of disappointment you're wearing right now." She came deeper into the room and sat on the edge of Hollis's desk, a high-heeled foot swinging as she tutted. "I figured you'd be freaking out about the press conference and having to stand up there with the brothers and, with the lack of replies to my messages, I came to see if I was right."

"It's not just that." Hollis tugged at his tie, not quite looking at her. "I mated with Taylin," he whispered, almost too afraid to say it aloud.

Monica fired off the desk and stumbled on her heels. "You did what!" she shrieked in alarm, eyes wide.

"Keep your voice down," Hollis hissed, blushing to the roots of his hair at her uncontrolled alarm and glad no one was there to witness it.

Would Taylin's brothers react in the same way?

Crap!

Ugh!

Panic rose and lodged right in his throat, making it hard to swallow when the thought stuck with all the others.

"How... no, scrap that." She gripped a hold of his arms and looked him in the eye. "Go you! I knew you had it in you to let go."

"Let go?" Hollis moaned. "I floated right out of my sanity, is what I did!"

"Ain't it cool," she fired back, looking so satisfied with herself, "you finally went after what you wanted and didn't think about all the damn consequences." She kissed him noisily on the mouth right as Hollis caught movement out of the side of his eye when the door opened unexpectedly.

His heart jumped with joy at the man moving swiftly into the room despite Monica giving him another noisy kiss, oblivious to the audience.

"What the fuck is going on here?"

Taylin's growl sent shivers down Hollis's spine and his cock awakened, jumping with excitement, exuding a large dose of pheromones to let everyone know exactly how excited he was.

Monica glanced sideways, appearing unconcerned by the sudden tension filling the room. Most of it was coming from the man stalking towards them with a look Hollis had only half caught when the alpha in the lift had challenged Taylin. It made him untangle himself from Monica because he liked his friend.

When that didn't appear to appease Taylin, who looked ready to rip someone's head off, Hollis got another jolt of desire at his territorial mate. He decided it was best to move in front of Monica regardless of how Taylin's display was making him weak at the knee. Categorically, if asked, Hollis would have said he didn't find this kind of behavior attractive, yet...

Taylin's eyes were blacker than brown and the glint in them was dangerous when he came to a halt.

"Nothing," Hollis replied breathlessly, avoiding inhaling when he was positive he was stinking up his own office with his lust.

"Is that right?" Taylin glared over the top of Hollis's head at the woman who remained behind him. "Then why the fuck am I smelling your arousal after she had her mouth on yours?"

His voice was more of a rasp and added to the swirling desire growing in the pit of Hollis's gut when it reminded him of how Taylin sounded after Hollis had fucked his throat.

So not helping!

It was impossible not to squirm as several things registered at once. His animal was preening. The ache in his chest was gone. Taylin was displaying a level of jealousy Hollis would never have considered him possible of, and Taylin had clearly read the situation all wrong.

"She kissed me to congratulate me on mating with you. The smell is 'cause of your reaction. This whole vibe you got going,"—he waved his hand in the air, feeling an urgency to explain—"yeah, it seems to be something I'm into."

Hollis, who hadn't cooled down from his earlier embarrassment, got so warm he tugged at his shirt collar when Taylin's gaze changed to predatory.

"That's my cue to leave!" Monica said, but Hollis didn't acknowledge her. He couldn't take his eyes off the man in front of him.

Taylin didn't look away at the sound of the door clicking shut. A strange tenseness came with Monica's departure. It buzzed against Hollis's exposed skin and heightened his awareness of every breath Taylin took when his thumb stroked over his parted lips, coming away with lipstick on it.

When Taylin sniffed the air in front of Hollis's face, the feeling intensified. "You're mine. I don't want you tasting of anyone but me."

The words held a boldness that got hard-wired to Hollis's cock. A submissive by nature, Hollis had no problem offering his mate whatever he needed to feel back in control. "Kiss me..." he paused and dipped his eyelashes, giving Taylin a begging look, "Mark me so everyone will smell you on me."

Devilish, the smile, when it came, did crazy things to Hollis when Taylin came closer and crooned, "Yes."

Hollis's groan got swallowed in the kiss that followed. It melted Hollis's bones. The kiss was punishing, bruising even, and contrasted with the gentle cupping of the back of his neck. Taylin devoured him, kiss after kiss until the world bled into a colorful array of desires, none of which were suitable in an office.

Did Hollis care...

Submissive in Taylin's arms, his cock leaked as his ass grew damp with his desire. The scent in the room held him in its thrall as Taylin sucked his bottom lip into his mouth and bit it. The coppery taste got a response from Taylin that rumbled deep inside his chest and left Hollis clinging on in desperation.

Were his ears ringing?

He blinked and moaned in complaint when Taylin dragged his mouth away from him. Hollis's cock throbbed hard enough that one more kiss would have sent him over the edge.

He was sure of it. "Just a little more," Hollis insisted, chasing the tasty lips of his mate.

"Christ, Hollis! You'd make the devil forget himself," Taylin panted, breathlessly. He glanced over to Hollis's desk and murmured, "Saved by the phone."

"Phone?" he asked stupidly. It made no sense why they needed to be saved by a phone.

"It's ringing." Taylin chuckled as ran his thumb over Hollis's damp lower lip. "Reminding me in the nick of time that we're at work and have a meeting to get to," he said with resignation while stepping back and checking his wristwatch, "in fifteen minutes."

"Fifteen minutes," Hollis repeated, like he was a speaking clock, his brain frazzled with how he wasn't anywhere near getting what he wanted.

"You're adorable like this." Taylin took another step backwards, then another. "You are definitely my temptation."

Hollis couldn't in his right mind see a problem with that, so he followed Taylin.

Strangled laughter boomed out of Taylin as he held up his hands as if in defense. "You gotta keep your distance..." he squeaked, making Hollis grin and take another step closer, feeling… very bold.

He liked it.

He liked it a lot.

"Seriously, my wolf's spirit isn't feeling in a very forgiving mood right now because I stopped."

"Neither am I," Hollis complained, though with the clouds of lust waning, he could—in a pinch—forgive Taylin for coming to his senses before him.

The phone, which he hadn't noticed had stopped ringing, started again. He adjusted his cock and reluctantly went to his desk, hoping reason would slap him in the face with how he needed to have his wits about him.

He was in so much trouble if he couldn't learn to control himself at work. Because his mate keeping his distance when he smelled like a little bit of heaven was for the absolute best if Hollis was going to have the ability to function at all.

It was!

"Hello, Mr. Adice here, how can I help?"

"Why aren't you in the conference room?" Silas snapped, helping to quell any lingering desire like a nuisance bug. "Have you seen Taylin? He's fucking gone walkabout!"

"He's here with me," Hollis answered truthfully, getting a hissed curse before he continued, "we were just heading to the boardroom."

This time he lied because Silas didn't need to know how close they'd come to missing the press conference if the phone hadn't interrupted them.

No.

No one needed to know how close a call that had been. Or that it wasn't Hollis being the sensible one. He couldn't quite believe it himself if truth be told, and he'd need to think about that later.

Chapter Twenty-Four

Taylin

His mind in a turmoil at his reaction to seeing Monica with her lips on Hollis, Taylin continued to battle the green-eyed monster. It was sticking like glue to his usual, even temperament as they left Hollis's office.

What had come over me?

Hollis, his wolf side pointed out with smug satisfaction.

Trying to ignore the pounding of his heart in his ears, Taylin shoved his hands into his slacks and prayed for some sort of miracle to cool his jets. He also couldn't help second guessing himself when Hollis remained silent, clutching the file he had collected from his desk.

Taylin strode down the hallway to the elevator with Hollis at his side, doing his best to keep his hands where they were. The scent of Hollis's pheromones, though not as strong as they were, lingered in the air surrounding them. It made it impossible for Taylin to think beyond what they'd been doing before they'd gotten interrupted. In the close confines of the elevator, a scene from another elevator played through Taylin's mind, making his teeth grind together as he held his breath at the intoxicating scent of his mate.

When was he going to catch a break?

He wanted to apologize for being such a barbarian and acting so out of character, but he wouldn't have meant it, so he kept silent. He also wasn't in the habit of lying and doing that with a mate was a big no-no. So, when the elevator stopped, he accepted that the tension would not budge anytime soon.

"Wait up, you two," came a shout from behind them as they started down the hallway to the boardroom.

Releasing a sigh at the sound of Jupiter, Taylin stopped and turned to see his brother loping down the hallway towards them. It was hard not to compare himself to the man in front of him. Stylish chic from head to toe, Jupiter exuded a confidence that very few knew was a wall that hid Jupiter's self-doubt.

Taylin caught a blur behind Jupiter, which turned out to be Wilder. His hair was a little wild, and he wore a pinched expression, which wasn't normal for the cute raccoon.

"I got caught up on a call and thought I was gonna be the last to arrive," Jupiter said, acting like Wilder wasn't there as they all continued towards the boardroom.

"You got caught up on shag, buddy," Wilder muttered crossly.

Whether or not he'd said it loud enough to be heard, Jupiter didn't so much as bat an eyelid or look in the raccoon's direction. Whereas Hollis slowed his pace and Taylin caught the way he was eyeing Wilder with concern and possible frustration.

Keeping his thoughts to himself, Taylin shrugged for something to do, feeling uncomfortable at the obvious friction between the two men. "We made it with plenty of time to spare, but it won't stop Silas from getting riled up."

"Truth!" Jupiter gave a dramatic eye roll as they entered the boardroom. "Nothing he likes more than riding our asses like his horses," he projected loud enough so no one in the room could miss what he'd said.

Those assembled in the boardroom glanced in their direction with varying degrees of interest and frustration. Monica was the only one grinning and Taylin was careful not to look directly at her. He wasn't sure he'd cooled down enough to be pleasant.

"I can only assume you're talking about me," Silas grumbled, taking a seat dead center of the smaller than usual table laid out with nine chairs behind it. Placed to face the rows of seats that had replaced the boardroom table in the middle of the room, it made what was about to happen even more obvious.

"Why would you think that, big bro?" Jupiter's laughter came out forced as he headed in the direction of Kodi and Kari.

Hollis grabbed Wilder's arm and dragged him off.

In need of a distraction to fight the urge to give chase, Taylin's gaze swept over Silas, who'd dressed to impress in a forest green cashmere suit, a cream shirt and a brown silk tie. He exuded power in the well-fitting clothes that revealed how physically fit he was from years of outdoor activities. His groomed, dark good looks added to the overall appearance of a high-powered executive. Only they knew Silas was a man happiest sat astride a horse.

Was he perfect to step into Dad's figurehead role?

Only time would tell.

There was tightness around Silas's jaw and years of living with his brother made it easy to see a hint of anxiety in his gaze as it swept the room to land on Ziggy, Silas's new PA. He stood alone, just off to Silas's left, looking watchful and ready to... strike?

The oddity of the feeling came and stayed as Taylin moved down the aisle left to get to the table. He continued to watch the exchange, his brows pinching together.

Intimacy.

The feeling struck Taylin because he'd witnessed it often between his fathers. There was a level of it in the exchange that only disappeared when Laken moved between the pair, and Ziggy glanced at Bowie, who walked up to him, speaking.

Taylin's gaze narrowed on Silas and he considered his brother's reaction to his mating announcement the night before. Was something going on between Silas and Ziggy?

Did it matter? It wasn't his business, was it?

Taylin shifted his attention to Ziggy, who he hadn't yet gotten a chance to get to know. He was in no position to judge or speculate.

Did that stop him?

No. Ziggy was an odd bod. His appearance came across as more 'alpha' than omega, however his behavior was definitely that of an omega. At least, what Taylin had witnessed of it up to *now*.

None of your business, he told himself as he returned his attention to the others surrounding the table. Rue was the second one to take a seat, only he chose the farthest end of the table.

Taylin cursed under his breath when Laken quickly followed suit and took the seat at the other end of the table, which he had considered taking.

The PAs migrated to gather in a huddle around Hollis, who looked to be having a serious discussion with how he was gesturing at them. Taylin forced his attention back to what was about to happen. Worrying about what Hollis was doing wasn't helpful.

He eyed the room, checking everything was as it should be. They often used the boardroom to accommodate large meetings of this type. This room, with the history of the rise of the company displayed on the walls, was all about how his parents had used their love to build something positive. Many would see it as a power play, showing off, but it had never been about that. Many of the people on the covers gracing the walls were those rejected by society and had succeeded despite that. It was a celebration of overcoming life's obstacles. Taylin had learned that at an early age. It was humbling to be part of it, and he had never thought differently when rejected by society and his biological family himself.

Counting six rows of ten seats laid out facing the table, which held water bottles, glasses, and microphones in front of each seat, gave his stomach a nasty jolt.

He stopped dawdling and went to take a seat next to Laken, wanting to be as close to the end of the table so as not to be in the direct line of fire.

Tugging the seat out, he sank down and avoided looking at all the empty seats. Nerves at what was to come turned his stomach into a washing machine, making the coffee he drank earlier swirl and slosh about.

"How many invites were sent out?" he questioned Laken, his attention refusing to refocus on anything but the rows of seats. If stepping into a room with his family hadn't worked to kill any remaining desire, those seats would, despite how Hollis's scent lingered in his nose.

"Sixty! Feels like Dad suggested we invite the fucking world and his wife. Christ knows why. When has the press ever held their water? One would be enough to get out what's officially happening and not some made up bollocks."

Taylin wasn't listening. Instead, he tracked Hollis who came along the back of the row of seats. Taylin didn't give him a chance to take another seat. He rose, pulling out the seat next to him while giving Hollis an encouraging smile.

When Hollis moved close enough for their jackets to brush against each other, Taylin went into protective mode. The move suggested Hollis was possibly as uncomfortable as Taylin at the prospect of facing the journalists. Taylin slipped a hand over Hollis's suit jacket to his lower back and let it rest there. The simple touch sparked off a giddy feeling. It was perplexing how euphoric he felt about something so basic. He was going to have to talk to his dad about it.

Taylin's instincts were wholly different from what he was displaying. In reality, he wanted to growl and bare his teeth at anyone who dared to look sideways at his mate.

Doing none of that, he came close enough to murmur in Hollis's ear, "I'm right here. If you need me, just squeeze my thigh." He didn't want to assume that Hollis needed protection, despite how he felt.

A jerky nod was the only reply from the ghostly-looking man at his side. He eyed his other brothers warily, seeing who remained standing. It took little to decide if it was safer to suggest Hollis take the seat Taylin had picked. After last night, leaving Hollis in the line of fire of Booker, Kodi, Kari or Jupiter felt unwise?

While he debated what was best, Hollis sat, then Booker parked his big ass next to him, leaving Taylin no option but to sit.

Booker gave Hollis a toothy grin, and Taylin pushed his clenched fists into his thighs in the hope it would stop the madness brewing inside him. After his reaction to seeing Monica touching Hollis, all bets were off about what would set him off, or so it seemed. This new aggressive side to him wanted to punch Booker's teeth down his throat for grinning at his mate in what felt like an overly friendly move to him and his wolf. The damn thing was there, egging him on.

Show them he's ours!

"As everyone is here, can everyone take their seats, so we can get this over with." Silas sounded like he was trying to break his teeth with the way they snapped against each other. The suggestion was not an actual choice with how he'd said it and it helped divert Taylin from doing something he'd surely regret... possibly.

"Please, can you all check the mics work," Monica requested when they were all seated.

Everyone obeyed without the usual grumbling at being told what to do, showing the mood in the room.

"Can you guys take seats at the back of the room?" Monica said to the PAs milling around the room. "We don't need any distractions once the vultures..." Monica giggled naughtily. "I mean, the press is let in here."

The guys laughed along with Monica as they made their way to the last row of seats at the back of the room.

Taylin would have much preferred them to be up front giving them some breathing room from the 'vultures'. It was a fitting nickname given the press liked to pick at the bones of whoever held their interest. Taylin had escaped—mostly—any direct attention from the tabloids. Jupiter was the one they loved to follow because he was so much more interesting.

Absorbing Taylin's focus, Hollis fidgeted with his glass and reached for a water bottle with a hand that wasn't quite steady.

"Let me," Taylin murmured, opening and pouring water into Hollis's glass.

He filled his own, then offered to fill Laken's and Booker's for something to do while Monica laid out press packs on the seats. The statement they'd be giving was in the pack, along with the business chart that factored in who did what in the company. There were glossy photos of them all together, as they'd decided none of them would pose for pictures.

"Thanks." Booker gave him an appreciative smile once Taylin placed the glass down. Then Booker pointedly gazed at Hollis, then back at Taylin. A second later, his nose twitched, and he leaned around the back of Hollis's chair, muttering, "You better calm your ass down or you'll be stinking up the place and causing a stir of a different kind."

His words, said low enough for only them to hear, didn't stop Taylin bristling at how Hollis dropped his gaze to his lap.

"Give fucking over, okay!" Taylin snapped, gritting his teeth and working on controlling his breathing. "It's not like we're doing it on purpose."

He picked up his water glass and drained it when Booker eased back, looking unconcerned at the rebuke. Feeling no better, Taylin refilled his glass, sensing everyone's eyes on him.

"Are we ready?" Monica questioned, her blood red fingernail rubbed at her lower lip. Nothing about the move was flirtatious but that didn't stop Taylin from objecting to the memory of lipstick traces on Hollis's lips after the kiss.

"Yes. Let's just get this over with," Silas demanded, diverting Taylin's attention when Monica stalked to the door on four-inch heels. Opening it let in a flood of noise.

A hand slipping onto Taylin's thigh was enough to get him to shift his attention to Hollis. The hand flipped over and Hollis wriggled his fingers. A little of the tension at what was coming eased as he placed his hand into Hollis's. Their fingers entwined and the tight clasp was uncomfortable and perfect.

The noise level in the room increased as folks vied for the best seats at the front.

"Monica wasn't wrong, look at them. They *are* a pack of vultures," Booker mouthed out the side of his mouth.

Hollis nodded, his gaze on the crowd.

"When have they ever been anything but," Taylin replied, mimicking Booker.

Taylin plastered a fake smile to his lips, praying for it to be over quickly. Being the center of attention was his least favorite thing. Jupiter, Kari, and Kodi were much more suited to this. But this wasn't about him, it was a show of solidarity. A united front.

It took way too long for everyone to settle, in Taylin's opinion, as he counted off the seconds clinging to Hollis's hand under the table. Assigned to the role of keeping everyone one in order, Monica encouraged everyone to sit. When that didn't work, she harangued folks into taking the unwanted vacant seats.

Monica held a microphone that was for the use of anyone that wanted it when directing questions. She coughed into it and stood directly in front of the table, holding up her hand once Ziggy had closed the boardroom door.

She waited until silence fell in the room. "Thank you. Before we start, there are a few rules to run through. I ask that you wait to ask questions until the board members have spoken. If you have a question, you will raise your hand and I will come to you with the microphone. If you choose not to follow these rules, you'll find yourself leaving without answers. Is that clear?"

If anyone was in doubt that she meant it, they were going to be in for a shock if they pushed her. Monica was a ball breaker. She had to be, working for years as Dad's PA.

An uneasy tension grew in the room as they each took their turn to talk about their individual roles and what, or how, that would change with their dads' retirement. Last night, there'd been some discussion about this meeting and Hollis's role in the new structure. A debate had ensued about revealing Hollis's role. Dad had pointed out Hollis was important to the company and therefore his role needed highlighting in the new structure.

A rigidness developed in Taylin's shoulders at witnessing the interest in Hollis when it became his turn to talk. They'd expected speculation, that was obvious, but as soon as Hollis revealed what his role was, the room erupted. People shouted over each other.

"Mr. Adice, did you have to interview for the role?"

"Mr. Adice, was it always your plan to join the board?

"Aren't you too young for such a position?"

"What experience do you have for this kind of role and responsibility?"

Then one brave—stupid soul fired out, "Has this got anything to do with the recent change in your relationship with Taylin Starling?"

Which led to the asshole thinking it was okay to continue. “Does your new role come with extra perks of *servicing a divergent alpha*?”

Taylin had respected the decision for Hollis to be present right until then. Whatever he’d experienced over Monica touching Hollis was nothing to the fury that came at having no way to shield Hollis. None.

As if expecting Taylin to stand, his brothers moved collectively, rising with him as he stood, fists clenched.

Booker, in a flash, lifted Hollis and the chair he remained seated in, looking poleaxed. His big, expressive eyes consumed his face when Booker placed it behind them, blocking him from sight as they closed ranks.

Fury came in white hot spikes at his own impotency to protect his mate from the implication that their relationship could be anything less than what it was.

“Enough,” Booker thundered before Taylin could find his voice past his anger when the questions kept coming. His roar made the hairs on the back of Taylin’s neck rise. “You will show respect.”

It wasn’t a request. Hell no.

Unable to see Hollis, Taylin easily scented the taint of fear. It was too much, and he pushed Booker aside to tug Hollis from his chair and wrap a protective arm around his middle. Keeping him close, he aimed daggers at all those who vied to get closer to the table, not getting just how dangerous Booker or any of his other brothers were to their health.

This was what Taylin loved about his family. When something was vital to one of them, it became important to all of them, especially when it came to threats.

"You were warned," Monica hissed, her sharp fangs gleamed in the overhead light. Despite her small stature, she gave off a 'don't fuck with me' vibe as she whirled around, hair flying, and swaggered to the man who'd offended Hollis. The way the guy winced suggested she'd dug in her nails. "This interview is over for you. Now get out."

The man, who Taylin hadn't ever met before, scowled at her, and attempted to rip his arm out of her grasp.

"Do as the lady says," Silas reiterated with a forcefulness that no one could mistake and the man stilled. Silas pointed at the others who'd been stupid enough to fire questions at them. "You lot, get out too. Make sure I don't see your sorry ass faces again or else..." The warning was obvious, despite it not being said aloud.

When the men and one woman reluctantly left, an uneasy silence followed and folks eased back, some sitting once more.

"The rest of you better sit your asses back down now and shut up." This came from Booker.

Once order had returned, and the security staff had escorted out the guy who'd continued to break free of Monica's grip, she reiterated. "Hold up your hands like I requested, *or you'll be blacklisted from any future events.*"

A hushed silence came as Hollis's seat was moved back into position. Taylin kept Hollis close, their hands clasped once more against his thigh. Taylin didn't miss how warily Hollis eyed the crowd.

The churning in Taylin's stomach was relentless at the unavoidable questions. They'd not talked about making their mating public. There was no way to ask Hollis in front of the audience what he wanted to do.

Argh!

He could see no way to avoid it without there being any backlash. Hollis's grip increased as Monica took the mic to a man with his hand held up. One Taylin had met once before. He supported 'divergent haters'.

Mic in hand, the dude came forward, a light in his eyes that caused Taylin's body to stiffen.

"So, is there any truth in the rumors about Mr. Adice and Taylin Starling having a relationship... sex? If so, how will this impact on decision making in the company? You say that there won't be any disruption to normal business. How can that be when a *divergent alpha* could become influenced by an omega shifter during those *intimate moments*?"

Said with pure disgust, the implied slur on his masculinity because he was a divergent wasn't what got Taylin snarling at the man, who looked too fucking pleased with himself when the room quietened enough to hear a pin drop. No, he got pissed that they'd call Hollis out on his professionalism.

Around him, Taylin didn't need to look at his brothers to feel their tension when every inhale burned his sensitive nose. Ready this time, Taylin placed their joined hands together on the table in clear sight of everyone. "Whoever your source is, they are incorrect." When none of his anxiety presented itself in his voice, he breathed a little easier and waited for the expected eruption.

"Bullshit," someone from the back of the room shouted.

The fingers clasping his crushed the bones together. Taylin didn't hesitate, he would not lie—he'd never dishonor his mate in that way—and lifted their joined hands. "Hollis, Mr. Adice, is not my bed partner, *he is my mate.*"

To make his point, Taylin tugged at his tie one handed and moved the collar of his shirt to reveal his neck.

He couldn't have stunned the crowd more, giving him enough time to glance at Hollis who wore a kind of dazed expression, blinking owlishly behind his spectacles. Unable to resist, Taylin gave in to the temptation and kissed his parted lips.

"Way to go on deflecting," Laken said, close to his ear. "But you'd better stop kissing Hollis before Monica goes all bitey bat on the press."

Taylin reluctantly stopped kissing a glowing Hollis to stare at the crowd swarming around them, some holding flashing cameras.

A sudden thought struck.

Had Hollis spoken to his parents about them?

Chapter Twenty-Five

Delicious & Vicious Chat

Frey: *Did you see what Booker did!!!!!*

Wilder: *We were right there, remember? Or did seeing the big bear getting all protective blow a fuse in your brain… or slacks…*

Ziggy: *I'm sure Hollis doesn't want to read a blow by blow account of the shit storm. He was front and center.*

Bowie: *I made banoffee cheesecake, do you think I should leave a slice for him in his office? They're all locked in the boardroom. Who knows how long that'll take?*

Lennon: *Rehashing and trying to figure who spilled the beans on Taylin and Hollis being together. Did anyone talk about it out of work?*

Ziggy: *Good point. I rarely mix with anyone out of work, so I know I haven't said anything.*

Frey: *I know I'm a gossip, but I would never speak to those assholes about anyone I work with.*

Monty: *Same. But I was thinking about what happened at the hotel. Could* *someone have overheard Hollis announce he was having his heat and Taylin was gonna help him? The place was busy, and Starling Enterprises is renowned along with the sons.*

Isley: *That's a good point. People can be so horrible. Did you see how shocked Hollis looked and how angry Taylin was? Do you think he'll take it out on Hollis?*

Frey: *Don't be silly. Taylin was mad at them for saying nasty things about him being a divergent alpha. Did you not notice the slur about Hollis being a shifter, therefore better than Taylin, and could manipulate him? What nonsense!*

Ziggy: *They're elitest assholes that know fuck all about it! And I'm sure everyone picked up on what that weasel was implying. I'd also say that no one could miss the measure of those men when they all stood with Taylin and formed a wall to protect Hollis.*

Wilder: *I suppose Jupiter gets some points for that.*

Frey: *Must I repeat myself… Booker being all angry bear… yummy!*

Isley: *Yes, we heard you. What about Taylin declaring being mated to Hollis? How romantic. The kiss… swoon!*

Bowie: *It was very swoony.*

Hollis: *I'm trying to concentrate on an important meeting and my notifications are blowing up. Bowie cake would be lovely and the rest of you… BACK TO WORK… NOW!*

Chapter Twenty-Six

Hollis

However Hollis had envisioned his day turning out, it wasn't being summoned by his parents after they'd received endless calls—his mother's words—since Taylin had declared they were mates to the world's press. He could feel their unspoken disappointment during the call he'd received, and he didn't blame her. He should have told them when he got home after his trip. Explained himself.

The problem with that was that he'd been unable to figure out himself how to refer to things between him and Taylin. He was the one to bite Taylin first... something that Taylin still hadn't rectified, even after he'd asked.

When did he have time? He's announced to the world we're his mate, what's wrong with that?

His animal was in his element, preening like a goddamn ballet dancer. He didn't care right now about whether they bore Taylin's mark, just that Taylin made such a bold move to the world's press. One Hollis remained conflicted about. He wanted everyone to know that they were mates. However, it didn't stop the worry about what it now meant after the press had made their feelings clear.

Priding himself on his professionalism, the implications and headlines, after today, would suggest to many that he'd slept with Taylin to gain a foot up in the business. The press was having a damn field day speculating nonsense. It wasn't about who was in charge of the company any longer. Taylin's forthright approach had made sure of that. They were more interested in how Hollis had *'wheedled his way into such a position of power'*.

'Shagged his way to the top'. That headline really irked. Online, some of the more hateful comments were about Taylin mating with a shifter. A divergent, not seeing his place in the pecking order.

It was fucking exhausting and soul destroying when Taylin had clammed up after the meeting they'd held post the fall-out. They'd hardly closed the doors on the press before they'd started picking apart everything that had happened.

The press manager, Rubin, who for some reason hadn't been present, had dramatically tugged at his hair when he'd explained that Taylin should have first discussed what he was going to say. Their press pack, he reminded them, was done for a reason, and they should not have deviated from it.

It was a moot point. They'd all gotten blindsided by the questions. Hollis mainly. He hadn't been able to get his dry mouth working.

This had brought about another heated discussion in private. Hollis had listened while the brothers, who'd shown how united they really were, argued heatedly around who the snitch to the press was. They wanted answers to who in the company was aware of the recent changes to Hollis and Taylin's relationship and would be so stupid to sell the information.

They cast their suspicion firmly in the direction of the PAs, though Hollis had no such conviction. He had skim-read the group chat that had vibrated so vigorously just minutes after they'd shut the doors, and added to his conviction his team of men—he would swear on his life—would not sell a story to the press.

Monty's suggestion that it could have been a random person because of Hollis, was a real possibility. But convincing the Starling brothers of that hadn't been his biggest concern when they weren't in the mood to listen. They were angry and deep in the blaming game.

Several hours on, starving after only having the piece of cheesecake—which was utterly delicious—his day had gotten no better when he'd had to go to Taylin and ask him to come meet his parents. He hadn't looked over-joyed and the silence between them since they'd gotten into Hollis's car was tense enough for him to feel like an over-tightened guitar string.

They should discuss how to approach this meeting with his parents. Only there was a barrier there. Real or imaginary didn't matter, Hollis was sure it was there between them. Was it him creating it? Was Taylin causing it?

Hollis wasn't rightly sure, or what it meant for them so early on in a new relationship.

Mates! You are mates!

Are you a broken record? Hollis snapped back and huffed out a breath at how the newness of this thing between them didn't prepare him for this. How could it when, in reality, they'd gotten naked and stayed that way for the five days at the hotel? Since returning—yesterday, how could it be only a day—they'd had little to no time to talk.

Whose fault is that?

Ready to start a fight with his animal because he really was in the mood for one, Taylin spoke and stopped him.

"Do you think they'll like me?"

Oh!

His pulse lept at the anxiousness he picked up. *Was this the reason Taylin was quiet?*

"Of course. Why wouldn't they?" He frowned, glancing at Taylin, his fingers clenching at the steering wheel at seeing doubt staring back at him. Returning his attention to the road, knowing their turning was coming up, he impressed upon Taylin what he knew about his parents. "My parents are nice people and are non-judgmental."

They were.

Possibly a little uptight, but nothing that would make him worry they wouldn't approve of his choice of mate.

Once, maybe twice, Hollis's parents had come to a work event, and he couldn't remember if he'd introduced them to Taylin. Had they somehow left Taylin with the impression they weren't accepting of divergents?

It was a question he'd never have considered in this context until he'd seen what they'd written in the tabloids. He was so distracted trying to think about anything his parents could have said to give that sort of impression that at the next turn, it didn't register why there were so many additional cars parked near his home.

"Oh fuck," Taylin ground out, jabbing at the windscreen. "Is that the weasel from today? Why can't we catch a damn break?" he said morosely, sinking down in his seat, pointlessly attempting to hide.

"Looks like." One sweeping glance at all the haphazardly parked cars and Hollis moaned. "Most of these cars don't belong to the neighbors' houses."

Hollis eased his foot off the accelerator, understanding there was no place to reverse and get out of there. They were going to have to run the gauntlet and he wasn't sure how he felt about that after what they'd gotten subjected to already.

"What do you want to do?"

Taylin's question took a second to sink in. Hollis became determined he would not run as he pulled past the cars to get to the driveway. "We go and introduce you to my parents, have dinner with them, and then go back to my place and do some of the things they printed so as not to make them all out to be liars!"

A rumble of laughter coming from Taylin released some of his worry, and Hollis grinned cheekily after parking behind his parents' SUV.

A flurry of people jumped out of vehicles and cameras got brandished about like weapons outside the windows, making Hollis's smile slip away.

"I should have used my car as a bowling ball and knocked some of these assholes over," he complained, giving thoughts to reversing over toes when his eyes danced with white spots from the flashes.

Taylin's laughter grew louder. "As tempted as I am to say yes, I much prefer there be no bars between us, love."

"I suppose—" Hollis blinked several times at the camera flashes and to check he was seeing correctly.

"Get out of here, this is private property," Hollis heard shouted from the man charging down the driveway wielding a broom at the people obstructing him from exiting the car.

All alpha, Hollis's dad was a good foot taller than Hollis, who took after his mom. He easily had people moving and jumping to avoid being walloped by the broom head.

"If you don't want a broom handle up your ass, I'd move quicker than that," he threatened, and caused Hollis to chuckle at the bizarreness of the situation.

His dad hated violence of any kind. He was a pacifist.

"Ready?"

"I'm not sure," Taylin replied warily, his attention on the man standing guard at the rear of Hollis's car.

"It's all show, he's a pacifist."

"Are you sure?" Taylin's brows arched as he reached for the door handle when Hollis nodded. "Then I don't suppose we can keep sitting here all night just to prove it."

Out of the car, Taylin waited for Hollis. Holding a grocery sack in one hand, he offered the other to his mate, despite the flashing cameras and questions being fired at them around Hollis's dad.

"I won't tell you again," Hollis's dad growled. "If you step on my land, you'll be needing surgery to remove this stick from places it wasn't meant for."

Hollis swallowed his giggles, hustling Taylin up the drive to the open door where his mother was waiting. She smiled and looked completely unconcerned by what was happening on her front lawn. Herbs and spices scented the air as they stepped inside.

Hollis had barely taken two steps inside before his mom was hugging him awkwardly, while trying to clap Taylin on the back in a soothing manner.

"Those horrible people. They haven't given us a minute's peace. And the things they've said about you both! Why, I could... do exactly what Hubert is threatening!"

It was impossible to keep the squeak inside when Hollis choked on his own spit at the tiny woman dressed in floral print using a broom handle in such a way. He'd never heard his mom threaten violence in his entire life. "Mom," he muttered, both horrified and a little proud she'd defend them both.

A second later, Dad was right behind them. "Move inside, boys." He nudged them down the hallway and closed the door with a snap. "We don't need those... those *pigs* taking pictures and shouting their filth at you both."

His dad didn't swear, but Hollis sensed today was a narrow escape by the definite hesitation and the way he'd looked at Mom before he'd finished speaking.

There was a moment's pause, as if no one could decide what to say next.

Hollis took charge and squeezed Taylin's hand before letting go. He walked to his dad when he placed the broom down. "Dad,"—Hollis looked at his mom who remained by Taylin—"Mom, I'd like to introduce you to Taylin Starling, my chosen mate."

His mom sniffed, and she reached into her skirt pocket to pull out a handkerchief to dab at her glistening eyes. "It's so lovely to meet you, Taylin. Let's go into the kitchen. I've made dinner."

She slipped her arm through Taylin's, giving him no option but to follow as she waved the hand holding the handkerchief about. "I hope you like chicken casserole, it's one of Hollis's favorites because I add pineapple. I hope you like pineapple. Fruit is one thing that Hollis will always eat." She sighed in such a way they couldn't miss her disappointment. "Vegetables, he was never very fond of."

"Mom," Hollis groaned, about to give chase when his dad laid a hand on his arm.

"Let her be." He smiled softly at hearing Mom continuing to fire questions at Taylin, not giving him any chance to answer.

"She's excited." He gave Hollis a look he knew well. A lecture was coming. "We both are. Why didn't you tell us, son?

We love you and have we not always trusted you to make the right choices for you?"

The internal sigh was all his animal. They both hated to disappoint their family. "It's a little complicated and very, very new, Dad. I would have spoken to you both... once I got my head straight."

Frown lines appeared as his dad's eyes narrowed. "Why did you need to get your head straight?" He lowered his voice, ensuring it didn't carry, but the concern was there.

"I bit Taylin only last weekend, and he hasn't bitten me back. We haven't really had any time to talk about what we both want next..." Hollis trailed off at his dad's wide-eyed alarm.

"Son... did you bite Taylin during your heat?"

Hollis had to work to hold his dad's gaze and not sag. "Yes... but it's not like that Dad. I've had feelings for Taylin for a long time... I just hadn't acted on them because of..."

"Work and you feared upsetting your structured life," Dad said, knowing Hollis all too well.

There was no point in denying it or explaining himself, his parents knew him. "He was—is my boss."

"And? If you love someone and they love you back, those things become unimportant." He ran a hand over Hollis's hair gently. "They shouldn't count, son. I blame myself for you being a little too work focused because I wanted you to succeed in a job you were passionate about."

"No, Dad, this isn't your fault. I got stuck in my head and couldn't figure out how to get out. Then Taylin presented me with an opportunity and, well... *things happened*."

A rosy color spread over the bridge of Dad's nose. "You love him, though?"

Back was the concern and, unsure this was the time or place to have this conversation, Hollis darted a look over his shoulder, listening out to hear Mom still peppering Taylin with questions.

When he looked back at Dad, he sucked in a deep breath and said in a rush, "Yes. I'd never have bitten him otherwise."

Relief came first before a smile appeared and Dad reached for him, giving him a bear hug. "Then you'll figure the rest out. I know my son. You'll work to find the answers."

He kissed the top of his head and Hollis burrowed his face into the warm scented sweater, inhaling and letting the familiarity remove the anxiety that had hounded him at disappointing the two most important people in his life.

"Hubert. Hollis. Where are you? I'm ready to plate up."

Hollis stayed put for another moment, appreciating just how lucky he was, then let go to step back. "Something I haven't said enough. I'm lucky to have you both. I love you, Dad."

His dad's smile stretched wider. "We are the blessed ones, son." His gaze traveled to where the voices were coming from. "Now we're doubly blessed. But let's not push your mom to call on us again. We don't want to go without dessert."

Hollis didn't laugh at the reality of her doing just that and swung around so fast his suit jacket whipped out like a cape before he scurried to the kitchen.

"Dessert could always get you to move faster!" Dad said through his laughter, hustling behind him.

"And what's wrong with that," Hollis said as they entered the kitchen to find Taylin minus his jacket with his sleeves rolled up to his elbows looking sexy, holding two full plates of steaming food.

Expecting panic, what he found was a relaxed man who looked right at home in Mom's kitchen. Hollis's heart felt like it rolled in his chest as Taylin strolled to him and kissed him. A gentle brush of lips that was barely more than a fleeting touch, yet it resonated deeply with how he was staring at him. "Which seat is yours?"

Were his glasses steaming up? Had his brain melted into goo? All good questions when he stared at Taylin cluelessly.

"Oh... look at that..." Back were the sniffing sounds coming from the direction of Mom, and it flicked a switch of alarm in Hollis's brain at how gooey she might get, dumping him back into reality with a big splash.

"Leave the boys alone, Miriam."

Hollis took the plates from Taylin, who remained looking relaxed with a glint of amusement in his gaze.

"Now Hubert, it's not every day our son brings home his mate. I'm allowed to get a little weepy. Just think, next there'll be grandchildren to spoil."

Hollis lost all color, his fingers cramping with how tight he held onto the plates when the impact of Mom's words brought with it a blinding reality of what he'd failed to do.

Holy fuck!

Holy fuck!

Holyyyyy fuck!

Chapter Twenty-Seven

Taylin

Taylin dragged himself into Hollis's immaculate kitchen and headed straight for the coffeemaker. It took two attempts to get the thing working with how sluggish his brain was. He scratched at his naked chest, which remained warm and smelling of Hollis. Taylin woke to find his mate sleeping in his animal form on top of him.

God, he didn't think waking up like that would ever grow old.

He opened cupboards in search of mugs, a smile curling the corner of his lips despite the raging hangover that gave him a set of tap dancers working at his temples. Once he'd placed two cups on the counter next to the bubbling coffee machine, Taylin went to retrieve the milk and see what there was to eat. He was in dire need of something to help get rid of the draggy feeling that came with drinking way too much.

The evening before, at least what Taylin could remember of it, was a success. It had to have been, otherwise there wouldn't be tubs of leftovers—enough for two—in the refrigerator this morning, would there? Unaware of what Hollis's parents would or wouldn't do, Taylin had to figure the fact Hubert hadn't torn him a new asshole had to mean something.

His chuckle was the only sound in the quiet house. Hubert brandishing the broom had definitely given off some ass kicking vibes. Tangling with him would not be on Taylin's to do list, for sure.

It was not the reason Taylin had drunk too much red wine. The shocker that had driven him to drink excessively was a reality check. One comment about grandchildren had railroaded itself into Taylin's head, ensuring he could think about nothing else except *the full box of condoms* he'd unpacked from his travel bags.

Was it a good thing he remembered little of the drive back to Hollis's home? He had a vague recollection of having a shower before collapsing into Hollis's bed. He slept right through, only waking up minutes ago with a banging head and all the questions he'd blocked out last night, which decided this morning to play the bongo drums in his brain in time to the tap dancers.

It drove him out of the warm bed once he had carefully moved the pygmy loris onto the spot he'd vacated in the hopes of not disturbing Hollis. The dark circles under Hollis's eyes the day before ensured Taylin had kept quiet, with it being the weekend. A heat was harder on the omega, in that they remained governed by their biological needs until it eased. Sleep and food were not their primary need during it. Hollis had to be tired.

Coward!

It was too early and not being caffeinated didn't prepare him to argue with himself.

He placed a carton of milk under his arm to grab a bowl full of fresh fruit, then collect a tub of yogurt, before knocking the refrigerator door shut with his shoulder. Back at the counter, he laid everything down and breathed in the fresh aroma of coffee like a dying man. Preparing a cup, he inhaled the rich scent before leaning back against the counter, sipping at the mug, waiting for the caffeine to hit his brain.

He stared out the kitchen window overlooking a tidy yard and small patch of grass that held two garden chairs and nothing else.

Why didn't I think to use protection?

You weren't thinking! His animal side stated gleefully.

Gods, I'm not in the mood for you. I blame you for this whole mess. His hand shook as he brought the cup back to his lips, drinking the hot liquid to avoid what was playing on his mind. *What if I've impregnated Hollis?*

And the issue with that is?

The snappy comment came with a dose of excitement that Taylin wasn't sure was the right response. He was afraid to join in when Hollis might hate the idea and blame him. He should have taken care of Hollis. It was the alpha's responsibility to protect their omega.

You want this!

"Stop telling me what I want," he fired back snappily.

"I don't believe I did," Hollis said from the doorway, in a formal tone Taylin had always hated.

His gaze darted to the man, who wore only sleep pants, looking gloriously rumpled and not wearing his glasses. "I was talking to my animal side," he explained hurriedly. "Do you want a coffee... some breakfast?" he offered lamely, waving in the direction of the stuff on the counter when Hollis squinted at him.

"Can your animal side... talk to you?"

Taylin nodded, then got the impression when Hollis squinted again he hadn't seen it, so replied, "Yep. Although some days I wish he couldn't."

Nice!

Bare feet moved soundlessly over the wooden floor, coming close enough to challenge the scent of coffee with Hollis's own sweetness. "I'll take a coffee, please."

Hollis moved past him to head to the tiny table tucked in the room's corner and pulled out the seat closest to the window. He plonked himself down, reaching for the glasses case sat in the center of the table Taylin hadn't noticed before.

Taylin watched in fascination as Hollis flicked open the box and pulled out a pair of bright red, square framed glasses and slipped them on. Such a simple act, yet somehow it gave Taylin's heart a jolt.

When Hollis found him watching, his brows arched up above the frame. "What?"

"You usually wear clear plastic, blue or black frames. I've never seen those before," he replied, for something to say when he couldn't explain how or why watching him felt so intimate.

Hollis shrugged, his gaze moving to the coffee pot expectantly. "These,"—he tapped the side of the frame—"I wear in the house or when I'm off. I like color, just not for work."

Taylin placed his mug down to prepare a coffee for Hollis. Taking it to him, he quirked up a brow. "Why no bright colors for work?"

Hollis took the mug and sniffed it before taking a sip. His eyelids flickered closed before he groaned. "Wonderful coffee." A teasing smile appeared. "You can stay."

Coming forward, Taylin bent down and moved the hand holding the cup aside to kiss the cheeky scamp. First came the taste of coffee, then mint, suggesting he'd brushed his teeth before coming down.

A moan reverberated through Taylin when Hollis wrapped both tongues around his, sliding, touching, and tracing over his tastebuds.

Careful of the cup Hollis still held, Taylin moved, sliding his hands up Hollis's throat and around the back of his neck, to tilt his head to get a better angle, deepening the kiss. Their groans matched as Taylin lost himself in the act of worshiping Hollis's mouth with his.

Whatever worries he had, they couldn't compete with the fluttery feelings that came with the simple act of kissing

Hollis. Years of wanting left him greedy. One breathless kiss led to another until their scent mingled with arousal, making Taylin tremble with the desire.

Talking first.

Talking needs to happen.

On repeat, because it was the last thing Taylin wanted to do, but eventually it had him ease back. Hollis's glasses were lopsided and the eyes behind the lenses appeared unfocused. He gave him one quick kiss and stepped back, his cock tenting the front of his boxer shorts.

"Breakfast," he said, more to himself, thinking that it would be too easy to avoid what he knew they needed to do... talk! "You need breakfast."

Hollis moved the mug closer to his kissable lips, looking over the rim, and gave him a look that was all challenge. "I thought I was having breakfast?"

Taylin shook his head, spinning back to the counter where he'd placed the yogurt and fruit. "I need to feed you and we should..." he looked back, wearing a serious expression which was hard with how delectable his mate was, "talk about..."

Nothing about Hollis changed as he took a sip of coffee, holding Taylin's stare as he swallowed. "About?"

Adam's apple bobbing madly, Taylin took a steadying breath. *Here goes nothing.* "The lack of care I took of you during your heat."

There was still no change to Hollis's expression and Taylin started to sweat, so he moved once more to face the man who was his everything.

"You took excellent care of me."

Was he being obtuse on purpose, or didn't he realize they'd not used any protection? "Condoms. I... didn't think to use them. I had them in my bag... not that I thought I was going to need them... I became distracted when packing and picked them out of my bedside cabinet..."

The more he talked the more amused Hollis got and Taylin couldn't seem to stop digging a hole he wasn't sure he could get out of. "Then I dropped them into my bag because Popi was there and I was holding the box, you see?"

"See what?" Hollis asked sweetly, causing the sweating to increase.

Taylin felt sweat gather under the hairline at the back of his neck, then trickle down the center of his spine. "That I wasn't bringing them because I thought I'd get to use them... it was reflex, is all."

"Reflex... I see."

Nothing suggested he did, and Taylin bit his lip to stop himself from saying more, instead he twisted back around to prepare a bowl of fruit for something to do with his trembling hands. "Do you want yogurt on your fruit?"

It was Hollis's scent increasing that sent up a warning flare before a chest pressed to Taylin's back. Silky skin slid against his flesh as hands crept around his waist, his pulse dancing with excitement when one slipped inside his boxers and fingers wrapped around the base of his cock. "Fruit and yogurt..." a nose touched his spine and sniffed. "Is that all that's on offer for... breakfast?"

Taylin's head hung between his shoulders as he fought the temptation to give in.

Hollis stroked his fist up his hard length and at the top squeezed, getting pre-cum to gather on the head. Another hand slipped inside the elastic, and he groaned low and needy at the fingertip sliding through the pre-cum and smearing it over the head.

"Hollis," he snarled, fighting himself.

A shiver ran through the man, who pressed his shaft against the top of Taylin's thigh, rocking. "I'm hungry..." teeth nibbled over his shoulder blade. "For you."

It was too much, and Taylin moaned in complaint even as he gave in and encouraged Hollis to continue. He clasped his fingers over Hollis's and helped to guide his hand up and down his shaft firmly. "What do you want?" he panted, his attention focused on the hands inside his boxers.

Sharp teeth grazed the top of his tricep while Hollis removed the fingertips teasing the head of his cock. There were sounds of material rustling as Hollis's lower body lost contact with Taylin. Hollis didn't lose focus on what his other hand was doing.

Taylin saw Hollis's sleep pants pool on the floor as they got kicked off. Before he could guess Hollis's intention, his mate's cock slid between his legs, nudging at his balls. "Have you ever let anyone..."

Taylin felt the tip of Hollis's cock graze his asshole, leaving a sticky trace, giving Taylin a wordless question.

He shuddered at how loud his wolf was yipping inside him. "No."

Hollis made a noise that sent a thrill through Taylin. Then two tongues moved over his skin, enticing a moan as they roamed over the top of his shoulders. Each flick sent curls of lust straight to Taylin's cock. The pressure around his shaft increased with each stroke, derailing any thoughts Taylin might be concerned with what Hollis wanted.

"Would you let me..." a tongue flicked down his spine, "fuck you? I want to be inside you when you bite me."

The animalistic sound that came out of Taylin was a raw need. His gums ached with the force of his imagination and the demand from his little omega. He was ready to bust a nut. His knot started to form, and Hollis shifted his attention. Tentative fingers roamed over the swelling and Hollis mewled, his pre-cum smearing Taylin's balls.

Way too much, the wet caress and Hollis's obvious enjoyment at touching his knot, Taylin lost his mind. He barely had the wherewithal to stop himself wrenching Hollis's arm from its socket with how fast he spun around. His cock slapping against his stomach as he picked up Hollis and without grace, threw him over his shoulder.

Giggles floated over his skin as Hollis wriggled and made his cock paint his upper chest, where it became trapped with his excitement. In the bedroom, Taylin dropped Hollis onto the unmade bed, tearing off his boxers, breathless with enthusiasm. The seam splitting didn't register as he flung them away, moving to reach for Hollis's leg as he rolled and crawled up the bed. "Where are you going?" he rasped.

"To get a bottle of slick."

If there was ever a time Taylin could come without anything touching his cock, it was then. Anticipation. It blazed there in Hollis's hungry gaze as it traveled over Taylin. His ass clenched at what was coming. "Where do you want me?"

Were they really doing this?

The bump his heart gave against his ribs answered for him when Hollis pointed to the covers. "On your back, there."

On his back, Taylin had no time to second guess what was about to happen when Hollis dumped a liberal amount of slick over his cock so that it dripped over his knot, down his balls, and dribbled down his taint to his asshole. The feeling was strange but not unpleasant, not when his mate chased it with nimble fingers, slicking everything he touched.

Cool slipperiness became warm with Hollis's teasing strokes as he watched with an avid interest his own hands making Taylin gasp and whimper in arousal. The ache of his knot pulsing hard made nothing else matter right until a slick fingertip touched the rim of muscle guarding his ass.

For a moment, the temptation to tell Hollis to stop despite how aroused he was, warred its own battle inside him. Then Hollis shifted his gaze to Taylin, who got lost under the spell of desperation etched in the tight lines of Hollis's wild expression. Taylin would never deny him.

Their gazes never moved away from each other as Hollis gently caressed, teased and worked to ease the tip of one finger into his ass.

His moan matched Hollis's as he breached him. The burning didn't last more than a couple of breaths and eased the rampant desire to come.

"Okay?" Hollis questioned through clenched teeth, skin glistening in the morning light with sweat, holding perfectly still.

His lips wouldn't unclasp, so Taylin nodded, doing his best to relax when the finger slid a little deeper. The burning sensation became much less and morphed into something that Taylin found unexpected. Need.

He wanted... more.

Whether it was how Hollis was staring at him or from his earlier arousal at the touch to his knot, Taylin didn't analyze. He wanted this. Desired to feel his mate inside him.

When one finger became two, Taylin couldn't tell anyone what his own name was. He bore down instinctively, his desperation to come making his body quake. Wanting Hollis to have what he craved, Taylin panted to hold off the inevitable.

"You need to hurry the fuck up," he demanded huskily when Hollis didn't seem to have the same level of urgency. The hands Taylin had interlaced and hooked under his head to stop himself from touching Hollis or his cock were cramping badly.

"You think you can take me?" Hollis's voice was hardly audible over the pounding of Taylin's heart. His whole body had become sheened with sweat. Right along with Hollis's. His cock looked red and angry, leaving strings of pre-cum on his thigh as he carefully removed his fingers.

The cock wasn't overly long but had some girth that would mean Taylin would feel every inch. "Won't know till you're inside me."

Hollis groaned, his head dropping between his shoulders for a moment, his body shuddering. "I'll go slow..."

An irrational spurt of jealousy came at the thought of his mate doing this with someone else. "Have you done this before?"

The head shake was immediate. "Never... never wanted to..." his gaze dropped to Taylin's splayed thighs, hard shaft and pulsing knot.

He licked at rosy lips and whispered, "Wanna see... and touch your knot when I'm inside you," like it was a dirty secret.

It triggered a vicious tug to Taylin's balls, and he grabbed for them, frightened he'd come, squeezing them painfully while he demanded, "Get inside me now!"

Between his thighs, Hollis came forward at the sharp command, his cock jerking as he moved to position himself. Taylin was forced to move his hands and sucked in a gusty breath when a second later, the crown of Hollis's cock nudged at his already sensitive hole, causing whorls of pleasure.

Screwing his eyes shut, he panted like an omega in labor and relaxed his asshole at the continuing pressure against the rim. Hollis's breath hit him in short bursts as he sank in slowly past the tight ring of muscle.

Expecting the burn didn't mean he was prepared for just how much more intense it would be. The wide stretch all but knocked the air from him. His lungs ceased as the pressure built in his ass, then Hollis changed the angle and the air exploded from him in a heady burst. Pleasure, the kind he didn't expect, came in a myriad of nerve endings dancing in sync. It blew his fucking mind.

"Do that again," he gasped desperately.

Taylin couldn't say if it was him or Hollis who growled with just how overloaded his brain was with all the competing sensations happening all at once. His cramping fingers flexed and caught some of his curls, adding a bite of pain while he kept his hips from jerking at the invasion. Unsure, despite how good he was feeling, he was ready to slam up onto the thick dick, burning a path of fiery pleasure to his knot. It increased in size and held all of Hollis's rapt attention.

A drip of sweat hit Taylin's nipple, then another as Hollis whimpered. "Your knot is huge." His arms shook on either side of Taylin's body. "Wanna touch it so bad."

Not thinking, Taylin parted his thighs further to grab Hollis's legs and lift them over his. Placing his feet on the mattress, he came up, thrusting the cock deep into his ass unintentionally. It stole his breath, while Hollis wailed, and wiggled to get closer.

It was wholly awkward with how Hollis's ass was on the bed to keep his cock inside Taylin. "Fuck, hang on," he gasped, his brain not functioning at the strain of doing shit that would end this far too quickly.

Hollis didn't listen and one hand grabbed Taylin's left shoulder to hold on while the other dropped between them, moving over his knot.

Taylin shuddered violently when those same fingers squeezed, and his vision turned white. Blindly, gums aching, he opened his mouth, and a second later blood filled his mouth as he bit Hollis's throat. The coppery taste didn't combat the sweetness of his mate when he swallowed, moaned, and sucked on the salty skin, eager for more. The small taste he'd had before didn't prepare Taylin for the explosion of whirling emotions setting light to every cell in his body. He quaked hard enough that Hollis rocked on him. The cock in his ass expanded further, forcing Taylin to shake.

Hollis's groans grew louder as his slicked fingers slid and teased Taylin's knotted flesh, and it was game over. His head arched back at the splendor of the moment, his blood zinging with the new life and he cried out when hot ribbons of cum burst from the tip of his dick, spraying them both and drenching the air with his scent.

"Yes... yes... cover me... mark me..." Hollis cried, panting as he pinned his body against Taylin, who rocked his hips hard enough the bed groaned under them.

"Want to feel your seed inside me," Taylin demanded mindlessly, lost in the throes of his passion. Lost to the need to please his mate.

"Anything for you, love... anything..."

Chapter Twenty-Eight

Hollis

Unable to move, Hollis clung to Taylin's shoulder with one hand and rested his head on the other. He dragged in the sex-scented air of their shocking antics and though his cock had done exactly what Taylin had wanted, it remained hard inside him.

Was that because Hollis remained in shock that first, he'd asked for this and second, Taylin had allowed it? Was it because he could feel where Taylin had bitten him?

All were a possibility in his dazed state.

Taylin's ass clenched and Hollis lifted his head to look at the sweaty, cum-covered man with a heavy-lidded gaze. "Want me to move?"

The position had to be uncomfortable now that Hollis could think beyond what they'd been doing.

He wasn't sure what had come over him—

Taylin came all over you, his animal said in a smug tone.

Hollis ignored his animal, watching Taylin closely to see if he'd start regretting what they'd done. He was aware alphas' didn't bottom, or so he'd always been led to believe. Not that he'd ever thought about it before today. He couldn't quite believe his own behavior when he'd got the need to push Taylin to see just how far the man would go for him. Thoughts of babies would do that to a mate, it would seem. He'd had lots of time to think about it while Taylin had fallen asleep before his head had hit the pillow.

Hollis suspected Taylin's drinking too much the night before was all about what his mother had said, and the conversation earlier suggested he was right. Only Hollis had ensured that the conversation got shelved for the time being.

"What's going on in your head?" Taylin asked instead as he stroked a hand over his cheek, making him realize his glasses were missing.

Hollis didn't move to search the bed, not when furrows appeared between Taylin's brows. "I disrupted the conversation you were trying to have," Hollis decided to confess.

Taylin's frown lines deepened. "Why did you do that?"

This was one of the things he loved about Taylin, he never shied away from hard conversations. "I'm not ready to think about the consequences that we're both responsible for."

Taylin's lips parted to suggest he was about to argue, but Hollis shook his head, desperate to finish now he'd started. "Don't say it's your responsibility alone. I didn't bring condoms with me, despite knowing how things could end up."

He'd concluded that at 2am before he'd shifted and moved to sleep on Taylin, exhausted but also resigned that it was an actual conscious decision he'd taken. The why... that was still debatable.

Everything inside Taylin lit up. He glowed brighter than the sun, and Hollis's heart swelled at how fucking lucky he was to have someone who would not condone his actions when they clearly could. "You want my babies?"

A chuckle bubbled up and before he could stop it, it escaped, followed by another, causing his cock to move inside Taylin.

The hand at his waist squeezed. "That's enough of that," Taylin said, squirming and shifting his ass back. "You might not be long, but I feel like I've ridden a damn pole. I'll be feeling you for days," he groused good-naturedly. "I suspect I'll be walking like one of Silas's cowboys."

Hollis's chuckles turned into full-blown gales of laughter at the backhanded compliment.

Seconds later, he lay sprawled on the mattress with an amused looking Taylin caging him in. "It's not funny." He attempted a scowl, then ruined it when his lips twitched.

"Absolutely," Hollis agreed, keeping the smirk off his face for all of a second.

Taylin growled and kissed him hard, leaving him wanting and panting when he rolled off the bed.

"Where are you going?" Hollis asked, suddenly not feeling quite as amused.

Taylin picked up his boxers and eyed them before he sighed at the torn seam, rendering them useless. "Well, I was going to get us something to eat." He twirled the piece of material around his finger. "Only these aren't fit for anything other than the trash can." He gave Hollis what appeared to be a speculative once over, his gaze lingering on his lower body. "Your underwear will not fit me and I only have slacks with me... so..."

Hollis sat up on the rumpled covers, shrugging nonchalantly. "Could be you need to bring some of your things"—*all your things*—"here?" He kept that thought to himself, waiting and watching the man still twirling his underwear around his finger.

"Are you asking me to move in with you?"

Hollis narrowed his eyes, squinting when his short-sightedness hindered him. Giving up, he glanced about the messy bed, looking for a slither of red. He'd never confess how many times he lost his glasses and part of the reason he chose red was because it was such an excellent color to spot.

There, tucked into the corner of the sheet. He reached over and grabbed them, slipping them on and returning his attention to Taylin.

"Your glasses... they're such a fucking turn on," Taylin said, like he was talking to himself rather than Hollis.

"I hate them, but I can't see anything beyond the end of my nose, so they're a necessary evil."

An unholy, devilish gleam appeared in Taylin's eyes. "At some point, I want to be the one to put your glasses on when I slip my cock inside you so I can see that sexy look you get become magnified."

Hollis fanned himself, sure he had suddenly stepped into a hot sauna. His cock twitched while his ass clenched at the idea. "Yes... erm... right... what were we talking about?"

Taylin let him off the hook and waved about his torn boxers. "You asking me to move in."

"We were?" Hollis questioned, still working to get his head to play catch up after the sexy movie his head was playing for him.

Deep chuckles accompanied the nod Taylin gave him. "You did and I'm saying yes." His nose wrinkled as he glanced down at his come and slick crusted skin. "But first I need to shower..." Hollis's stomach chose then to make a loud gurgling noise, "and feed you. Then I'll take you to introduce you formally to my parents."

"What... why? I know them," Hollis squeaked in alarm, not sure he was quite ready to face either Lane or Derick after yesterday.

"I met your parents officially. Now it's my turn." His tone suggested refusal was futile. Then he spoiled it by adding, "Please?"

Swallowing back a sigh of frustration at just how that request melted his heart, Hollis rolled off the bed. He pointed a finger at Taylin. "I want pastries for breakfast, lots and lots of pastries..." he sailed past Taylin, "and I'm having the first shower."

A grin formed at the complaints that followed him into the bathroom to switch on the shower. He waited Taylin out as the shower warmed up. His animal side fed him playful ideas, all of which meant Hollis would get little choice in saying no. Playing along, Hollis cocked out a hip, recalling just how Wilder did it to get his own way countless times, and fluttered his eyelashes at Taylin. “You could shower with us?”

Taylin stepped forward, then paused. “Us?”

A second later, Hollis was in his animal form at Taylin’s feet, then he climbed slowly up his leg, his tongues licking at the hairs as he acquainted himself with the taste of Taylin. When he reached Taylin’s upper chest, the remaining cognizant part of him witnessed the alarmed expression.

About to shift back, his animal kept control. *Don’t you dare, I want some time too.*

In the shower… it’s a step too far. Even as he said it, Taylin’s expression softened, and he cupped a hand under his furry bottom, holding him carefully as he got into the shower. “So, do you like soap or shower gel?”

Hollis’s morning euphoria disappeared the second he pulled into the driveway of Lane and Derick’s home. He regretted the last pastry he’d eaten as the door opened and Hollis got the impression that Taylin had texted Lane to let them know they were coming.

Dressed more casually than Hollis had ever seen his boss, Lane hustled to the car door before Hollis could throw an accusing look at Taylin.

The door opened and Lane's preferred aftershave greeted him, and he didn't have time to move before Lane hugged him hard enough that Hollis worried for his ribs. "Hollis, you don't know how happy you've finally made me," he whispered in his ear.

Huh?

Finally?

What did that mean?

He didn't get time to think about it when Lane eagerly pulled him from the car. "Let's get inside, it's warm but not warm enough to stay out here." Lane also gave him no chance to reply as he continued. "I've let Bessie know you'll be joining us for dinner. She's cooking up a storm in her excitement at one of her boys bringing home a mate."

Giving Taylin a bemused 'help me' glance, Hollis didn't get the opportunity to see his reaction as he got ushered into the divine smelling house.

"Popi, give him room to breathe," Jupiter said, sauntering towards them, wearing black sweats and a T-shirt that was full of rips. "You'll frighten him with your over eagerness."

"Don't be silly. Hollis knows me by now and as he's the first boy that Taylin has brought home to meet us. I'm going to treasure the moment."

An eye roll that was better suited to a teenager got aimed at Lane's back when he faced Hollis, radiating happiness. "My boys don't get how monumental this is for me. Taylin hasn't dated for over five years, and I've waited for him to see what was right in front of him."

Huh?

Five years...

Alarm came and went and matched the look that Jupiter now wore as he narrowed his gaze on Lane. "Popi, were you playing matchmaker all this time?"

Taylin's loud "fuck," caused them all to look toward the doorway. "What... what are we talking about here?"

Boisterous laughter burst from Jupiter as he pointed at Taylin. "You've been played," he said with difficulty through the raucous noise he was making.

Hollis glanced between the men, his gaze lingering on a very flushed looking Lane as he scowled at his son.

It didn't take a genius to figure out what brought Booker down the stairs or Silas from a room off the hallway.

"What did we miss?" Silas questioned, coming to a halt next to Jupiter.

"Popi played matchmaker for Taylin and Hollis."

"I did no such thing," Lane replied indignantly, his cheeks glowing. "If I had, they wouldn't have taken five years to figure themselves out, now would they?"

Hollis wasn't sure that was a valid argument when he couldn't decide if Lane looked guilty or not. He definitely wasn't acting himself, that was for sure. He was fidgeting, something Hollis had never seen him do before.

"What's all the laughter about?" Derick asked when he came down the hallway after Silas and Booker joined in with the laughter.

Taylin, dressed in the rumpled suit he'd worn the day before, slung his arm around Hollis's shoulder, casting a look at his family Hollis couldn't read.

"Dad, these assholes believe Popi was playing matchmaker."

Having turned his attention to Derick, Hollis caught a flash of something that to him appeared to be amusement before it was gone. "Popi wants you all mated, he's made no bones about it. Did you pick Hollis on your terms?"

It was Hollis's turn to blush at who made the first move as he tensed, waiting for Taylin's answer.

"Absolutely, and I'd pick him every time."

"Gawd... you're such a sap," Booker muttered under his breath.

Silas slapped Booker's shoulder. "You got that right."

Derick's blue eyes were icy when they shifted to his two sons. "You know karma never misses..." His grin was one Hollis was pleased wasn't aimed in his direction when he shivered at the intensity, "and neither does Fate."

On that, Derick walked to them and held out his hand to Hollis. The warmth he displayed was wholly different than that of moments ago. Hollis blinked owlishly.

"Welcome to the family, Hollis. I'm so happy for you and Taylin's..." The bridge of his nose wrinkled, and a smile transformed his entire face. Hollis got a little star struck. "True mating."

Freezing up and forgetting himself for a second, Taylin had to give him a hip bump to get Hollis reaching for Derick's hand.

"Thank you." What else was there to say?

"Shall we move into the sunroom? Silas, can you get a bottle of champagne to celebrate. Oh, and some of that chocolate cake Bessie made? Also, grab your brothers so we can all celebrate together."

"Cake and wine?" Silas asked, sounding anything but convinced the two went together.

Booker made a noise at the back of his throat that sounded decidedly like a groan.

"Cake goes with everything," Hollis answered, while Derick released his hand to take a step back.

At the same time Lane said, "Cake goes with everything, you silly boy."

Laughing, Lane tucked his arm through Hollis's, tugging him artfully away from Taylin.

"Alphas." He rolled his eyes heavenward. "They know nothing when it comes to cake. Now let's get comfy and you can tell me what plans you have for the wedding."

There were groans, only Hollis couldn't tell if one came from Taylin as he was already being encouraged to go with Lane.

"Better you than us, Taylin." Jupiter's voice carried to them, along with his chuckles.

Terrified, Hollis didn't hear Taylin's reply and went meekly with the force of nature that was Lane, unsure if running and hiding in some out of the way place was possible.

Wedding... who said anything about a wedding?

Chapter Twenty-Nine

Alphaholes Chat

Taylin: *You're all a bunch of assholes encouraging Popi about this wedding shit.*

Taylin: *Stuff!*

Jupiter: *You just remembered Dad can see the comments, didn't you? LOL*

Taylin: *Fuck off!*

Laken: *You should be more worried about Popi seeing this. He was in his element at the weekend, despite how weepy he got to see you packing your bags to leave.*

Taylin: *Weepy was not what you guys were… overjoyed was what came across with how helpful you all were to shove me out the door.*

Silas: *Of course we're overjoyed, one less person to create noise! And if I read it right, Hollis looked as terrified as you. Is he actually speaking to you? LOL I bet he isn't…*

Taylin: *Silas, you can fuck all the way off too.*

Booker: *Why are you taking this out on us? You're the one who mated with an omega and brought him home to meet the family. We're just showing our support.*

Taylin: *You talked about fucking outfits for the groomsmen! What fucking possessed you? And don't get me started on Rue talking color themes for flowers.*

Booker: *Popi possessed me. His enthusiasm was contagious. He was so happy, why wouldn't I want to encourage that? Show how happy I am for my baby brother to get Hollis in the sack… oops I mean your HEA.*

Taylin: *You wait… I'm gonna be front and center when you mate and then we'll see whose so fucking smug!*

Kodi: *Come on Tay, give it up. You secretly played out in your head, you waltzing* *down the aisle with Hollis. Wasn't it you that did that whole wedding plan thing with a designer when you were like seventeen? It was him, wasn't it?*

Kari: *Yep… I think Popi kept that big folder Tay had. If it's still in the house, it'll be in the basement boxed with a bunch of other stuff. I'll go look for you, Tay. I'm sure Hollis would enjoy your attempts at planning a wedding… Didn't you do it for a boy you were crushing on?*

Taylin: *Christ, how the fuck do you remember this stuff? And you dare Kari, and I'll search out the pictures of you holding that Ken doll you loved to sleep with.*

Silas: *Are we back in middle school? We all have skeletons in our closets we don't want paraded in front of others.*

Taylin: *Scared Silas? You got something you wanna tell us?*

Silas: *Stop deflecting, Tay.*

Rue: *My chat is blowing up, why can't you do this at a more reasonable time?*

Jupiter: *Tay is having a mini meltdown about how supportive we all were about his wedding.*

Taylin: *I never asked Hollis to marry me, assholes.*

Dad: *Taylin, you can say no to Popi… possibly… maybe if you do it now… As for the rest of you, stop winding Taylin up. He's in love and it changes everything as y'all will find out…*

Booker: *Nope.*

Rue: *That's a hell no!*

Jupiter: *Too many gorgeous men out there to limit myself to one!*

Kodi: *Who needs a mate to be happy? Not me. I love my life.*

Kari: *I second that!*

Laken: *I'll sit on the fence.*

Silas: *Laken, be careful you don't get a splinter in your ass. Mates… after witnessing Tay boo hooing like a baby…*

yep, you can keep that shit. I'll stick with my horses.

Dad: LOLOLOLOLOLOLOLOLOLOLOLOL *as if you have a say!*

Chapter Thirty

Taylin

The desk in front of Taylin remained cluttered with paperwork, even after he'd diligently worked through several piles that required his attention. His secretary had long since gone home and, judging by the stiffness across Taylin's upper back, it was late.

Placing down his pen, he checked his wristwatch, confirming his suspicion. Groaning at just how late it had gotten, he rolled his shoulders and stretched his arms above his head. How was it nearly ten pm?

He paused and a niggle at the back of his mind morphed into a deep dread when he tapped at his computer to look at his calendar.

"Argh!" He rubbed at his face in frustration at what he'd forgotten. He'd promised Hollis he'd be home by seven so they could have dinner together. He even put it in the calendar so he wouldn't forget.

How did that work for you?

"Why can't I get my act together?" he grumbled aloud.

Three weeks under the same roof and all the high hopes of getting to spend lots of time together had yet had to materialize. So far, they'd managed two evenings together and an uninterrupted Sunday. It wasn't enough, which was why he'd purposely penciled in time.

"How shit of a mate am I? Can't even damn remember to go home on time!" he muttered crossly, under his breath. It was frustrating how life conspired against them with deadlines and trips away. It was why he'd promised Hollis this evening before the next trip, requiring him to leave the next afternoon.

Taylin eyed his silent phone and reached to check it for messages.

Nada...

Was Hollis pissed? It was a stupid question when he would be mightily pissed if the tables were reversed. He blew out a gusty breath and stared at the screenshot of Hollis he'd taken when he'd just slipped on his red framed glasses two weeks ago.

Should I ring now?

Give him time to have a rant and calm down before I get home?

A warmth came at just how Hollis's house was home and that layered on the guilt because Hollis didn't—hadn't—complained once about how little time they spent together. Did that mean something?

The wedding Popi had decided they needed, thankfully, hadn't gotten mentioned again. However, that could be because they'd had no time to see Popi. Hollis hadn't mentioned it when they'd got back to his, with all of Taylin's things.

Did it mean he wanted to get married? It was a question Taylin had no answer to because he was too chickenshit to ask and it had the oddest habit of popping into his brain when it was least convenient to think about. It was alone now, having dealt with the question about an unexpected pregnancy.

Taylin hadn't, as yet, processed his mixed feelings on that issue. As Hollis had little to no clue about his species and pregnancy, they'd done some research together and Taylin hadn't admitted aloud he'd been a little disappointed to discover that July to October was when pygmy loris's were fertile. That meant there was absolutely no chance Hollis was pregnant. Now that they had this information, they could avoid getting pregnant.

A planned pregnancy...

Admit it, you want little pygmy lorises to cuddle.

There's no guarantee with my genes.

His wolf side snorted, and it felt like he'd given him the finger.

Listen, with how things are right now, and we aren't even in the busiest part of the year, my workload is already insane. This madness and *babies... they'll need their parents there for them. When I'm home, Hollis isn't and vice versa. That's not conducive to having babies.*

It wasn't... was it?

Of late, they were all getting a true insight into what an amazing job Dad and Popi had done with juggling work and their private lives with eight sons. They did it, but it was exhausting thinking about how they'd achieved it. Taylin acknowledged he needed to find his groove before his life changed again.

He blinked the calendar into focus as he shoved aside those worries for another time, considering he should get his ass home. He leaned closer, his eyes narrowing on the screen.

"You motherfucker, Booker!" There, added to the trip away with Booker the next day, was an extra full day of appointments, eating into his weekend.

All thoughts of getting home to Hollis disappeared when he searched his contact list for Booker's, hitting dial the second he found it.

"Yo," Booker answered on the first ring.

"Don't yo me, asshole. Why is there another day added to the trip? I have fucking plans with Hollis this weekend," he shouted, not worried anyone would hear him when he was probably alone in the building.

Taylin ran through their plans and could see no valid reason as to why they'd need another full day and night away to finalize the commissioned pieces they'd finally agreed on. He rubbed his fingers in a circle on the left temple, doing his best to hold onto his temper, waiting and counting three seconds of silence Booker made him wait for a reply.

"You finished throwing your hissy fit?"

"You did this on purpose!" he snapped back, in no way finished.

“Did you read the content of the appointments?” Booker replied lazily.

He hadn’t, and Booker damn well knew that by his self-righteous tone. He reached and clicked the mouse to open the extra appointment, his anger waning—a little.

“That’s why, you dick,” Booker grumbled after a moment. “We have to go back and kick those alphas out the door of the factory we now own. Dad sent me the confirmation of ownership an hour ago, and that was when I added the extra day to your calendar.

“We need to act now before they get wind of who has taken ownership of the place. With how the press has been over your mating *and* the changes at the company, we’re under a lot of scrutiny and there’s a chance things could blow up if we aren’t careful. It’s slim, granted, but it’s a risk I’m not prepared to take when it comes to those omegas. Dad was on board with that and as we’re not that far away with our current plans, I saw no reason we couldn’t extend the trip instead of making an additional trip after the weekend... *just so you can get your end away.*”

He'd cooled down as Booker explained, then the fucker had to hit him with the jab at the end. His brothers' teasing and what felt like obstructions to Taylin’s personal life was getting to be a real fucking pain in his ass.

“You’re an asshole, you know that, right?” Taylin would love to say he’d been getting plenty of hot sex, but with his late nights and Hollis’s, one of them was usually asleep before the other got in bed. Taylin wasn’t a selfish prick who’d wake Hollis for sex. Waking with his little pygmy loris curled on his chest was extremely satisfying... it was. Just, hot sweaty sex would be nice too.

"Trouble in paradise already?" Booker teased.

"No!" Taylin became convinced Booker heard his teeth grinding together when his brother chortled.

"How's the wedding plans going?"

"I'm hanging up." He heard the belly laughter as he hit 'end call' to slump in his chair, pouting. It was a common occurrence these days with how his brothers had ramped up the teasing.

His stomach snarled a reminder it had been hours since he'd last eaten and pushed him out of his seat. Phone tucked into his slacks, he reached to switch off his computer, then the lamp on the edge of his desk, casting the room into moonlit darkness. He grabbed his suit jacket, slipped it on and headed out the door.

He didn't breathe any easier in the car when he exited the parking lot, cutting down a near empty main street. Driving through nearly deserted streets, Taylin drove through the part of Hazardville that came with memories he had shut in a box years ago. Only, with those boxes being pried open by the press daily, it was hard to shut them again.

With Hollis's home on the far side of town, Taylin had to drive through the neighborhood he had called home briefly. It brought with it nightmares for all those who weren't as lucky as him. Homelessness was something Hazardville council pretended didn't exist because those on the streets were mainly divergent.

Forms skittered back into the shadows as he drove by and his hands tightened on the steering wheel as he felt a stab of pain for those who were hiding, hoping to evade those who prayed on the weak and vulnerable.

A desperation to get home to Hollis came with such velocity Taylin couldn't catch his breath. He increased his speed, hoping to outrun the shadows of his own past. Booker wasn't wrong. The press had become relentless since they'd invited them in. Wrong or right, they were stuck with the consequences. Taylin's biological parents and siblings had cashed in, selling their story for everyone to read about *his family's pain at finding their offspring was divergent.*

He'd seen the headline this morning and stupidly read the article, then buried himself in work to hide from his own pain. It was the reason he'd lost track of time. That he'd allowed it to interfere with his life left his mood hitting the rocks just as he pulled into the drive.

He had the wherewithal to check no one was lurking before he got out of the car, striding to the house. His inner turmoil was riding him so hard he felt like he'd snap in two. His hand shook as he attempted to fit the key in the lock.

The door burst open before he could turn the key. Hollis took one look at his expression and whatever he saw there caused him to leap at Taylin. Arms and legs wrapped around him as he caught his mate and buried his nose in his neck, releasing a pain ridden breath. "I missed dinner, I'm so sorry."

"Shush, it's fine."

Aware that anyone could see them, Taylin stepped into the house and used his shoe to kick the door shut behind him before giving into temptation. The kiss was hot and needy.

Both were breathless and flushed when Taylin stopped to move them from the hallway up the stairs to their bedroom. Eating was no longer a top priority. He wanted to forget. He wanted to immerse himself in his mate.

"I missed you," he murmured against Hollis's smooth throat, kissing down to his mating mark to nibble on the scarred flesh.

"Missed you too." Hollis shivered, his legs clenching around Taylin as he rocked his erection against Taylin's suit jacket.

The sleep pants Hollis wore were no barrier to Taylin's wandering hands. He slipped them past the elastic waist and over the fleshy globes of Hollis's bare ass. Hollis moaned and tilted his pelvis to rock against Taylin.

The slick coating Hollis's asshole made it easy to slip two fingers inside and widen them. Taylin knew how much his mate loved the burn.

An unholy moan followed the muscles clenching around his digits. "Another," Hollis gasped hotly, his breath coming in small pants.

Taylin did as ordered.

Squelching, moans, groans, and whimpers added to the urgency for Taylin as he stumbled toward their bed. He only had the ability not to crush Hollis when they hit the covers, his fingers not leaving his mate's ass.

"Enough, want your cock," Hollis whined through kiss-swollen lips.

Blood pounding hard enough to make his ears ring, Taylin yanked off Hollis's sleep pants and jerked at the zip of his suit pants, clumsily tugging out his throbbing cock. A second later, he thrust deep inside the hot, convulsing channel that squeezed hard enough sweat broke out over Taylin's body at how close it brought him to climax.

"Fuck, you're tight... am I hurting you?" he rasped past the dryness. Holding completely still, which went against every nerve ending inside him that wanted him to move, sweat slid down his hairline.

"No... more... fuck... move... please," Hollis demanded breathlessly.

With a mindlessness that was more suited to insanity, Taylin thrust into Hollis, who begged for more. It was a hard, dirty fuck, and it did what nothing else could have; it closed down Taylin's brain.

Unsure how much time passed before he howled his release after Hollis's clenching hole alerted him Hollis had climaxed, Taylin rolled and collapsed onto the mattress utterly wrecked.

When his brain came back online, it came with a huge dollop of guilt. He placed an arm over his eyes, dragging in a deep, sex scent breath.

A hand crept up over his suit sleeve. "That was amazing... Give me five minutes and let's do it again."

Taylin lifted his arm and glanced sideways at the man wearing only his t-shirt covered in cum, who looked utterly pleased if the smile aimed at Taylin was anything to go by. "You liked that?"

"Hell yeah. What's not to love about hot, sweaty, unbridled sex?" Hollis asked in a way that suggested Taylin was mad if he suggested otherwise.

Fuck, he loved this man.

Taylin sat up and removed his jacket, throwing it on the floor, then did the same with his shirt and tie. He eyed his spent cock poking out of his slacks and gained back his sense of humor. "Slacks on or off?" he asked Hollis, shifting his attention back to his mate.

The wickedness to the smile went straight to Taylin's cock, which twitched at how Hollis was eying him. "Most definitely on."

In a fast move, Taylin rolled back on top of Hollis, pinning him to the bed. "On it is!"

Chapter Thirty-One

Hollis

Hollis wanted to sulk after the glorious evening they'd had the night before, as he listened to Taylin explain that their weekend plans were going to have to change.

"Booker added the extra day to the trip last night. We're close enough not to have to add in an additional trip away and waste time on dealing with the situation at Design Detailing & Co now it's confirmed the company sale has gone through." Taylin, carrying shirts and underwear, gave him an apologetic smile, going to the open suitcase on the bed. "He wants to do some ass kicking. I get it, but fuck, I'm sorry. I know we were going to have a proper date night Friday and a weekend of lounging in bed binge watching movies, eating takeout."

Worry, it was there in the taut lines around Taylin's lips as he cast another look at Hollis before resuming his packing.

Hollis slipped on his shirt, buttoning it up as he kept his disappointment out of his voice when he answered, “He’s right. It’s silly to come back when you’re close to the factory. And those alphas could be doing who knows what to those omegas during this transition period.”

They had talked about him going, but Taylin didn’t need Hollis present for the meetings with Brand Alliance and the lawyers to iron out the last few details before the contracts received their full approval. His sensible side had taken hold with the list of ever-growing demands the other brothers threw at him, so he’d acted like the professional he was and had forgone his urge to say ‘fuck it’.

The ‘fuck it’ was getting much harder to ignore and it worried Hollis that his sensible side was disappearing with each passing day because of the sexy hunk who’d taken up residence in his heart.

Taylin folded another shirt and added it to the pile, then glanced up at Hollis. “I’m disappointed. I meant it last night, I miss you.”

Sincerity and disappointment reflected at him helped, it did. So did how sore his ass was and how he’d be feeling just how much Taylin missed him for days. A dopey grin appeared. “Then you’ll need to demonstrate again when you get home on Saturday night.”

A light of interest came over Taylin’s sexy grin. “You could be asleep?”

Finished with buttoning up his shirt, Hollis slinked around the side of the unmade bed and ran a finger down Taylin’s naked chest until it reached the belt buckle, where he tapped at it. A vision of Taylin last night popped right to the forefront of his mind.

"I've never had anyone attempt to seduce me while I'm asleep..." he cupped Taylin's cock, feeling it swell under his hand and getting an extra thrill. "That could be fun, don't you think?"

The huskiness in his voice wasn't put on, not with how dry his mouth got at the flare of desire and the hard shaft doing its best to poke through the zipper.

Taylin's groan sounded painful as he placed his hand over Hollis's, cupping it and pressing it more firmly against the hard shaft beneath his clothing, the scent of arousal warmed the air. "If you keep that up, you'll be face down on the mattress with my cock in your ass..."

Hollis, never a flirt, fluttered his eyelashes at Taylin, tempting the sexy beast inside his mate he had discovered. Last night... yeah, he wanted a lot more of that side of Taylin unleashed on him. "I don't see any problem with that... I mean, you are the boss."

"Fuck..." Taylin cursed, his gaze roaming the bed as his phone chirped madly. "Brothers! Cock blocking fuckers," he growled, moving, forcing Hollis to let go so he could search the covers for the offending item.

Hollis decided moving far away from Taylin was for the best. Aroused enough to want to consider jumping Taylin and to tell him to ignore work was not a good thing for a man in his position. Something he had to remind himself of repeatedly as he finished dressing, only half listening to Taylin.

He left him in the bedroom when the conversation continued, and he wasn't sure he had talked himself around from his current 'fuck it' moment.

He had waffles and fruit plated and coffee percolating by the time Taylin appeared dressed, his suit jacket in place giving Hollis a sinking feeling in his gut.

"Sorry." Taylin eyed the table and sighed morosely, adding to Hollis's conviction they wouldn't be having breakfast together. "The plane is booked for a damn service back here tomorrow, so we have to leave now. Booker will be here in a minute."

Hollis's face fell, despite understanding. "Can't you at least eat a waffle? You ate so little last night," he fussed, picking up the warm waffle and offering it to Taylin.

His expression softened and Hollis's breath caught in his throat at the love he was still getting used to seeing. "I love you," Taylin said, taking the waffle from him and swooping down to kiss him hard.

Breathless and the world beyond his glasses wonky, Hollis whimpered at the loss of Taylin's hot lips when he stepped back, saying, "That'll be Booker."

"Huh?"

Taylin grinned cheekily, pointing to the doorway with the hand holding the waffle. "Ringing the doorbell," he explained.

A blast of heat filled his cheeks as he coughed in embarrassment at having heard nothing. "Oh... okay.

"You're fucking adorable." Taylin kissed him too fast for Hollis to do more than blink. "I'm gonna have to go, I'll ring you tonight."

Seconds later, he heard the door slam and Hollis remained standing in the same spot, his lips still buzzing and his body too hot for comfort.

"That man is lethal!"

Isn't it great?

Hollis couldn't argue with his animal, not one little bit.

He took another minute to revel in his reality that, despite how busy they were over the last few weeks, he continued to wake daily to find himself curled up on his mate. He was pinching himself on an almost daily basis, just to see if he would wake up from the dream he was in.

Not tomorrow or the next day or the day after that, his animal sulked.

Stop being greedy. He wasn't sure if he was actually talking to his animal or himself as he felt his animal flounce about inside him, ignoring him.

Thirty minutes later he entered his office, having eaten standing at the counter, before collecting his laptop, which he brought home daily to work while waiting for Taylin to come home. It was that or pace, and that wasn't nearly as productive.

He placed the bag on his desk, barely having time to shed his suit jacket, when the door burst open and Wilder ran in, tears glinting in his eyes.

"What did he do now?" Hollis asked, walking to close the door before guiding a now sobbing Wilder to the chair in front of his desk. Hollis caught a whiff of melon and something sweeter when Wilder didn't let go and clung to him, forcing him to crouch next to the seat.

"I'm sure he's doing it on purpose now!" Wilder whined.

"Doing what?" Hollis asked, none the wiser. Jupiter, it appeared, was making it his life's mission to make Wilder as miserable as possible. Why, Hollis hadn't figured out.

Wilder relaxed his grip on Hollis to reach into the breast pocket of his shirt, pressing at the screen of the phone he now held. He held up the screen to Hollis, while his other hand scrubbed at his damp eyes. "This!"

"Wilder, you will refrain from calling the men who contact you by a number or else I will need to consider your suitability for the position of my PA," Hollis read aloud.

"He's going to fire me!" Wilder cried, his dark eyes swimming once more.

Hollis sucked in a breath, getting a tickling feeling at the back of his throat when it sank in exactly which men Wilder was using numbers to remember. The conversation he had with the little raccoon only two days ago ran through his mind, and the tickle increased.

Wilder had literally taken Hollis at his word when he'd innocently suggested that Wilder add numbers to the men who called and wanted to speak to Jupiter when Wilder kept getting the names mixed up, setting off Jupiter to rant at him once again.

He ran a hand over his mouth and worked to keep his reaction to himself, when it was to laugh inappropriately at how Wilder had handled the long list of men who Jupiter dated.

"He can't fire you, Wilder," he said to allay that fear first, because Wilder was an excellent PA and only had issues with Jupiter. "I'm the only one who can do that. I told you to read your contract, didn't I?" he said gently. "Your roles and responsibilities fall directly under my remit. If Jupiter has issues with your work, then he should be addressing them with me."

"He can't?"

Hollis shook his head, trying to get a read on what was running through Wilder's head with the thoughtful look he now wore. To date, it had only been Wilder who'd come to visit Hollis with problems. All of which related to non-work problems.

It was time to pay Jupiter a visit, one Hollis did not relish after the fun the other man had at his expense over a wedding that he hadn't actually had a proposal for.

Wilder sniffed huffily, rubbing at the tip of his nose, drawing attention to the gleam that appeared in his eyes that set off a warning bell inside Hollis. "Whatever thought has just ran through your head, don't do it." Wilder was the cheeky one of the group. He acted impulsively most of the time. His adorability meant that he got away with his silliness—until Jupiter.

"I don't know what you mean," he replied innocently.

Hollis rose and shook his head, pointing at Wilder, who tucked his phone away. "This is me you're talking to. I know you. You are excellent at your job, but your impulsiveness could land you in more hot water with Jupiter." Hollis thought for a second. "Maybe it's time to consider switching you with one of the other PAs." It was the safest option when none of the others had complained about working with Jupiter in the past.

The speed with which Wilder left the chair left Hollis wide eyed. "No. It's my area of expertise. Why should I be the one to get punished for his behavior?"

"He's upsetting you on a nearly daily basis, Wilder. How is that punishing you?" Hollis let out a little of his frustration. "The file notes I have from your frequent visits to my office are bigger than that of all the other PAs put together."

Wilder's little nose rose in the air. "He's a... he's a... well, I don't know what he is. It doesn't matter... you don't need to worry about it, I'll fix him... it." He quickly followed up with a reassuring smile that did nothing to allay the feeling Hollis had that things were about to go from bad to worse.

"Wilder, I'm warning you, *please* don't do anything stupid. I don't want to have to do what Jupiter is threatening because you did something to rile him up." He was wasting his breath, he could see it as Wilder nodded but didn't lose the glint of devilment Hollis was familiar with.

God save me from sassy raccoons!

Chapter Thirty-Two

Delicious & Vicious Chat

Lennon: *What's with the outfit Wilder? Isn't that a little too racy for a work day?*

Ziggy: *You didn't wear it to work?*

Bowie: *What am I missing? Wear what?*

Lennon: *Yes he did…*

Bowie: *Wear what? Will someone tell me, come on?*

Wilder: *A purple lacy corset that Ziggy suggested I buy to make me feel better after Jupiter threatened to fire me*

Bowie: *I'm lost. When did Jupiter threaten to fire you? And if it's a lacy corset… isn't that more a girl thing? I don't think I've seen boy ones. Do we make those? If so, can someone send me the link? I'd like to see. Duh… I could just go to Wilder's office*

Ziggy: *Dare I ask how Lennon can see it?*

Lennon: *He's not covering it up! Gotta say, he looks hot as fuck in it!*

***Ziggy:** Words fail me, Wilder*

***Wilder:** Good, that means when a certain someone sees me, then they'll also be at a loss for words at our next meeting… together*

***Hollis:** Wilder… tell me you don't look indecent for the important meeting with the organizers and models for the Milan fashion show!*

***Wilder:** Of course not… everything is appropriately covered… I swear*

***Lennon:** He's covered for sure… in lace and silk!*

***Hollis:** Do you want to turn my hair gray, Wilder? Put a picture in the group chat.*

I want to see exactly what you have on before I get in my car and come across town to wring your neck for worrying me

Lennon: *Don't worry boss, he's got a fitted white shirt on under it*

Hollis: *Thank you Lennon. Wilder, I'm not finding any amusement in this…*

Wilder: *Spoil sport, Lennon. Boss, I'm just asserting myself and showing Mr 'you look like a bargain bin reject' that I can make a fashion statement just like his model toys!*

Hollis: *That thudding that can be heard all over town is me banging my head on the wall*

Wilder: *Sorry boss* ⊠

Chapter Thirty-Three

Taylin

Missing Hollis enough to prevent him from sleeping, Taylin had encouraged his brothers to cram in meetings despite how exhausting it was. It would allow them to fly home Friday evening instead of Saturday, giving Taylin the chance to claim back a little of his weekend. He'd kept quiet and not told Hollis in case something disrupted the plan.

Taylin felt the adrenaline pumping through him, removing some of the dragging tiredness when they pulled up outside Design Detailing & Co's factory.

The place looked no different from the last time they visited over a month ago, except for the car lot outside full of expensive vehicles. Taylin would bet his last cent on none of them belonging to the omegas inside. They had requested, or the subsidiary company they owned had requested, a meeting, insisting all staff be present Friday morning.

Taylin suspected Amatus, because they'd not bothered with a site visit before the purchase, was feeling pretty secure that those who'd bought the company wouldn't be concerned with the appalling conditions. Because who in their right mind bought a business sight unseen? Not anyone who was concerned about the conditions the omegas were forced to work under, he'd suggest.

"Looks like a full house." Rue, the first to speak, cracked his knuckles. His rhino's presence was visible in his eyes when he turned his attention to Taylin and Booker. Jupiter, Silas, and the twins wanted to come today, but other work commitments in Hazardville prevented it. Laken was out of the country and had complained bitterly to be missing out on 'head bashing', as he called it.

Taylin suspected Popi had stopped Dad from coming after the conversation they'd had on FaceTime last night.

"Looks like," Booker replied brusquely, his interest going to the large stretch hummer that pulled up next to them. "Security team are here."

Booker opened his door and got out, visibly vibrating as he tugged his suit jacket into place. No suit could mask the animalistic nature of Booker's bear, no matter the cut or expense.

"Remember to keep it professional, Booker," said Taylin as he and Rue followed, watching Oakland, a huge tiger shifter, exit the hummer. Exuding power that left no one mistaken that the guy wearing all black wasn't someone to tangle with unless they had a death wish. Taylin could still recall the first time he'd met him ten years before. His coal-black eyes held a predatory danger that warned others to be careful. Taylin never changed his opinion.

Those coal-black eyes swept the area and Taylin figured the man missed nothing when he returned his gaze to the other men filing out of the stretch hummer.

The decision to bring their personal security team had come from Dad. Not that any of them argued when they were unaware of what they were going to face once inside. Keeping the omegas safe was their priority. Despite Booker being more than capable of sorting out a few alphas that stepped out of line, as were Rue and Taylin, guns were different. None of them were invincible to bullets, so they'd brought men trained in arms along with many other weapons.

They hadn't gotten to where they were by being stupid, and as much as the reason they needed the armed men galled them, they accepted it. What was about to go down wouldn't be easy, but it could be quick and without casualties, if played right.

"I've gone over the schematic of the building with my men, having considered what you remember of the placement of those carrying weapons. Holt, Legacy, and Rana will guard the exits. The rest of my team will take point once we have eyes on where the armed men are," said Oakland. Not one for wasting energy, he signaled to his men as he spoke and seconds later, they were all walking toward the factory.

Purposefully early to get the element of surprise, Taylin rolled his shoulders and whispered, "Be prepared for the smell." It was all the warning he gave, inhaling the fresh air before reaching for the handle on the door in front of him.

The smell was worse than last time. Taylin gagged on filth, blood, and what smelled like shit. Voices carried over the sounds of activity.

"Remember, you fucking runts, one word and you'll regret you were born," came from an alpha that Taylin hadn't seen before, who was stationed up on the upper floor watching over the factory floor. Amatus stood at his side, none of the pleasantries he'd put on for them evident.

Both the gun and the vicious look the alpha aimed at the omegas made Taylin's heart speed up at the implication.

An unnerving quiet followed. Oakland's men moved so silently, it took Taylin a moment to realize they were no longer behind him but had dispersed around the factory.

It took several more seconds for the alphas in the place to notice something amiss due to their attention focused on the men working hard and, Taylin suspected, doing their level best to be invisible.

It sickened him and his anger surfaced when he caught Amatus nudging the armed man next to him. The gun was now trained towards them.

Show time.

"Hello Amatus, good to see you again," Taylin snarled, all wolf, prowling closer to the workbenches to be heard.

The omegas close by reeked of fear, stabbing Taylin's heart and adding to the anger morphing into rage. He kept a tight grip on it when these men had more than their fair share and didn't need his, too.

"What... what are you doing here," he snarled back, his voice carrying in the open space, as he moved quickly to the metal staircase that led to the factory floor.

"No pleasantries today?" Taylin's grin was all teeth. "I mean really, is that any way to speak to the new owners of Design Detailing & Co?" He tilted his head, arching a brow. They had previously decided he'd do the talking as the more level headed of the group. Taylin suspected that might have been an error.

He watched as several emotions ran over the other man's face as he stalked across the factory, unaware of the men close by cringing away.

Disbelief won out as he came to a stop in front of Taylin and the tense atmosphere in the factory increased. "What nonsense. I have the emails from Starling Enterprise advising you had no interest in working with us. Your loss," he sneered. "We had a better offer." He came closer to Taylin and spat, "Divergent."

Booker's growl was ominous, echoing in the cavernous room.

"You're trespassing on private property, you need to leave now, before..." At the unspoken threat, an armed alpha came up behind Amatus to drive the point home, lifting the gun in their direction.

Booker's aftershave alerted Taylin to him moving. Booker came to stand close enough to Taylin's side that their suit jacket's touched. Taylin didn't take his furious gaze off Amatus when Rue came and flanked his other side.

"The only people trespassing are you and those fucktards aiming guns at the omegas." Taylin came forward, getting a hit of Amatus's stale breath as he got in his face. "You're all fucking fired, every damn one of you, *now get out.*"

"Totally professional, bro," Booker muttered, sounding extremely amused.

The alphas didn't move, but the omegas did.

"We don't mean you guys." Booker walked towards the work benches and approached the nearest, trembling man, keeping his voice soft.

Taylin suspected they thought they had no choice. They were dead wrong. "Listen to me. Every omega here, if you wish to stay and work for a company that will take care of you, then you can. No one is going to be forced into anything." Taylin didn't need to see skepticism, because who would believe them after what he could only imagine they had suffered at these asshole's hands. "I know it is hard to believe right now—"

Movement out of the corner of Taylin's eye at a brave omega moving from behind his work station came with a loud crack and something whistling through the air. The following scream stopped Taylin cold.

Barely registering he'd swung to charge in the direction the cry had come from, there was a thwack and cry of, "Who the fuck do you think you are?"

Taylin hadn't seen Oakland move. The man had the whip wielding alpha by the throat, dangling effortlessly. One side of his face was swelling up and blood dripped from a cut to his eyebrow down the skin where the bruise started to form.

Oakland now held the whip in his other hand, looking ready to attack anyone who moved.

He wasn't looking at the fucker he held but at the tiny omega with matted hair, bleeding from his cheek where the whip must have sliced his skin from bone. "Brier, get the Medi pack from the hummer for me."

A man whom Taylin assumed to be Brier left wordlessly.

"We'll take care of you, little one," Oakland murmured, almost sweetly to the dumbfounded looking omega.

"You will?" he squeaked.

Taylin was as surprised as the omega. Oakland was a badass who never came across as having a softer side.

"Yes," Oakland answered, his gaze shifting to the alpha, who dangled and kicked out, struggling to escape his hold. "Move again and I'll fucking snap your neck."

Ice coated his voice and Taylin felt the change in the atmosphere from that one threat aimed at an alpha instead of an omega. It felt like the omegas all took a collective breath together, then Amatus fucking spoiled it.

"I don't know what the hell is going on here. You can't come in here and threaten my men when they are only protecting the omegas."

"Bullshit," Booker rumbled out.

Amatus raised his hand and made a circling motion with his finger.

Whatever that signal meant, it didn't get the desired effect. Moments later, he spun around looking up, only to come to a stop and make a gasping noise.

Oakland's men were there, their guns aimed at the heads of the alphas, who were minus their weapons.

Taylin reached into his suit jacket and pulled out two envelopes. He offered one to Amatus, who stared at it with trepidation. Yeah, be scared fucker, because he was fucking done and if Taylin had his way, the guy would never get another job. "This terminates your employment effective immediately and that of all the assholes wielding weapons."

"You can't fire us!" he blustered, fear shining in his eyes.

Taylin's toothy grin was back. "You should have read the small print, dickhead. We can and we have. The company buyout contract," he held up the second envelope, feeling a satisfaction at wiping off the self-righteous prick's smile, "gives a large percentage of the profits to the omegas who have worked to build up the reputation of this firm."

Taylin waved it high in the air, ignoring the man going a shade of red that clearly wasn't healthy, who foamed at the mouth in front of him. "We will compensate you all for the distress you've endured while working here. We'll pay your bills for any medical care you require, assisting you in recovery. It's all written here, and I've copies for all of you."

"Noooo," Amatus cried out.

"Yes," Booker replied, grabbing the ass by the throat and lifting him effortlessly. "Just be fucking thankful getting fired is all you're getting today." Booker threw the other man towards the door. He landed in a heap, hard enough to rattle his teeth. "Now get the fuck off our land."

"Oh, and one last thing," Taylin said, his wolf practically purring. "There's something else in the fine print that you should be aware of. It's a standard clause in all Starling contracts, but it's one of my favorites. It's buried in there, amongst all the boring legal mumbo jumbo, but basically it says that if we discover any kind of foul play perpetrated by the previous owner...that would be you...then all monies involved in the deal are forfeit. So, not only are you not going to get a single cent, what would have been your money is actually going to go towards righting all the pain and suffering you've inflicted here."

Almost like the omegas had been unleashed from their chains, whimpers, sobs, and giggles came from everywhere.

Taylin grinned happily at Rue, paying no attention to the protesting alphas. “This is a fucking good day!”

“No, this is a great day.”

“Time to clean this place up!” Booker marched to the alpha who’d stood behind Amatus. “You aim that thing at me for a second longer and you’ll be wearing my fucking fist.”

He snatched the gun from the alpha’s limp hold. Booker’s hands shifted into great enormous paws and crushed it like a twig, throwing it back at the alpha, who stood dumbfounded. “Scram,” he growled.

Protesting voices gave Taylin a boost as he pulled out his phone and, as promised, recorded the alphas’ getting their asses kicked and catching the glimmer of hope coming from the omegas as they watched intently what was unfolding before them.

He turned the camera to catch his own grinning face. “Make sure to share this with Frey, Monty and Lennon.”

He stopped the recording a moment later and sent it to Hollis.

"Come on, Mr. Unprofessional," Booker called, shaking his head at Taylin. "There's work to be done, so stop staring at yourself on camera and start figuring out who needs what."

Taylin gave him a salute and, despite the awful smell, took a deep breath, walking to the nearest omega. "Hi, I'm Taylin Starling. What's your name?"

Several seconds passed when the dirt covered omega finally brought a pair of stunning, bright green eyes up to look at Taylin. "Aven," he murmured quietly.

Taylin held out his hand, keeping his movements slow so as not to scare Aven. "Nice to meetcha."

When the work roughened hand slipped into his, Taylin kept hold of his smile, even as he witnessed the scarring on the thin arm protruding from the threadbare t-shirt.

"Same," Aven replied softly. "Will... will we have to stay... in the basement... when you leave?" Big green eyes ate up the tiny face of the omega. "I'm frightened of the dark."

Chapter Thirty-Four

Hollis

"I don't think this is a good idea," Hollis protested, dragging his shoes over plush carpet into the swanky club Frey felt was appropriate Friday night fun. The strange way they'd had to come in gave Hollis pause. Why were there three sets of heavy doors into the place?

Inside, classical music played in the background and didn't disguise the low hum of noises filtering out from the booths sitting back against the walls.

Goddamnit!

Hollis's gaze skittered around the decadent black, gold, and red... *sex club*. His nose twitched at the powerful scent of sexy pheromones. Black padded leather booths lined three of the walls in the large space. The middle of the room held chrome and glass topped tall tables where folks mingled, drinking and watching those in the booths who were...

"Jeez, is that alpha getting..." Bowie coughed violently, looking at Hollis with alarm as he went seven shades of red.

Why did I moan about my canceled plans with Taylin?

Why?

Frey's styled blond head fired around to look at Hollis. "We're not leaving. We just got here, and this is a great idea. No one has to do anything except drink and watch the fun. That's what the information on the website said." He pointed to the large dudes situated around the room, watching the crowd. "They'll stop anyone from doing something we don't want."

"Are you sure about that? That alpha over there, sitting alone... he's staring at us!" Bowie mumbled with uncertainty as he clung to Hollis's arm, looking around like he might get attacked at any moment.

"I heard Jupiter talking about this place to one of his playthings," Wilder added. "It's teeming with hot alphas who just want to have fun. We need some of that in our lives."

"Speak for yourself," Hollis murmured, doing his best to untangle himself from Bowie, who was attempting to climb him like a tree. Something he would never achieve with how much bigger the highland cow was than Hollis.

"Watching can be fun," Ziggy reiterated, staring at Frey fixedly before he took hold of his elbow to guide them to one of the few free center tables.

"Have you been here before?" Hollis asked, perplexed at the feeling he was missing something between Frey and Ziggy. Seeing no choice when Ziggy didn't answer him and continued on toward the free table, Hollis went after him, bringing Bowie with him. Truthfully, he had no choice in the matter when Bowie refused to let go of him.

Hollis did his best to avoid looking at the activity in the booths, experiencing his face flame when some things were harder to look away from than others. What the heck had he gotten talked into?

No one paid them any real attention. *Why would they when they were getting a free show?*

Hollis shuddered involuntarily, considering how to explain coming to a place like this to Taylin if he ever found out.

"Drinks. We need drinks," Frey announced, using his phone to scan the QR code on the top of the table they were gathered around.

The team had all been at a bit of a loose end after their monthly catch up had run longer than expected. The video Hollis had received from Taylin had caused a bit of a shock so Bowie had suggested they all go and get something to eat together.

Somehow, seeing how much worse the place looked than Hollis remembered didn't help with Frey's tears and Lennon's quietness. Hollis had planned on heading home straight after they'd finished their burgers. An evening of wearing his pajama's and feeling sorry for himself had been curtailed when he allowed Frey to talk him into continuing on to this place.

"Can I have a cocktail?" Wilder asked, peering over Frey's shoulder at the screen of his phone.

“I’ll get us all a cocktail, as this was my idea.” Frey didn’t look up when he spoke, reeling off all the different choices on the menu.

“Oh... oh, I’ll have the cherry one,” Wilder said excitedly.

“Me too,” Lennon interjected, looking at Frey.

“Sounds good to me, too,” Monty added distractedly, his attention held by the alpha in a booth off to their right. “Shit. Is that Jupiter?”

Wilder spun in a circle. “Where?”

Lennon pointed at a booth tucked into the far corner of the room. The dim lighting made it hard to make out the two figures doing...

Hollis’s hands shook as he removed his glasses, tucking them into his pocket, feeling it was the safest place for them, and his brain. There was nothing on earth that was going to possess him to watch Taylin’s brother get his groove on—*in public*!

“Let’s go say hi,” Wilder suggested, sounding nothing like himself.

Without his glasses, Hollis had no clue what Wilder’s expression would give away but there was no way in any universe they were going anywhere near Jupiter, which would require Hollis putting his glasses back on to avoid tripping over someone. There was also the slight problem he might consider telling Taylin of this adventure on the wild side. Again, he didn’t want to have to explain how he’d gotten talked into this. His willpower was zero and it was not something he wanted to think about. “No. We are staying right here, having one drink and then we are all leaving *together*.”

"Spoilsport," Wilder moaned. "Hey, where's your glasses?"

"In the safest place. I do not need to see my mate's brother... doing whatever he's doing... in public."

"Isley, what do you want to drink?" Frey questioned.

"I'll have the cherry thing too."

Frey nodded. "Hollis, Ziggy, what about you two?"

Resignation came with the understanding that the quicker he got a drink, the quicker they could leave. "I'll take the cherry one, too."

"Might as well make that a full house," Ziggy supplied, coming closer to Hollis.

"Great," Frey murmured. "I'll put in the order."

"Frey needs this." The words whispered in his ear by Ziggy caught all of Hollis's attention. He cursed his lack of glasses as he squinted at Ziggy, trying to make out his expression. Frey had been quiet in the group chat the last couple of days, which wasn't like him, and Hollis had made a note in his diary to catch up with him on Monday to check in.

"I am missing something?" Hollis asked, keeping his voice low and doing his best to be vague in case one of the others heard him. Whatever the reason for Frey's recent unusual behavior, it appeared Ziggy might have the answer.

"He's having a rough time personally, that's all I can say. I'm sure he'll tell you in his own good time."

The reply didn't help the ball of anxiety forming in the pit of Hollis's stomach at what Ziggy wasn't saying. Frey, for all his flirtyness and gossiping, was a dedicated employee and good friend. Hollis's protective side surfaced. "Should I talk to him... now?"

"I don't know if that's a good idea or not. He's fragile right now and..."

"Is he getting his cock sucked?" Wilder exclaimed loudly, derailing Hollis's conversation.

"Dear gods, he is," exclaimed Bowie. "Is that even legal?"

"The club has a license that permits it. A bit like the places omegas can go to and hire an alpha to help with their heat, I suppose," Ziggy answered Bowie.

A smartly dressed guy carrying a tray with pretty glasses filled with their drinks brought the conversation to a halt. "Good evening gentlemen, your round of cocktails. I'm Enzo, your server for the evening. If you require anything more, just signal to me." He smoothly deposited the pink, frothy drinks on the glass tabletop.

Frey held out a hand to the guy and Hollis assumed he was tipping him when seconds later he said, "Thank you," then sailed away.

"He's sexy," Monty whispered. "Got a kind of movie star vibe."

"Yes, I'm sure," Hollis said, having no clue. "I think we should all keep our eyes on each other, have our drinks, then get the hell out of here before Jupiter sees us!"

"I think the only thing he can concentrate on is the guy blowing him!" Isley murmured, his head turned towards where Jupiter was.

Hollis moved to block Isley's view after picking up a glass and handing it to him. "Drink up."

“Holy cow, look at that alpha with the omega sat on his lap!” Frey exclaimed, so loudly, Hollis choked on the cocktail he’d picked up to take a sip of.

“Please, keep your voice down,” he hissed once he stopped coughing.

“No one’s paying us any attention,” Frey hissed back, sounding miffed. “Stop being a killjoy, Hollis. I just wanna see... how alphas behave with omegas.”

His phrasing set off alarm bells, but Frey turned his back on Hollis before he could ask what he meant.

Ziggy put a restraining hand on his sleeve when he went to get Frey’s attention. “Let him be for tonight.”

Hollis blew out a frustrated breath, conflicted by his need to take care of Frey and not wanting to interfere where it wasn’t wanted. “Okay... but on Monday I’m going to find out what the heck is going on.”

“Fine.”

“What’s happening on Monday?” Isley questioned, sidling closer to Hollis, side stepping Bowie, who had finally relaxed enough to leave Hollis alone and was staring at one of the booths.

“Nothing. Now let’s drink up,” he said gently, doing his absolute best to keep the concern out of his voice.

He breathed a little easier when Isley didn’t question him further. However, like the others, he watched what was happening around them rather than drinking his cocktail.

This is going to end in disaster!

A few hours later, Hollis felt like he’d fallen down a rabbit warren and was searching to escape the maze when one drink turned to two, then three at Wilder's and Frey's begging pleas to stay. As their boss and the responsible one, he couldn't leave them and go home.

Now, his head was swimming from the potent cocktails and the sexy fragrant air he couldn't escape every time he took a breath. Hollis couldn't decide if he wanted his willpower back or not when Ziggy ordered a fourth round of drinks, and the alcohol haze numbed the ache he worked hard to pretend wasn't bothering him. At home was a lonely bed that would make the ache in his chest worse.

Staying isn't so bad, is it?

Unsure if it was him or his animal asking the question, he grinned drunkenly at Ziggy when he handed Hollis a tall, chilled glass with several pieces of fruit floating on top.

"What's this," he slurred, eyeing the fruit with delight despite the fact that he couldn't tell what was what.

"Paradise passion… you said something about fruity, didn't you?"

His slurred words made Hollis giggle. "Fruit is my favorite."

Wilder slid an arm under Hollis's suit jacket, hugging him while resting his head on Hollis's shoulder. "We know you're a fruit lover… or is that a Taylin lover?" His soft chuckles brushed against Hollis's neck, tickling. "Is it wrong, I wanna be the omega getting to have fun with Jupiter, even though I can't stand him? I think there's something wrong with me." He sighed dejectedly.

The drink in Hollis's hand splashed over his clothing as he jerked away from Wilder when his words penetrated the alcohol bubble, heart skipping to a tempo that made it hard to stop his hand shaking. "Noooo, lalalalalalala… I can't hear you," he exclaimed in a drunken panic at what might come out of Wilder's mouth next.

The man in front of him, who'd let go, wrapped his arms around his waist, rocking and howling with laughter. "Lalalalalalalala… are you singing to me… Hollis," Wilder gasped through laughter that got louder.

Hollis raised the glass, fighting his way to the edge to swallow down the contents when he felt, more than saw, that they were gaining far too much attention. The potent liquor burned a path straight to his brain as he tilted his head from side to side, attempting to get his eyes to work. "Why do they make glasses so you can't get your fingers into the bottom?" he complained after three attempts. When he looked up, the others were all laughing… at him… possibly.

"Time to go!" he announced huffily, or he would have if he hadn't slurred his words or wobbled as if someone had added curves to the underside of his shoes. Going to place his glass down, it hit the edge of the table. Hollis squinted, coming so close to the table his nose was touching it as he placed the glass down safely, nearly going cross-eyed with how he had to focus to stand straight.

"I'll help you home," Bowie offered, slipping an arm through Hollis's when he shook his head, attempting to rectify what was happening with his eyes, only he made matters worse when the room titled weirdly.

"Why are the walls moving?" He wasn't sure what he was asking as he weaved his way outside.

Fresh air hit like a hurricane, making him reel backwards into… Ziggy.

"Oops… sorry, Ziggy."

"Has someone ordered UberX for us?"

Hollis attempted to get his lips to move together instead of independently of each other, which was how it felt when he was sure he had the answer somewhere hiding in his brain. "Home… need… home." Yeah, he was sure his lips would find their way back to him then.

Chapter Thirty-Five

Taylin

Exiting the car, depressing thoughts and exhaustion weighing him down, Taylin stopped to stare at the house in total darkness, getting a feeling of its emptiness. He shook it off, aware that Hollis had no plans for the evening, and put it down to the harrowing day.

Nothing could have prepared them for what they'd found in the factory's basement. A shudder ran through Taylin, pursued by another when the scent of degradation clinging to his clothes wafted up to his nose. They'd called in the police upon discovering the chains and handcuffs used to keep the omegas captive. When Aven had asked about returning to the basement, it had opened up a whole can of nasty. It took six of Oakland's men to hold Booker back from ripping Amatus's head from his body.

Amatus and the other alphas were all locked up in jail, spluttering about injustices that fell on deaf ears. Taylin had put in a call to Dad that, using his many connections, would hopefully see that they'd stay there. He wasn't stupid enough to believe that justice always worked in the favor of the innocent.

Taylin ran his hands over his tired and achy eyes, trying hard not to think about how, when they'd switched to video chat, Popi had wept inconsolably at what he'd seen. Shaking off these maudlin feelings as best he could, Taylin walked to the trunk, hoping not to rehash it all—when they'd done that throughout the flight home—with Hollis. Tiredness had him hesitate, fatigue making him consider leaving his things right where they were until tomorrow.

He released a gusty groan and popped the trunk to grab his suitcase and laptop carry bag. Hollis liked things orderly and wouldn't be happy with him for leaving his things in the car. Coming out to get them, once inside, wasn't part of his plans.

Clicking the key fob, lights flashed and then moonlight guided him up to the front door. His thoughts went back in a direction he didn't want but couldn't avoid with the day clinging to him like glue, forcing him to repeatedly relive what none of them had been prepared for. There was no hiding what they'd discovered. Those omegas deserved to be heard.

Flinching as he remembered that they'd left all those omegas in those conditions, at the hands of those barbaric assholes, after their first visit, Taylin consoled himself that what they'd achieved today changed things for those men. They were no longer trapped in that hell.

Oakland's team would see to that. They had stayed behind to escort the men to a swanky hotel they'd booked out to give them some privacy and safety. For now, Oakland's team were staying put. The factory was closed until the omegas healed and decided what they wanted to do. Whatever that was, Starling Enterprises would honor it without question.

Quietly, Taylin opened the front door and slipped silently into the house, just taking the time to lock up then going straight to the stairs. He left the lights off, having quickly become familiar with the layout, and tiptoed up the bedroom.

He stopped outside the closed bedroom door, getting a whiff of himself. Quickly changing direction, he went to the empty room next door. Switching the light on, he waited for his eyes to adjust. He placed his things down and stripped where he stood. Walking naked into the bathroom, he didn't wait for the water to heat as he stepped into the glass shower cubicle, determined to wash off the stink. He gritted his teeth to keep the curse words for escaping as he shivered, reaching for the shower gel on the shelf.

The water hardly had a chance to get steamy before he was turning off the faucet to step out and grab a towel. He slung it around his shoulders, using it to dry his hair first because the thick curls took a while. Disregarding the water dripping down his body and onto the tiled floor, he avoided looking at himself in the mirror above the sink.

Rubbing vigorously, he touched the ends, satisfied he wouldn't soak the pillow. He left the towel hanging around his neck and reached for a larger towel to rub off the moisture clinging to his skin, then he draped it around his waist.

Lastly, he took the one he used for his hair to mop the floor, using his foot to move it around and soak up the water.

Done, he dropped that towel into the laundry basket, walking out of the bathroom on legs that suddenly felt filled with lead. In the hallway, his hand on the handle of the bedroom door, he stilled.

His eyes narrowed when he picked up the sound of an engine idling right outside of the house. The hairs at the back of his neck prickled, and he was heading down the stairs a moment later, uncertain why, but driven by a feeling something was off.

Had the press discovered where Hollis lived?

He'd barely hit the bottom stair when the door in front of him opened with such force it bounced off the paintwork with a resounding thud. His heart did something real similar as it thumped painfully against his ribs at the sight in front of him.

"What's you do that for," Hollis slurred to the man who stood with his arm around his waist, looking to be holding him up.

"'Cause you're wobbling, and I fell," Bowie said, sounding as drunk as Hollis.

Taylin stared at the tableau the men made, completely unaware of his presence as they glared at each other.

In his tired state, it took a moment to notice Hollis was missing his glasses. He crossed his arms over his damp chest. "What's going on?"

Two sets of eyes shifted in his direction, only one held Taylin's full attention. Hollis gave him a beautiful, if not lop-sided and smashed grin. "You're home."

"He's home," said Bowie gleefully, all but shoving Hollis towards Taylin. "Now you can stop complaining you'll be alone."

Hollis missed the step and lurched forward towards Taylin, who reacted on pure instinct to catch him before he fell on his face. The towel around his hips slithered down his legs to pool at his feet.

"Shit!"

Bowie and Hollis both groaned at the same time. Taylin wasn't concerned about Bowie or his nakedness. No, it was Hollis's wandering hands as he cooed, "Nakey mate."

"Thanks Bowie, see you." On that Taylin slammed the door shut, not in the least bit sorry when Hollis latched his two tongues around his nipple and wiggled them playfully. Regardless of how tired he was, his cock twitched.

He dragged in a deep breath, then exhaled quickly to take another breath when he scented... "Where the fuck have you been?" he demanded. "You smell of sex!"

The last thing he expected was for Hollis to giggle, his hands clumsily roaming down Taylin's naked body.

"Jupiter...

"Jupiter what?" he rasped past the dryness in his mouth at the many things his brain conjured up that his brother was capable of.

"Sex... club... doing... sexy st..." Hollis slumped against him and a split second later, released a soft snore.

"Hollis." He gave his mate a little shake. "Hollis... wake up."

He didn't so much as raise an eyelid as he groaned and snuggled his way back into Taylin's body, highlighting once more what Taylin had scented coming from him.

He growled, scooped up Hollis and marched up to the bedroom, leaving the towel. He took his time stripping Hollis, and, seeing no evidence of anything that would have him done for murder, he coaxed him to drink some water before tucking him up in bed.

Satisfied he'd taken care of his mate for the time being, he stomped out of the bedroom to retrieve his phone from the spare room, a full head of steam building as he opened up the group chat.

Alphaholes Chat

Taylin: *Jup, what the fuck have you been doing with my mate at a sex club? You better fucking answer me, or I won't be responsible when I get my damn hands on you.*

Silas: *Why are you messaging at one in the morning?*

Silas: *Forget I asked, now I've got my eyes to wake up.*

Booker: *Why would Jup take Hollis to a sex club? I'm confused.*

Kodi: *Not the only one bro… are you guys home?*

Rue: *It's too sordid a story for now, will catch up tomorrow. But yeah, we got home an hour ago.*

Taylin: *Jup, answer me!*

Jupiter: *Keep your fucking hair on, I was busy…*

Taylin: *I'm not in the fucking mood Jupiter. Why did you take Hollis to a sex club tonight? What the fuck were you thinking? Did someone touch him? He reeks of sex.*

Jupiter: *I did no such thing! They were all there at Sinful. Hollis and the other PAs getting drunk and having fun watching what goes on in there. And I wasn't paying attention to what they were doing, I was preoccupied.*

Silas: *All of them?*

Booker: *What's this shit?*

Laken: *Why is it that I'm figuring preoccupied means having someone bounce on your balls in a public place?*

Jupiter: Don't knock it till you try it bro.

Kari: *We aren't all as kinky as you.*

Jupiter: *You sure about that… Daddy…*

Kari: *Fuck you!*

Silas: *We don't care what y'all get up to. More importantly, what were the PAs doing in the club, Jupiter?*

Jupiter: *How the hell would I know? Having a good time, I suspect, away from you boring alphaholes. Now leave me the fuck alone because whatever they were or weren't doing has nothing to do with you lot. Or me!*

Taylin: *Hollis is my mate!*

Jupiter: *Then, if you take a damn second to pull your head from your ass, you'll know he's incapable of doing anything because you're mated! Now if you lot have finished the Jupiter bashing part of the night, I'm going to finish living my goddamn life the way I choose.*

Booker: *Anyone know if we could find out if the others got home safely?*

Kari: *I'll reach out to Bowie, he'll have been sensible.*

Taylin: *You couldn't be more wrong. He was as drunk as Hollis when he was here.*

Kari: *Is that right?*

Kodi: *What's with you, bro? Something I'm missing here?*

Silas: *We're all fucking missing something… our damn sanity since we got assigned these PAs!*

Taylin's lips quivered, and he shook with laughter not a second later at how right Silas was as he closed the group chat, noticing that he was standing naked in the middle of the room and feeling much better than he had.

Jupiter made a valid point, Hollis was his mate, and Taylin became embarrassed he'd jumped to conclusions. He could only put his reaction down to the shit day and shock at seeing Hollis drunk. It was a day of firsts!

If there was one consolation, Hollis hadn't seen him acting like a jealous ass. After his day, that was a win.

He put his cell on the dresser and left it there so as not to be disturbed by the chat. He got the impression the others wouldn't drop the topic of whether the PAs got home safely. Which was interesting, but didn't warrant him losing any sleep.

When he slipped quietly between the cool sheets, Hollis rolled straight into him, giving him a sense of peace that had been missing since he'd left him. Hollis wriggled closer, moving until no one could get a hair between them. A sigh followed, then came the soft snores.

Taylin buried his face into Hollis's hair until he found a spot that was pure Hollis and inhaled. He laid an arm over Hollis's body and shut his eyes.

Tomorrow... they would talk about visits to sex clubs... without him.

Chapter Thirty-Six
Hollis

The gentle thud of a heartbeat under his ear left him confused as Hollis surfaced from sleep. He flicked his tongues over his teeth, hating the furriness he encountered. Opening gritty eyes, Hollis peered up at the man he was lying on.

Huh?

What day was it?

What had he missed?

Hiding was the only thing Hollis considered when he caught a whiff of himself and the pounding at his temples brought with it a flicker of a memory of the night before. Had Taylin come to the door naked?

Hollis wasn't sure, but he got the impression he was going to find out. Question was, how much trouble was he in.

The way he smelled...

"I can hear you thinking. And judging by how your heart rate has just picked up, I'd say you're recalling some of what happened last night." Hollis couldn't decide if the rumbly voice vibrating against his ear sounded amused or pissed.

Chancing another look at Taylin, he gave him his bestest smile, although he wasn't feeling it with how hungover he was. "I… it was… you see…" Hollis groaned and buried his fiery face in Taylin's chest. He'd never been good at evading.

"You went to Sinful and got an eyeful while getting drunk. That about sum it up?"

Was that amusement?

He peeked at Taylin, searching his expression. "Yes," he whispered. "Are you mad at me?"

The grin Taylin aimed at him took away the panicky feeling wanting to take hold. "I was at one o'clock when what you said implied Jupiter took you to a sex club. Smelling as you did, it was touch and go as to how fast I could find my brother and rip his head off."

Hollis squeaked. "No… Jupiter didn't take me there. Frey did."

Taylin's brow quirked up. "I should have suspected he'd be the one to encourage you." He ran a finger down Hollis's nose and tapped the end. "I wasn't aware you liked to frequent places like that. Are you interested in voyeurism?"

When Hollis shook his head, he groaned at how it made the thumping at his temples increase. He shifted to sitting so he could rub at the sore spots. "Frey didn't mention what the place was before we went. As soon as I figured it out, I was clear, one drink, then we were leaving together…"

"How did that work out for you, love?"

The light dancing in Taylin's eyes made Hollis bury his head in his hands, muttering, "They wouldn't listen to reason, and I couldn't leave them alone."

"They have you wrapped around their fingers." Taylin chuckled, stroking his fingers over Hollis's hands. "You're a soft touch, and they know it."

Hollis dropped his hands and scowled, or he would have if it didn't hurt. "I am not," he replied indignantly.

"Whatever you say, love." Taylin came up to sitting and effortlessly lifted Hollis onto his lap, nuzzling at his neck.

He growled and quickly pulled away. "You need a shower."

"Could you make me a coffee first?" he fluttered his eyelashes. "Please."

Somehow it worked and, caffeinated thirty minutes later, he was feeling more like himself and smelling of fresh lemons from the shower. He walked into the bedroom where Taylin had dressed casually in jeans and a black sweater and was sorting through his suitcase. Now his head was clear, Hollis frowned. "I've just realized it's Saturday, how did you manage that with your schedule? Not that I'm complaining." Obviously, having Taylin home was amazing.

Taylin stopped what he was doing and his grim expression caused a ball of dread to form in Hollis's stomach. "We managed to fit in more than we planned, and two canceled meetings led us to rearrange the trip to Design Detailing & Co. The video I sent was before... before we found the basement."

Hollis walked to Taylin as the tension rolled off him. It was as if he was looking through Hollis and he shivered in the room's warmth. The robe he wore did little to combat the chill as Taylin continued.

"They chained them down there... kept them against their will." His hands formed into fists. "Beat them and treated them like they were worthless."

When Hollis touched Taylin's hand, it was icy cold. Much like his eyes when they stared at Hollis. "They're all divergents. Every last fucking one of them." His voice broke and tears tracked down his cheeks as Hollis came forward and hugged Taylin hard.

It took a second for his arms to move and for Taylin to hug him back. Then he crushed Hollis to him. "We had to hold Booker back, it took six men to restrain him. Only he wasn't the only one who wanted to kill those cunts. Wanted to rip out their black hearts and fucking burn them alive!"

Violence, the kind he'd never suspected Taylin capable of, was there in the depth of his emotions, none of which he held back as he clung on to Hollis as if afraid to let go and do exactly as he threatened.

"What happened to them, the alphas?" Hollis whispered, almost too afraid to ask.

A shudder ran through Taylin. "Arrested and placed in jail for now. I'm sure they'll get some slick divergent hater to get them out. But we have the evidence, all of it. We made sure to get pictures and video evidence in case they have someone torch the place."

Hollis looked at Taylin's taut features, tear stains gracing his cheeks. "You think they'll do that?"

"They might. Who the fuck knows? Dad suggested collecting as much as we could to validate the statements and conditions of the omegas."

Hollis swallowed the bile burning the back of his throat at what that was. "The omegas, they're safe, right?"

Taylin gave him a grim smile. "We found a hotel close by to the factory and booked out every room solid for the next six months. They'll stay there if that's what they want. Get whatever they need to help them heal. If it's at all possible."

"What about their families?"

The severity of Taylin's changing expression gave a wallop to Hollis's gut better than a mule. "They're picked based on being rejected by their family because of who they are. The animals sold it to them like they'd be their new family."

Horror swarmed through Hollis and the coffee made a hasty retreat from his stomach and up his throat. His mouth watered as he gagged. He spun out of Taylin's arms and darted to the bathroom. He barely made it as the coffee reappeared in a violent gush, splashing the toilet bowl. Tears streamed down his face at such evil.

Large hands stroked up his back as he heaved and cried into the toilet, unsure how to process the information when his animal was in total accord with him—devastated. Utterly devastated at how those omegas had continued to suffer after their visit a month ago. A month. Thirty days. How hellish would that feel?

Hollis couldn't even contemplate it. He had no point of reference. None.

"Don't blame yourself," Taylin murmured, more in tune with Hollis than he'd possibly given him credit for.

He coughed, spat, and wiped his mouth with the back of his hand, glancing back through blurry eyes. "How can we not? We left them there," he rasped past the awful taste in his mouth. "The suffering…" he sobbed.

Collected in Taylin's arms, he found himself cuddled, sitting in his lap on the bathroom floor.

"I know." Sadness dripped from his words. "But we can't go back and change what's happened. We can only move forward from here. Give them opportunities to flourish without the oppression."

Hollis's blurry, tear-drenched eyes met Taylin's, begging. "You promise?"

Taylin rested his forehead against Hollis's, making it easier to see him as he cupped Hollis's face, gently. "Yes, love. Those men now have Popi and Dad fighting in their corner. They can't lose with that."

On Monday morning, Hollis strolled through the reception area with Taylin at his side, holding his hand, giving the few people milling around that early something to look at. Hollis had more pressing things to be concerned about though, and folks gossiping wasn't anywhere on his agenda.

They'd spent the rest of their weekend eating far too much cake and binge watching box sets on the TV. Most of that time, they'd stayed close, holding or touching, appreciating the closeness. Neither wanted to dwell too much on the reasons why.

Both of them had avoided news channels on the TV that could alert them of the ongoing situation which had erupted like a volcano around the omegas. The only updates they'd received were from the brothers. They did their best not to sink too deep into the 'what ifs' they'd chosen to bench talking about when it upset Hollis.

Today had rolled around far too fast and with it came the reality they were going to have to deal with the horrors and Hollis was going to have to watch the video footage Taylin had mentioned. But first, he would need to deal with the Wilder and Jupiter situation before talking to Frey. Hollis continued to get flashes of the evening, which added to his worry list.

The elevator opened in front of them and Taylin released his hand, moving it to the base of his spine to guide him in. The silence between them wasn't uncomfortable and Hollis felt no need to break it. Breakfast had been a quiet affair, as had the commute to work, both lost in their thoughts.

Hollis's floor came first and when the doors opened and the first person he saw was Wilder, he had to control the urge to sigh at not getting a cup of coffee first to fuel him for the conversation.

Taylin hadn't shared what he'd gleaned from Jupiter about Friday night, and Hollis wasn't sure he wanted to know. There were still a few blank spots and filling them in could wait.

Taylin's hand moved around his hip and before he could utter a word, he became glued to Taylin's body and a hot, hungry mouth claimed his in a kiss that short-circuited millions of brain cells.

Hollis couldn't remember what he was supposed to be doing when Taylin withdrew and, after a couple of seconds, nudged him out of the elevator. "Have a good day," he said just as the doors shut and he disappeared.

"Wow, he sure looks like he knows how to deliver a kiss. I thought I was going to have to get a bucket of water to cool you both down."

Wilder's voice was enough of a bucket of water to remind Hollis he was at work and that for a brief moment, he'd forgotten the other man was watching.

"Yes... what... can I say," he said, stumbling over his words, blushing hard enough he sensed he was glowing sufficiently to get used on an airport runway to guide a plane in for landing.

Wilder slapped him playfully on his shoulder. "You're so lucky."

Hollis eyed the sullen expression that came with those words, and this time he did sigh. “Let’s go to my office.”

They walked silently down the passageway, passing no one on their way to Hollis’s office. Inside, Hollis slipped off his suit jacket and hung it up, rolling up his sleeves while Wilder went and perched on the seat opposite Hollis’s desk, giving him worried glances. His gaze darted between his hands and Hollis repeatedly.

“You remember what I said on Friday night?” Wilder started as Hollis sat.

“Yes,” he admitted.

“I didn’t mean it. I was drunk,” he rushed to say, his gaze not quite meeting Hollis’s, one hand going to rub at the leg of his sage green slacks, the other forming into a fist that rested on the arm of the chair.

“I see,” Hollis murmured, staring at Wilder, showing he wasn’t fooled, not in the slightest.

“You’re fantastic at the look,” Wilder said, slumping in his seat as he circled a finger in the air. “Like a parent who knows their child is telling fibs.”

Resting his elbows on the desk in front of him, Hollis came forward to place his chin on his knuckles, continuing to hold Wilder’s gaze. Seeing no way to avoid this, he considered how best to broach the subject. “If you want to lie to me about your personal situation, that’s up to you. Dealing with Jupiter, that is where I come in. You are his PA and whatever is going on between you—”

“Nothing is going on,” he replied, jumping up out of his seat to pace in front of Hollis’s desk. “He’s an insufferable asshole. Demanding and picky. Forcing me to act like his personal secretary for dealing with the substantial number of men he bonks." He swung to face Hollis, eyes blazing with a wildness that caused a knot of tension to gather at the top of Hollis's shoulders.

"Do you have feelings for Jupiter?" he asked, against his better judgment.

Emotions too varied for Hollis to guess at, flashed over Wilder's expressive features. If Wilder did indeed have feelings for Jupiter—which Hollis suspected was the case—this was going to end in tears for the little raccoon. Jupiter was a playboy and Wilder was way too softhearted for his own good.

What looked like resignation came when Wilder came to a halt. "Maybe... I don't know. He makes me so mad I wanna punch him... then..."—he blushed a deep shade of red—"I get these urges to jump his bones when I see something beyond the asshole he comes across as most of the time. It's making me crazy."

Never having had the same compulsion, or not to the same degree as Wilder, Hollis struggled to find the right reply that would help. "You know Jupiter's reputation..."

Wilder plonked himself back in the chair, groaning. "Yep... and that's without what we witnessed on Friday night." He ran his hands through his dark locks, disturbing them. "See, this is why I came to talk to you. You always tell me the truth I need to hear."

Hollis didn't correct Wilder about what he'd not seen on Friday. "I can't tell you what you should do in your personal life," Hollis murmured, thinking on what he'd decided as the best way to handle this situation. "I can only do that with work."

Hollis's anxiety at what he was about to do got him up and around his desk to crouch next to Wilder. "As I suggested before, swapping you to a different Starling brother is the best solution. It would give you some breathing room to gain a better perspective, so to speak."

This time, Wilder didn't make any objections. Instead, he did something that made Hollis's worry increase and nodded slowly. "Maybe that's for the best."

Chapter Thirty-Seven

Alphaholes Chat

Jupiter: *Tay, what did you say to Hollis to make him decide Wilder shouldn't be my PA any longer?*

Taylin: *No clue what you're talking about? When did this happen?*

Jupiter: *Today! Don't act like you didn't know. You're sleeping with Hollis.*

Taylin: *First off, he's my damn mate, not my bed partner. There's a difference. And why would I act like I don't know for any* *other reason than I don't? You should point your bony finger at yourself. I'm surprised Wilder hasn't asked to escape sooner. What's it been six weeks… that has to be a record for a relationship… even a work one for you?*

Jupiter: *Fuck off, you smug shithead. Admit you're pissed at Hollis enjoying watching me at the club last Friday.*

Silas: *Do I need to come and bang your heads together? I thought we'd addressed what did or didn't happen at the club a week ago? Also Tay, the question is valid when I've somehow ended up with Wilder? I was cool with Ziggy.*

Taylin: *ASK HOLLIS! He's in charge of the PAs, not me. He doesn't discuss his work decisions with me, and neither should he just because we're mated. He didn't do it before then, so why should it be any damn different now? Get over yourselves and man up. What's wrong with having Wilder, Silas? He's great at his job.*

Silas: *So was Ziggy!*

Booker: *Hollis better not be planning on messing things up for us all. It's taken me long enough to break in the PA I have.*

Rue: *Break him in? Silas is really rubbing off on you.*

Kodi: *God, let's hope not, cause that's just wrong on so many levels.*

Kari: *They aren't blood brothers, so what's the issue?*

Laken: *Why is this conversation veering off in a sex-related convos?*

Jupiter: *'Cause no one is getting enough sex.*

Taylin: *You speak for yourself.*

Chapter Thirty-Eight

Taylin

Second guessing himself, after the week of haranguing his brothers had given Hollis for switching Ziggy and Wilder, Taylin had planned a day date picking fruit. Jupiter had laughed his ass off, and his other brothers weren't much better when he'd stupidly told them what he was going to be doing today.

Hollis needed something to put the smile back on his face and Taylin was going to do his best to achieve that, despite what his brothers thought was lame.

"Will I need a warmer coat?" Hollis asked, lifting the light jacket he held.

Eyeing the soft blue sweater Hollis wore, Taylin shook his head. "That should be fine. I checked the weather forecast, it's not gonna rain."

A furrow appeared between Hollis's brows. "So, are we going to be outside?"

Taylin gave him a nervous smile. "Yep."

Hollis's head tilted to the side and he waited with a look of expectation. When Taylin grinned but said no more, Hollis slipped on his jacket and made a huffing noise. "So it's a secret," he muttered impatiently, heading off towards the door.

A chuckle tickled the back of Taylin's throat as he went after him, clutching his own jacket. "Don't you like surprises?"

At the bottom of the stairs, he turned to look up at Taylin and shrugged. "No one's ever arranged a surprise for me before, so how would I know?"

Finding out he was the first, Taylin wasn't sure if he should be jumping for joy or be terrified if what he had organized fell short of Hollis's expectations.

He came down and stood in front of Hollis, reaching to straighten his glasses. "I've never done it before, so it'll be a first for both of us..." he came forward and kissed him. "So please be gentle on the feedback."

The lips under his trembled as they curved up. "Ok... I'll dust off my rating system."

"You're not funny," Taylin replied, taking in the gleam of delight behind Hollis's glasses.

He reached up and touched Taylin's lips. "Then why are you grinning at me?"

Taylin took the hand, slipping it into his to tug Hollis to the door. "'Cause I get to spend the day with my temptation."

"Good answer." Hollis's giggles were a pleasure to listen to and continued long after they pulled away and were heading to the Hillcrest Orchard.

The place was several miles away and offered the opportunity to pick different varieties of apples they grew: Rome Beauty, Golden Delicious, Granny Smith, Goldrush and Yates. Hollis loved all fruit but had a thing for apples, especially in cake. There was a bakery at the orchard too. Taylin had checked with Bowie to see whose turn it was to bring in cake on Monday. It was Hollis's, so he had the option to select something for work too. Although Hollis in an apron, elbow deep in flour mix, was a sight that got Taylin a little hot under the collar—weirdly.

"Is the heater too hot for you?" Hollis questioned, his hand pressing the dial to lower the heating settings.

The blush warming Taylin's skin upped in temperature as he swung a quick glance at the man eyeing him.

"Nah, I'm..." Taylin caught Hollis's nose twitching out the corner of his eye and he bit his lip at how his arousal was filling the interior of the car. "Behave," he finished instead.

"Me," Hollis asked innocently, his hand landing on Taylin's upper thigh, close to his groin. "I'm not the one having... inappropriate thoughts."

"I'm having no such thing," Taylin argued for form, loving this cheeky side of his mate more and more.

Hollis's fingers skimmed the crease of his thigh, inches from his cock. "Oh... what a pity." A throaty chuckle came next as the fingers retreated.

"Put that hand back," Taylin challenged, laughing when Hollis made a point of folding his two hands together and placing them in his lap.

"You're driving and we don't want any accidents."

His laughter increased as he changed gears and slowed, seeing the sign that told him to take the second left turning. "I can always stop and turn around."

"Don't you dare. I want my surprise date!"

He hoped it wasn't a disappointment. Taylin had read there was a petting zoo and a farmer's market with other fresh produce. If the fruit picking was a total bust, then at least they could see some cute animals and grab treats for the rest of the weekend! This was what he continued to reinforce to himself as Hollis switched his attention to look out the window.

Taylin navigated the traffic and wasn't sure what to make of the odd squealing noise when they passed the large sign telling Hollis where they were.

Too busy looking for a place to park with how full the car lot was, Taylin couldn't take the time to really gauge how Hollis was feeling about their final destination.

"Over there," Hollis said, pointing to a car pulling out, bouncing in his seat. "Quick, before that other car swings back around."

Was he excited?

Taylin focused on parking, before he finally chanced a look at Hollis, who was already undoing his seatbelt, reaching for the car door. He flashed Taylin a wide grin full of happiness. "Can I pick the apples? It said on the sign we could. Did you organize for us to do that too? I want a large wicker basket. I'm sure I saw a dude with one of those. Do you think they have more?"

Hollis was already out the door and Taylin chuckled at getting no chance to respond. He got out, smelling the sweetness of fresh fruit, and came around the hood.

Hollis paid him no attention, his head swiveling this way and that, trying to mimic an owl.

"Yes I did, but I've no clue on both counts." Taylin said, working through Hollis's unanswered questions.

Hollis glanced at him, wearing a look of confusion. "Huh?"

"I'm answering your questions," Taylin explained, doing his best to hold back his laughter.

"Oh, yeah, right." Hollis reached for Taylin's hand and started to drag him towards the building. "Can we get two baskets, one each? I don't want to share."

The laughter came out this time. It didn't stop Hollis in his pursuit of dragging him as quickly as he could to the entrance. "You can have whatever you want."

Hollis fired a smile at Taylin that hit dead center in his chest. "Good, because I want everything." He stopped to reach up on his tiptoes and gave Taylin a wet kiss, then let go of his hand to skip excitedly through the door.

How could he not love him?

Basket in hand several minutes later, with instructions on which orchards held the apples Hollis favored, they headed off. The weather was perfect, not too warm, just pleasant enough to feel comfortable walking, and it was dry.

Taylin wandered behind Hollis, happy just to watch him take the less busy paths and fastidiously pick his apples. His two tongues got busy, appearing repeatedly as he sniffed at the apples, sighing in contentment as the pile in his basket grew.

When the sun glinted off the dark strands of Hollis's head, it revealed a couple of leaves that had landed there. He made for a pretty picture. His glee at seeing his basket overflowing, standing amongst the apple trees, the leaves in his hair adding to the overall effect.

"Here," Taylin said, offering his empty basket when Hollis' was too full to take any more apples. His fingers itched to reach for his cell phone to catch how Hollis looked.

Hollis bit the corner of his lower lip, sucking it past his teeth and shifting his gaze from the basket to Taylin and back.

He was too fucking adorable wearing a look of conflict as he stared longingly at the empty basket, then at his full one. "I won't eat them."

Taylin worked to keep his face straight at the look of relief that came at him guessing exactly what was running through his mate's mind.

When the swap happened, Taylin reached up and picked out the leaves. Hollis squinted as he looked up to see what Taylin was doing. "You've got leaves in your hair," he explained.

Hollis ran a hand through his hair, impatiently displacing them before Taylin could, then he was off once more in the direction of the next group of trees, labeled Golden Delicious.

"These are good for baking, as they're really sweet," Hollis said, eyeing the apples intently. "I could make some apple cobblers for Monday." He eyed the basket Taylin held critically. "I might need another basket. I want to make jam too and apple slices... oh, and maybe apple flapjacks. Then of course there are Danishes too, for breakfast."

The basket was not small and the weight he held told Taylin their current hall would be plenty, if not a little too much.

Did he say that aloud?

Of course not, he smiled dopily at Hollis. "I'll go see if I can swap out the basket for an empty one."

"Make sure they don't give my apples to anyone else," he called after Taylin when he headed off in the direction of the main building.

He lifted his empty hand, shaking with laughter at his own worry that Hollis would think this idea to visit an orchard would be lame. And they hadn't even visited the bakery yet.

Chapter Thirty-Nine

Hollis

Stiff and more than a little achy after the vigorous reward he'd given Taylin for the best date he'd ever been on, Hollis shuffled into the kitchen Sunday morning with ideas about how to use his vast haul of apples. He'd left Taylin asleep when his animal had actively encouraged him to come and bake.

They were both eager to get started. His week had been difficult, as he'd held his stance on the decisions he'd made. This was the perfect antidote to moaning alphas. The dull, gray sky he could see beyond the window as he came into the kitchen reinforced it was the perfect day to mess around baking.

Before that, he needed a caffeine hit. He set up the coffee machine, then leaned against the counter, waiting. He ran a hand over his bristly jaw, eyeing the three boxes filling his kitchen table.

Had he gone a little overboard?

Hollis used baking—and cake eating—as a de-stressor. A way of emptying his head of any and all worries. This morning, he had no such issue after yesterday. Today he wanted to bake for the pure pleasure of making something tasty for Taylin as a thank you for giving him such a wonderful day date.

Who'd have thought a visit to an orchard would make him so gooey inside?

Me.

As if!

You know I'm always way ahead of you.

Oh... is this a competition?

It can't be a competition when I'm right.

Hollis sniffed indignantly and reached for his full, steaming mug and doctored it with creamer and sugar. He took a sip and waited a beat for the caffeine to wake up his sluggish body.

One mug emptied, he filled it again and left it on the counter to wash his hands. He eyed his sleep pants and baggy T-shirt and shrugged. They would do. He went to pluck the apron from the back of the kitchen door and tied it around his waist. Then he went to search his cupboards for all the things he needed.

Flour, brown and white sugar, baking powder, cinnamon, nutmeg, corn starch, eggs, milk, butter, vanilla, and finally salt. He laid them all out while considering what he should do first. Apple Danish twists for breakfast would be perfect.

He grinned to himself at how his stomach rumbled in anticipation.

Hollis got to work on making the filo pastry. It was a lot of work, but he wanted everything made from scratch. He hummed to himself, losing track of time as he followed the steps in his cookbook.

The kitchen had become scented with apple, nutmeg and cinnamon by the time he slipped the tray into the stove and set the timer.

When he turned to go to the sink, his heart jerked hard in his chest at the sight of Taylin lounging against the door frame, wearing only his sleep pants, which sat low on his hip bones, showing off his abs.

"I didn't hear you come down." Hollis blushed at the lazy, sexy grin Taylin aimed at him.

"You were humming and having fun. I could watch you all day," Taylin replied, straightening and coming towards him.

The lights he'd switched on beamed down on all the naked flesh that rippled and his hunger for the apple Danishes became secondary to the need for Taylin. Some days Hollis didn't know how he'd resisted for so long... *or why*.

Arms slipped around his waist and moved down to cup his ass. "Do you know that I've a fantasy about fucking you wearing this apron?"

Hollis gasped at the imagery Taylin's words conjured in his mind. "You do?"

"I do," he murmured against the side of Hollis's neck a moment before he licked at his beating pulse, moving down to the claiming bite mark to nibble on the flesh. It had a direct line to his cock and Hollis felt faint with how fast he hardened.

Despite how sticky his hands were, he clutched Taylin's wide shoulders, groaning at the hands wiggling into his sleep pants and pushing them down.

"We can't do this here..." Hollis moaned when a thick finger made what he was going to say a lie as it sank into his slick ass. The squelching noise revealed the effect Taylin had on him. There was no hiding from what he craved.

Teeth at his bite mark bit harder and, panting hard, Hollis parted his thighs and thrust against the man wrecking him. Taylin claimed his mouth and Hollis lost any hope of being sensible.

Lifted, his ass hit a cool wooden surface, and then the apron got shoved off to the side as there was some fumbling. Hollis mewled into Taylin's mouth as the head of his cock touched his slick hole. The pressure was intense at the lack of prep. He wanted to feel him, needing it more than taking his next breath, so he titled his hips up in invitation.

He captured Taylin's guttural moan in his mouth as it joined his own when Taylin did as Hollis encouraged. The burn was expected, as was the fullness that came as Taylin sank deep, not stopping until Hollis felt the bulge of his forming knot.

"All of you," he begged.

Taylin's knot fascinated Hollis and, if he was honest, he was a little obsessed with how big it was and the feeling of it expanding inside him. Each time, he craved it more than the last.

"Are you sure? You're so fucking tight, love." Taylin's restraint was much better than Hollis's. His whole body was tight with tension as he searched Hollis's expression for signs of distress.

"Need it," Hollis stated truthfully.

The growl was pure wolf when Taylin thrust in those last few inches, his hands at the base of Hollis's spine keeping him in place. "You asked for it."

His husky voice and the roguish light dancing in Taylin's eyes sent shivers of lust through Hollis. His ass bathed the shaft splitting him open, while his cock leaked its approval over his stomach.

He reached to thread his sticky fingers through Taylin's hair and cling to him. The wood beneath his ass moved at the force of the first thrust. Wood scratching on tile barely registered beyond his desire. His heart beat for the passion Taylin unleashed on him and all he could do was hold on.

His heart had awakened to this love and Hollis wanted to sink in and wallow in its beauty. In its power. Bathed in the heat of it, he felt the moment Taylin lost control and gave into madness. To his passion for Hollis. It was the best feeling and Hollis wanted to experience it again and again until he took his last breath.

His brain closed off and he sank into the depths of his feelings. How much longer it was before Hollis blinked the room into focus, he couldn't say. Everything looked to be on the tilt, and it took way too long to figure out that his glasses were lopsided.

"What happened?" he rasped, unsure exactly whether he was lying or sitting... on the table.

"I'm not sure if I should be insulted or proud you don't know we made out on the kitchen table?" The dry chuckle tickled the damp skin of his throat before Taylin shifted against him, easing back enough to look at him.

Hollis's ass clenched at the semi-hard dick he remained impaled on, explaining exactly what had happened. "Proud," Hollis said, feeling more than a little hot with embarrassment at his own behavior. He moved to fix his glasses and then wished he hadn't at the sight of Taylin covered in a floury mess. His dark curls were speckled with white flecks and what looked like bits of apple.

The alarm on the cooker chose then to rescue him. Then he registered the scent of the pastries. The Danishes were indeed ready.

Hollis shoved at Taylin's chest when he made no effort to move. "Move, or my pastries will burn," Hollis exclaimed, wriggling back and getting a grunt of complaint from Taylin, which he ignored.

He hadn't worked hard to make breakfast to let it burn. Off the table, Hollis's embarrassment went up a notch, feeling the cum sliding out of his ass and down his inner thighs. He acted like he wasn't an absolute mess and showed off his bare ass as he reached for the oven mitts, bending to retrieve his Danishes.

They looked and smelled delicious. He held up the tray, grinning at the man tucking his cock away. "Ta-da, breakfast!"

"I thought I just had breakfast." Taylin's lips made a smacking noise when his gaze swept over Hollis, straying to his lower body and staying put as his eyes sparkled with amusement.

Hollis glanced down and groaned in complaint at the apron sat off to one side. His cock hung out for all to see, along with the cum smeared on his baggy T-shirt. "It's all your fault," he accused, stomping to the worktop to place the tray down.

A hot body pressed against his back and pinned him to the center aisle. Hands landed on the countertop, trapping him while warm lips nuzzled at his ear. "If I take full responsibility... and be a good boy." The sticky head of his cock brushed against the crack of Hollis's ass, and he bit his lip to keep his moan from escaping. "Do I get some of those Danishes?"

"Uhuh," Hollis mumbled, working to hold still and stop himself from being a wanton hussy. Something Hollis had never been in his life—until Taylin.

You always were. His animal wasn't shy to point out. *You just pretended you weren't. But your sex toys prove differently.*

Why don't you just shut up!

Chapter Forty

Taylin

One week slipped into the next and Taylin wasn't sure he could remember what his life had been like before he had mated with Hollis. His days began and ended with Hollis... mostly. He sighed once more at how his thoughts had turned to his mate and their time together when he'd seen Booker's message. Trips away—which were necessary—without Hollis, put a hitch in his perfect life.

He got up from his desk, deciding that it would be quicker to walk to Booker's office than reply to the message, which would only generate more to-ing and fro-ing. He needed to triple check that he absolutely had to travel. At his appearance, Alma glanced up from her computer, her hand automatically moving her glasses back up the bridge of her nose where they slipped when doing computer work. "Need me?"

"No. I need to talk to Booker." He paused and scratched his cheek. "If Annalise arrives before I get back, there's a file on my desk marked with her name. She can get started on running the numbers for the sales from Hales department stores over the Midwest."

"Are they as projected?"

Taylin gave her a wide grin. "Better. There's a six percent increase in sales on the fashion accessories we trialed in Hales stores. The work we did with Kodi on marketing has worked well enough that we can repeat it in the bigger department stores like Riles next."

"See, this working closer together isn't as bad as you thought it would be."

Taylin kept his thoughts on that to himself and nodded, taking his leave quickly before Alma read his concern. For him things were fine, but the alphahole group chat since the swap over of Ziggy and Wilder would suggest otherwise for Jupiter and Silas, who were at each other's throats more often than not of late.

Outside Booker's office, he found his secretary's desk empty, so knocked on the door and waited for Booker to call out.

At the gruff shout letting him know he could go in, he stepped inside Booker's office and got hit by the fresh scent of chocolate and spice. He glanced at the seats, expecting to find Frey, who often smelled of those things.

"Who you looking for?" Booker questioned, sitting back in his seat, making it creak.

"You," Taylin replied, shutting the door behind him. To test the water and the theory he'd been harboring after hearing a snippet of heated conversation between him and Silas over Frey, he added, "Although it smells like Frey in here."

Booker fired forward in his seat, his dark eyes narrowing on Taylin. "He works alongside me and what the heck do you think you're doing sniffing at him?"

Taylin chuckled and held up his hands at the angry glare that could chop a man off at the knees. "I don't sniff him. It's just impossible to ignore him when he smells of chocolate and spice, isn't it?" he asked innocently, waiting for Booker's reaction.

When Booker rose to his full height, his eyes shooting daggers, what Taylin suspected became a firmer reality.

"You've got the hots for Frey," he accused, holding back his amusement, and going to take a seat, not worried when Booker towered over his desk looking no less angry.

"Give the fuck over. 'The hots'? What the hell kind of adult thing is that to say?"

He gave a nonchalant shrug, enjoying himself immensely now the shoe was on the other foot. He'd taken a lot of abuse over his relationship with Hollis, pay back was way overdue. "The only kind that fits with your over the top reaction."

Booker's weight when he sat made the chair groan and he didn't mask the strangled noise that came out of him. "What do you want?" he asked testily. He started to tap the pen he was holding on the arm of the chair, revealing more about Booker's agitation than he'd probably noticed.

Taylin—feeling a little bad—dropped the subject of Frey and referred to the message Booker had sent. "The trip back to the hellhole, is it necessary?"

It had been four weeks since they'd returned. Oakland and his men remained in Minnesota, along with the additional legal team Dad had flown there to work on protecting the rights of the omegas when Amatus and his men got bailed from jail.

That little tidbit of information continued to infuriate Taylin, even when he'd suspected it would happen with the divergent haters supporting those fuckers.

"Unfortunately, yes. They want us back there to go over our statements in person. Amatus' lawyer is requesting in-person meetings with me, you, and Rue," he threw the pen on the desk. It hit the computer and ricocheted off the desk, falling to the floor, unnoticed by Booker who had reached to pick up a sheath of papers and wave them at Taylin angrily, temper flashing in his eyes.

"We don't have to go," Taylin pointed out. "Legally they can't make us."

"No, they can't, or not yet. But..."

"It's the right thing to do," Taylin finished for Booker, resisting cursing when he could recall far too easily the conditions those omegas had lived in, some for years.

"I'm arranging for the jet to fly us tomorrow morning, as we have this family thing tonight."

Taylin frowned at Booker. "Family thing?" he questioned, trying to recall what Booker was referring to. "I wouldn't call dropping off some baked goods that Hollis made for Popi tonight, a family thing. Hollis could do that himself, without me." Not that Taylin would suggest such a thing when time out of work together was precious.

Booker burst out laughing. In fact, he laughed so hard his eyes streamed with tears as Taylin stared at his brother, confused as fuck. “What am I missing?” he asked when Booker continued to laugh—at him, evidently.

“Popi invited Hollis’s parents over for dinner to get to know them and to talk about how cute you two are together,” he choked out, continuing to roar with uncontrollable laughter.

How cute they were together, was that code for something else?

Out of the chair in a flash, Taylin didn’t even bother to respond to Booker as he headed right out of the office door. He could hear his brother’s laughter ringing in his ears as he marched to the stairs to go to Hollis’s office, not prepared to wait on the elevator. After that unforgettable night where Popi had mentioned a wedding, the conversation had gotten dropped.

Had it?

Am I overreacting?

Had Popi said something to Hollis? He’d not once mentioned anything to Taylin. Was this panic driving him to see Hollis because he wanted to... *propose?* Hollis was his mate, a wedding would just be the icing on a very delicious cake.

Out of breath, he marched into Hollis’s office only to come to a standstill when the group of PAs sat in seats surrounding Hollis’s desk all glanced in his direction.

Hollis rose, tugging at the end of his tie, his shoulders rigid when he met Taylin’s gaze.

“Is there something *important* you need, Taylin?” His head inclined toward the men who watched Taylin with undisguised interest. "As you can see, I'm in the middle of a meeting right now."

"Did you know we were having dinner with your parents and mine tonight to talk... about how cute we are together?" he stated distractedly, his brain two steps ahead of his sensibility with all the different scenarios running through his mind at possibilities for their future. Evidently, talking about it took precedence over an audience listening to the conversation.

Giggles from the assembled PAs got drowned out when Hollis squeaked, "What!" His cheeks paling. "When... what..." He sank into his seat and covered his face with shaky fingers. "Ugh, parents!"

"Out," Taylin stated firmly. "All of you leave now."

He didn't so much as take his eyes off Hollis, who continued to hide his face in his hands, shoulders slumped.

When the door closed softly, Taylin walked around Hollis's desk and crouched down on one knee. He licked his dry lips and released a shuddery breath when he took hold of Hollis's trembling hands and he acknowledged why he'd come in the first place. He didn't want to play pretend. Marrying Hollis would be a dream come true.

"I'm sorry."

"For what?" asked Hollis, his brow crumpling and his eyes shining.

"For spouting off in front of an audience. For my interfering parents. Because if Popi is having your parents over, then Dad knows and must be humoring Popi." He blew out a breath. "And for not planning to do this in a more romantic setting, because I don't want to wait."

"Huh?"

Back was the adorable confusion looking at him from behind the red frames Taylin had encouraged Hollis to wear because he loved them. "I love you Hollis Adice. Mating with you is one of the most special moments of my life." He brushed his lips against Hollis's quivering ones. "I want a life full of adventures. I want children. I want everything. And I want it with you. I would be honored if you'd agree to be my husband. I'll love and cherish you forever, I swear." The kiss was deeper, lasted longer, so he was breathless when he stopped because he needed air and an answer.

His heart shuddered in his chest as he used the pad of his thumb to collect a tear rolling down Hollis's cheek. "What do you say?" he whispered.

Taylin toppled backwards at how Hollis launched himself at him before he could react. They landed in a heap of legs and arms as Hollis showered his face with kisses.

"Is that a yes?"

Hollis giggled and laid his cheek against Taylin's. "That's a yes. A hundred times yes, a thousand times yes. All the yeses in the world," he cooed delightfully.

Taylin's facial muscles ached at how wide he smiled up at the ceiling, wrapping his arms around Hollis and holding tight. He didn't care that he was lying on the carpet in Hollis's office and someone could come in at any moment and find them like that.

"Do you think this will make our parents happy?" Taylin asked, feeling very giddy. Like a child on Christmas morning, waking to discover a stocking crammed full of presents.

"Mom and Dad never mentioned anything about the invite for dinner tonight, either." His sigh held a world of frustration. "So we should make them wait… at least an hour tonight before we tell them the news. No matter how damn cute they think we are!"

Taylin snorted in disagreement. "Only an hour, I'd say at least two." He rolled them over and looked down at a tousled looking Hollis. "We don't want to make it too easy on them if they've been chatting about us. Who knows what else they've talked about."

Hollis dragged his head down until they were barely an inch apart, a cheekiness coming through that set Taylin's heart racing. "So… when do I get to pick my engagement ring?"

Chapter Forty-One
Hollis

How he'd finished the meeting that Taylin had disrupted, Hollis never knew.

"Why are you grinning like that?" Frey looked at Ziggy. "He never smiles like that when he's talking spreadsheets. I mean, does anyone else think it's odd?"

Frey glanced at the other men, and Hollis rolled his eyes heavenward. "Can't someone be happy at work?"

"There's happy... and then there's *happy.*" Ziggy's chuckle quickly became matched by Bowie's and Lennon's.

Hollis pointedly looked at his watch. "Haven't you all got more important things to do than sit here and gossip... *like work*?"

The tug to the cuff of Frey's sleeve as he eyed Hollis showed he wasn't about to give up. "I wasn't gossiping, I was making a valid point about you giving a happy vibe over spreadsheets."

Hollis's sigh held a depth of acceptance because secretly he wanted to talk about Taylin's proposal. He'd been wrong about the romance of it. It was pretty perfect for Hollis. The place didn't matter, the intention behind his words did.

Love.

He was loved.

We're loved.

Semantics.

"I'm getting married," he announced excitedly before getting into it with his animal side.

Frey bounced on his seat right along with Isley.

"I told you guys, didn't I," said Isley, who was now out of his seat, wiggling his tiny butt.

"Alright," Wilder grumbled. "You got it right. But I said first that Taylin bursting into the room meant something epic was about to happen."

"You thought they were gonna get naked and do it on Hollis's office desk," Bowie supplied, blushing as he grinned shyly at Hollis. "You wouldn't do that, would you!"

The way he said it was more a statement than a question and wasn't something Hollis was going to touch with the longest stick in the world, especially given how he had become disappointed that the kissing and hugging on the floor had stopped.

"When are you going to go ring shopping?"

Frey's question brought about more enthusiasm as the conversation steered in a direction Hollis was happy to talk about.

Then Monty got out his cell phone. "Ohhh," he cooed, "let's look for jewelers in town!"

Hours later, Hollis's gaze traveled to the back seat of the car where he'd placed the apple cobbler, tarts, and Danishes he'd made the night before, then back to his hand. His stomach did a weird flippy thing when he stared at the platinum band, inlaid with pink diamonds.

When the shop assistant had laid several trays on the counter for them to look at, Hollis had known in that very moment that he wanted it. When Taylin had slipped it on to his finger and it fit perfectly, it was all the sign that Hollis needed. A whole ten minutes after entering the shop, they'd left with Hollis wearing the ring, categorically refusing to take it off his finger.

It winked in the overhead light and Hollis glanced out the window, realizing they'd come to a standstill and Taylin had opened his car door.

Taylin's laughter said he'd caught him once more daydreaming over the ring. "I suppose making them suffer for a little while is out of the question when it means taking off your pretty?"

Lane's call the previous night came with a story of how he was jealous of not getting some of Hollis's baking efforts. He'd played Hollis, he could see it now when Lane would know that Hollis would offer to drop some off. The invitation he'd accepted for this evening definitely had included no information about his parents coming for dinner. He had to give it to Lane, he really wanted them all to be one happy family. When he'd then rung his parents this afternoon on the pretense of organizing lunch to see if they'd mention anything, his Mom had been very enthusiastic about the evening.

Hollis had to acknowledge he was impressed with Mom wanting to meet Lane and Derick when she was normally a little more reserved. Was that because she'd talked about grandchildren and was looking for an ally who would be on her side? Lane would definitely be that, Hollis was sure.

As he admired his ring, he decided that how he felt about all that could take a back seat to the overwhelming merriment at Taylin's proposal. He was a traditionalist. He was raised that way and although he'd never actively push for marriage, delight came at the prospect nevertheless and he'd never be able to conceal that. The spontaneity of the proposal made his heart so fucking happy.

"I take it that's a definite no then?" Taylin's voice pulled him from his thoughts and back to the fact he'd not answered him.

He stared at his parents' car parked on the driveway. The scent of spiced apples, some of the ones he had cooked and frozen—after admitting that he had indeed collected too many from their trip to the orchard—filled his nose when he inhaled to stem the bubbly feelings. "I'm not taking my ring off, not for anyone."

"Love, that's fine with me. I want the world to know you're mine."

"You know that sounds very macho possessive?" Hollis outright laughed at Taylin when he shrugged and gave him a 'do I care' look.

As Taylin got out of the car, Hollis noticed that the front door was open and Lane was making his way towards them, Mom right on his heels.

He didn't hear what Lane said to Taylin while he watched Mom smile at him. He got out more slowly, his facial expression neutral, and put his hands on his hips when she came to him.

"So... are you and Lane best friends now, Mom?" he asked sweetly, titling his head, his eyes narrowed on her. "Because if I hadn't rung you today I'm guessing you wouldn't have told me you were coming here tonight?"

Lights poured from the windows behind her, casting a shadow around her, but Hollis didn't miss how color crept into her cheeks, staining them a deep red. "Lane called us at the last minute to invite us over and I thought isn't that nice. I get to see my son, who I've not seen in weeks, and meet Taylin's parents at the same time. I told you this afternoon how excited I was," she said with a hint of defensiveness.

"You were seeing us on Sunday, Mom," he pointed out, not letting her off the hook quite yet.

"Yes, but I wouldn't have met Lane and Derick, now would I?" She looked in the open door. "Oh, you have been busy. Did you use the new cook book I bought you?"

One look at her guileless expression and Hollis shook his head, huffing loudly. "Mom, you really need to work on your diversion tactics. You suck at it."

"This is all your mom's idea," Dad said, appearing with Derick, clearly having heard what he'd said.

Dad strode to Hollis and gave him a hard hug that made his woes always feel a little less weighty. "Don't be too hard on her," he whispered in his ear.

Hollis held on for another second, then his excitement got the better of him with his parents right here. As they separated, he lifted his hand, saying nothing, just waiting for the reactions. He didn't have to wait long.

"Oh Hubert, look!" Mom sniffed loudly, snatching Hollis's hand. "He's engaged!"

She said it so loudly, Hollis wasn't in the least surprised when Silas, Booker, Kodi, and Laken came rushing out the door in a pile of bodies and crunching gravel, vying to get closer.

Taylin stood next to Derick, grinning foolishly at everyone. "You need to thank Booker"—he looked directly at him—"for spilling the beans about tonight."

"Jackass," Booker grumbled when Lane spun towards him, tutting and wagging his finger.

"Were you trying to cause trouble, young man?"

"He always does," Kodi supplied, laughing.

"Shut up." The look Booker cast at Kodi held the threat of violence.

Lane stepped between them and hooked his arm through Booker's as if to hold him back. "For that naughtiness, you can help me bring in what Hollis made, which you won't be getting any of."

"What?" spluttered Booker, doing as Lane directed without quibbling.

Hollis heard him arguing when they walked back into the house carrying the trays and boxes he'd brought. "Isn't it supposed to be a celebration? I mean, maybe I pushed Taylin to pop the question, isn't that what you've been angling..."

"As Booker has finished setting the cat amongst the pigeons, shall we all go inside and eat?" Derick suggested, his normally hard features softening when Taylin rested his head on his father's shoulder.

"You were humoring Popi, weren't you? I expected better of you, Dad." If he aimed for grave, he failed when his amusement danced in his chocolate eyes.

"Me too," he replied, and everyone laughed, even Hollis's dad. "But none of us are any better at resisting Popi. He just wants one big happy family. However it comes."

"That's the truth!" Taylin laughed.

Fawned over and the ring discussed in great detail by Lane and Mom, along with the proposal over dinner, Hollis was a little relieved when he could escape to the kitchen to plate up dessert at Lane's suggestion.

Mom and Lane came with him into the kitchen. They had bonded over their love of a fashion designer that they both insisted would be perfect for making the wedding outfits.

There was no sign of Bessie, the housekeeper, who'd made their delicious meal.

"It looks like Bessie has set everything up for us," Mom said, going towards the platters laid out on the counter. "She's a veritable treasure, Lane."

"I don't know what I'd have done without her with eight boys to feed and care for."

"How long has she been with your family?"

"She's a gem."

Lane nodded at Mom, his eyes revealing his emotions. "She is, and I could never repay her for what she's done for my sons. All of them. She's more a mother to them than those that birthed them..." A small gasp for air came from Mom, and Lane turned his full attention to her. "It's the truth. Some families don't deserve the precious gifts they're given."

"But you do," Hollis said, stepping closer to Lane. "They are the men they are because of the love you gave them. You and Derick. Your adopted sons aren't the sum of their pasts. They've become so much more than that. Anyone can see it. They are brothers in every sense that counts," Hollis murmured quietly, a little embarrassed by his own outburst, but feeling compelled to say what was on his mind. Taylin was an amazing man, and Lane and Derick contributed to that.

A gentle hand squeezed his shoulder, and he turned slowly, already knowing who was there by the subtle fragrance Taylin wore.

Love. It sparkled at Hollis, lighting up his insides as the hand touching him moved and fingers teased down the side of his face until he reached his chin where Taylin pinched gently, holding his gaze. "This is why you're my temptation." He brushed their mouths together and Hollis let out a breathy moan. "My love, how could I not be tempted by you?" His mouth lingered longer on the second kiss, making Hollis's toes curl in his shoes before he heard Mom.

"Don't they look cute smooching?"

Hollis pulled back in alarm, his eyes widening on Lane and Mom. "Mom," he exclaimed. "Really!"

"What, you are cute," she answered, not sounding at all concerned, looking directly at Taylin.

"Give in, protesting is futile. I learned from the pro there, looking just a little too satisfied with himself."

Lane jiggled his arms, plates clicking together as he clutched at them and did a poor job of hiding his quivering lips as he looked away, in Hollis's opinion.

"Is it too late to change my mind about the wedding?" Hollis asked tongue in cheek, deciding if you couldn't beat them, then he'd join in.

"Yes," Mom was quick to say.

"Of course," Lane supplied, not sounding as confident as he eyed Hollis, searchingly.

"Too late now." Taylin tapped at the ring on his finger. "Didn't you read the terms and conditions?" The wicked smile got Hollis's blood pumping. "That ring is legally binding. Non-returnable. I'm also sold as seen, no refunds." His nose touched Hollis's, and he beamed. "You're stuck with me."

Hollis held back his grin for all of two seconds before it slipped free. "I can live with that."

Read on for a snippet of what's coming next for the Starling brother!

Bonus Scene
Booker's Bliss
Frey

"I can't stay for the meeting with Sawyer's lawyer, I've an appointment. I'll only be gone for about an hour."

Frey knew that the energy Booker released could fluctuate dramatically with his mood, so he had learned to read it like a barometer. It was the only way to try and get a feel for what might come his way. Right now, it told him that there was a storm brewing, and it was heading right for him. Why couldn't Booker, just for once, check his calendar in advance?

"What do you mean you've got an appointment and can't stay? It's your job to be here for these types of meetings." Booker's snappy growl was enough to bring a burning to Frey's nose. Yup, he had totally pegged Booker's mood.

Everything he feared about this appointment and what it meant for him was ready to pour out of him in a flood of

tears that Booker would absolutely hate. Frey was struggling more and more with his emotions, just as his doctor had said would happen if he continued taking the heat blockers beyond their recommended five years.

He sniffed, just once, but it was more than enough to get Booker out of his seat, towering over his desk. His hands slammed down on the papers scattered over it and he shook his head, making his dark waves move. "Not in here... you hear me? No tears... this is a workplace... not a... not a nursery for sniffling foxes."

Frey wanted to see the funny side of the absolute panic coming off the enormous bear at the mere threat of a tear. Only he couldn't. There was nothing funny about his situation and he needed to attend his appointment. He had to look at least partly in control if he wanted to argue his case for continuing the drugs. They had become his lifeline to continuing the pretense that all was well.

He sucked in a shaky breath and boldly looked Booker in the eye. "I never cry at work," Frey insisted, because in the past this was the absolute truth... not so much of late. "And I put this appointment in your calendar last week so you would know in advance I wouldn't be available."

He sniffed again, this time more in indignation. "It's not my fault you didn't check it and as I said, I'll only be gone for about an hour. I'll be back in plenty of time for the four o'clock meeting with Laken."

Met with suspicion at the crack in his voice, Frey chewed on his lower lip, holding Booker's gaze.

Booker thumped his ass into his seat and jabbed a finger at Frey, looking less than impressed. "Make sure you are."

Frey didn't wait to see if he was going to say more. He darted for the door and slipped out, closing it behind him and carrying on down the corridor. He avoided making eye contact with anyone, trying his best to give off the vibe he wasn't in a hurry.

He didn't breathe easy until he was in the underground car park and headed to his car. The lights flashed as he approached, signaling the doors had opened. The fob in his pocket automatically did its job when Frey couldn't get his mind to work in any semblance of order. He slipped inside, hands trembling.

He did everything on automatic pilot, his mind utterly chaotic, making focusing on anything impossible. Panic did that to him and it was probably best when thoughts of what would come in the doctor's office would be something that could derail the life he had created to hide the truth about himself.

Shivers came as he started the engine and headed to his appointment.

Exiting the car park, he groaned at the heavy rain bouncing off the hood. The sky was dark and moody, matching his mood perfectly. Rain lashed down on the windscreen, ensuring he took his time and paid attention to what traffic there was.

The doctor's building was five minutes by car from his office and traffic was light. Frey suspected that was due to the storm that had blown in that morning, as the weatherman had predicted.

Parking in the near empty lot next to the two-storey office, Frey didn't bother grabbing his umbrella when the wind would whip it inside out in seconds. No one wanted to look like Mary Poppins flying with an inside out umbrella, despite how cute he'd look in his sparkly sneakers and bright pink raincoat.

He darted for the door and even though he was but two or three seconds outside, his hair became plastered to his head and rain had seeped down his collar, wetting his sweater. The receptionist, Clare, glanced up from the computer screen with a ready smile. She'd worked here as long as Frey could remember. And since he'd been coming since he was a toddler, it was a long time.

"Frey, so lovely to see you." She glanced at the window, furrows appearing between her brows. "It's wild out there. I can see the rain hasn't eased at all. Do you want me to get you a towel to dry your hair?" Up out of her seat before she'd finished speaking, she skipped to a cupboard that Frey knew held all manner of things a person might need.

It never failed to make him smile the way she moved. Frey long since convinced himself she put springs into her shoes to make her bounce that way.

"That would be great," he replied, although she was already grabbing him the towel.

"Dr. Hockings is on time, so he shouldn't keep you waiting more than a minute or two. His last patient left ten minutes ago, so he'll be writing up his notes." She handed him the towel, offering him a sympathetic smile.

Two swipes to catch the offending drops, he returned the damp towel to her waiting hands, then Frey sat in one of the comfy leather chairs that had originally been a weird mustard color but were recently updated to the classy brown they were now.

He cast an eye over the varied selection of magazines on the coffee table in front of him. Most came from Clare and her husband, he had learned in one of the many conversations he had with her when the doctor ran late. An eclectic taste from motor mechanics, muscle cars, fashion and beauty, along with one or two on planes and trains.

Clare, if not busy, would sit and gossip with him about models. He could see today wasn't one of those days as she went back to work at her computer.

Too nervous to bother to read, Frey pulled out his iPhone and scrolled through Delicious & Vicious group chat, finding none of the usual humor at reading the threads of conversation.

The phone rang on Clare's desk and Frey swallowed hard, figuring out it was to say he could go on up and see the doctor. He got up when not two seconds later Clare said, "Yes, your next appointment is here, I'll send him right up."

Frey smiled his thanks and walked to the door leading to the second floor. The smell of the place, a little disinfectant and a lot of air freshener, didn't help with the nerves doing a swing dance inside him when he reached the second floor.

Hyperventilating, his hand continued to tremble. Frey quickly tapped on the white door, like ripping a plaster off just to get it over with.

It opened to reveal a gray-haired and bearded man with a weathered face that spoke of the many hours Dr. Hockings spent outdoors. He loved to keep fit through cycling and hiking.

As usual, Dr. Hockings wore a gray suit and white shirt. Not once had Frey seen him in anything else in all the years he could remember. It was like that was his doctor's uniform instead of a white coat. Which Frey didn't mind, not one bit as it made the doctor appear more human and allowed Frey to usually feel a little more relaxed. Today, that was not the case.

"Hi, Dr. Hockings. It's good to see you," he lied. "You must be glad to be working inside with how awful the weather is out there today."

Frey knew he was waffling, but his nerves wouldn't let him stop as the doctor stepped to the side to allow him into the consulting room.

An examining couch, a chair, and a desk with a computer on it were all the furniture in the room. The pictures on the cream walls were all of body parts and descriptions of how they worked. On the one large window sill below the frosted glass window sat a hip, a knee and a spine model.

"You too, Frey. Take a seat and let me pull up your blood work."

Frey sat fidgeting with the cuff of his raincoat, determined not to jump to any conclusions about the results and whether he could persuade the doctor to give him more medication. He'd spent most of last night stressing about it and hadn't slept at all. Something Booker noticed this morning and pointed out.

"So, I'll get to the point of why I asked you to make an appointment." Dr. Hockings reached for the cup of water on his desk and took a sip.

Frey didn't need the doctor to tell him the blood results were bad. Dr. Hockings only ever took a drink of water when he was collecting his thoughts on how best to deliver news that was mostly unpleasant. Everyone thought Frey was flighty, which he was, to a degree, but his past also meant that he was excellent at reading people. It was a knack, and if he was correct, Dr. Hockings was worried.

Glass down, he wet his lips and gave Frey a sympathetic smile. "As I explained last time you were in, it's been nearly six years since you started taking the heat blockers. You have all the literature on the side effects, so I won't bore you again with those." His expression became very serious. "My problem, Frey, is that I was right to worry about continuing with the drugs after your insistence last time. What I hoped wouldn't happen... has. Your hormone levels are very low. So low that I'm doubtful they will return to a level that would allow you to conceive when you choose to find a mate."

Frey blinked slowly, digesting what he'd secretly worried about for the last six months. "I won't ever be able to get pregnant."

"I can't say never, but with your blood picture and your long-term history of taking the drugs to prevent your heat, I'd say it's unlikely. I'm sorry."

"It's not your fault. It's mine. I knew the risks." Saying it aloud made reality sting like he'd stumbled into a bee's hive. "Does that mean I won't be able to have any more? Drugs, I mean?" This was Frey's biggest fear.

Pregnancy. A person had to be having sex with an alpha for that to happen. He had no alpha nor was having sex of any kind, even alone, so it was a moot point.

"You are now susceptible to other ramifications such as mood swings, emotional outbursts, decrease in sex drive to name but a few if you continue to take the drug. In good conscience, I am no longer able to prescribe them for you."

Even knowing it was coming didn't help the physical blow those words landed and he jerked back in his seat. Horror etched into his features as the first tear rolled down his pale cheeks.

Dr. Hockings leaned forward and patted his knee. "I can refer you to a therapist... to talk about your past so you can—"

"No." He sniffed and scrubbed at his wet face. "I've had therapy and their suggestion to... yeah, I can't do what they want." He could, but only with one person he trusted implicitly—Booker. And Frey didn't have the courage to ask the bear to help when he really wanted... *more than someone to help him through a heat without scaring the hell out of him.*

Ask him.

No!

He rose, needing out before he broke down and begged when he already knew that was useless. "I'll figure it out."

His fox remained pushy and focused on the bear. *He's interested, I know he is.*

Booker would never want us.

Frey quashed the idea even as his fox made a rude noise.

The gentle bear would never be interested in a defective fox, not in a million years.

How do you know if you don't ask?

Standalone

When Fake Changed Everything

Christmas beyond Christmas

The Elves and the Bondage Daddy (Grim and Sinister Delights Book 5)

Agrippa My Heart

His Boy to Tease

Headshot

A Brat For Kinkmas

Hanging With Daddy

A Little Christmas Matty Secret

A Little Christmas Terrence

A Sucker For Christmas

Music & Dreams

Magic Demon & the Hunter

Series

Assassins To Order With Lisa Oliver

Marvin – Marvin and Ajani

Ben – Ben, Teilo & Nico

Duron – Duron & Beaumont

Conrad – Conrad & Kylo

Dancing With the Devil – Wyatt & James

Tangled Tentacles Series with Lisa Oliver

Alexi #1

Victor #2

Todd #3

Markov # 4

Kelvin # 5

Little Paws Haven Series

Little Treasure he Hides

Weird & Wacky Shifters

All He Wants For Christmas is a Fingerling

Alpha's Fingerling Surprise

A Boy Called Blu

The Potters Creek Series

A Christmas Wish (book one)

The App Series

The App: Daddy kink (book one)

The App: Littles (book two)

The App: Puppy play (book three)

The Flamingo Bar Series

Always More (book one)

The Little Side of Me (book two)

3 Is the Magic Number (book three)

La Trattoria Di Amore Series

Puzzle Pieces (book one)

Dominated but not Subdued (book two)

Made to Submit

The Playroom Series

Mine, Body and Soul: Part One

Mine, Body and Soul: Part Two

Mine, Body and Soul: Part Three

Ferron's Journey: Damaged Part One (book four)

Ferron's Journey: Hidden Part Two (book five)

Ferron's Journey: Revelation Part Three (book six)

Mine, Body and Soul Trilogy

Ferron's Journey Trilogy

Spinoff Love's Heart Print

Dark River Stone Collective Series

The Light Beneath the Dark (Book One)

When Darkness Turns to Light (Book Two)

Running From Darkness (Book Three)

The Billionaire Playground Series

Property of a Billionaire (Book one)
Reluctant Billionaire (Book two)
Billionaire's Muse (Book three)

Heart Stones Series

Blood King

The Manx Cat Guardians Series Where it all Began: Origins (Book 1)
Seeing Beyond the Scars (Book 2)
Destiny Collides Past and Present (Book 3)
Searching for a Soul to Love (Book 4)
The 12 Disasters of Christmas (Book 5)
Laws of Attraction (Book 6)
The Teacher's Boy (Book 7)
Boxset

Audio Books
Mine, Body and Soul, Part One: The Playroom Series
Mine, Body and Soul, Part Two: The Playroom Series
Mine, Body and Soul, Part Three: The Playroom Series
Daddy Kink: The App (book one)
Always More: The Flamingo Bar (book one)
When Fake Changed Everything
Ferron's Journey: Damaged Part One
Ferron's Journey: Hidden Part Two
Ferron's Journey: Revelation Part Three

Romance books in a mixed series of M/F and M/M by the Author under a different pen name Jayne Paton

Smith's Corner
Delilah & Dallas (book one)
Layla & Levi (Book two)
Ash & Alora (Book three)
Fox & Faith (book four)
Storm & Stone (book five)
Hunter & Holden (book six)

Crime and Thrillers by the Author under a different pen name J Paton

Headspace
Chozen: Dark MM Crime Drama (Headspace Book 1)
Chozen: Dark MM Crime Drama (Headspace Book 2)

About the Author

Eccentric cake lover who has a passion for words of all kinds. I'm Jayne or JP, I live in the Isle of Man. A tiny place in the Irish sea where all the magic happens. I'm a confessed bookaholic and if I'm not writing I love to snuggle with a book or two...if you catch my drift.

If you're interested in keeping up to date, then I've a few places you can do that, and they're listed below. My website is where you'll find all the different Me's there are, LOL. As I travel this path into the future, I'm going to be writing in different genres so to stop there being any confusion I'll be writing under different pen names.

If you would like to give me any feedback or just have any questions, go ahead and friend me on Facebook, and I would be happy to answer anything. I hope you enjoyed this book and if you would also like to leave a review, then I would love to read your thoughts. Even if you just want to rate it, I'll be grateful

Thank you for being a part of my dream.

Newsletter Sign up

Goodreads

Tumblr

Bookbub

Instagram

Twitter

Facebook

Website address

Facebook Author page

JP Manx Minx's

Patreon

Printed in Great Britain
by Amazon

45228171R00233